BILLY QUIZ AND MISSION TO MARS

CHRIS RICKABY

OW

Acknowledgments

Firstly thanks to, to the amazing Gill Foreman and One Word for championing and publishing this book.

Also, to Carrie Plitt who gave excellent editorial feedback during various initial iterations. To fellow students on Curtis Brown Creative's writing course who pitched in enthusiastically with thoughts, critiques, and advice on how to improve the narrative, and Anna Davis and Jake Arnott who taught so insightfully upon it.

A word, too, to Barney Thompson, my writing partner for the upcoming City of Ghosts under the pseudonym Ben Creed, who waded through an early draft and injected the requisite amount of optimism into my editing process.

I'd also like to mention Mick Hall, who gave me some down-to-earth insights into working in Newcastle's post office in the 1970s (No one does down-to-earth quite as well as Mick). Cora Phillips for the brilliant cover design, and Toni for her meticulous proofing.

Finally, to my wife, Sue, who gave me unwavering support

on the long road to publication, my mam (she'd prefer mum) who encouraged my early love of reading, and my granddad who was a postman and also wrote beautiful letters.

For Sue

A Note on Dialect

For readers outside the UK, Geordie is the dialect of the city of Newcastle upon Tyne in the north of England. A simple way to familiarise yourself with its unique rhythms and cadences is to watch the video 'Call Me Da'lin' (a quirky cover of Carly Rae Jepson's Call Me Baby) by local band May Arcade on You Tube. It's great. Or, as we would say in Newcastle, 'dead canny, like.' Korean Billy (You Tube) also delivers an excellent basic primer.

There's a glossary on page 322.

Noctis.
Monday, June 14th 1976.
35 days until Viking 1 lands on Mars

Chapter One

Me mam's dead. It was two years ago when she went. An accident, the Newcastle coppers said. I thought about it for a long time, afterwards. Every single day, in fact. And, after a while, I realised it was the size of the cheese and pickle plate she chose that killed her.

They did a cheese and pickle plate at Walker Comrades – the working men's club she went to on Sundays, after mass at St Jude's – and she liked them. So, I suppose, that's why she stayed a little longer. I mean she wasn't a drinker like some of them. She just liked the taste of cheese when pickle was also being offered. That particular combination, like. I've thought about the plate a lot as well. The size of the plate they might have given her. A bigger plate and she might still be with us. A smaller plate and the same thing applies. It was a medium plate she'd opted for. I checked that with the steward at the club afterwards. You can fit about eight crackers on the medium plate. Four on the small, twelve on the large but a medium plate takes eight.

Then I did the obvious thing: got meself a stopwatch and did some cracker consumption tests.

They only confirmed what I already thought. It takes a normal person, like me, about 24 seconds to scoff a Ritz cracker covered in Branston Pickle and cheese. You do the maths. That's say 4 x 40 seconds for the small plate (I used 40 seconds as a multiplier because me mam had a dead lady-like bite.) 12 x 40 seconds for the big plate. And 8 x 40 for the middle. The one she actually chose. The way that all works out is this: small plate consumption time: 160 seconds. Big plate consumption time: 480 Seconds. Middle plate consumption time: 320 seconds.

That makes 160 seconds, either way, the difference between life and death. The difference between crossing Scrogg Road, on the fourth of August 1974, without a hitch, or crossing Scrogg Road and being hit by Mr Pontefract, the insurance salesman, in his 1972 Hillman Imp.

It scared me a lot, back then, when I worked that out. Made me fourteen-year-old head hurt just thinking about it. Does Destiny choose you? Or do you choose it? I don't know. I'm not certain. What it does mean though is that every tiny choice you make – every little this and that, what seems like nothing at all at the time – well, any one of them can kill you.

Chapter Two

Me bedroom door rocks on its hinges and cracks against the wall. The light switched on slaps me brain awake.

'Come on Billy Quiz. Wakey, wakey, it's time for worky, worky. This is how it's going to be for today and the rest of your natural. You can think of this morning as "Your starter for 10."'

Me dad picks up me new grey uniform off me chair and throws it onto the bed.

'You dropped out of A Levels, and now you're going to find out exactly what you dropped into.'

Dad does up the top button of his own grey uniform jacket, then runs a comb through what remains of his thick, dark 1950's quiff. His smile is as white as the smiles on the Colgate toothpaste ads on the telly. And his face is all nice lines, all grinning symmetry. It's a bit like being woken up by a working-class Hughie Green. He can certainly talk as much as the cheesy presenter on the telly.

I sit up in bed and stare at the Tin Tin alarm-clock me mam

bought me when I was little. One of Captain Haddock's arms is pointing at the six. The other one is pointing at the four.

'It's half-past four in the morning dad? Half-past four in the morning!'

Me dad's grin spreads so wide it looks like the corners of his mouth might push his ears up around the back of his head.

'I know because I'm there already. It's called the Real World, Billy Quiz. All that stuff you've got stuck inside your head. All them facts about this, that and the bollocking other, they won't help you now, son.'

He pops the comb back into the top pocket of his own grey uniform.

'Welcome aboard Her Majesty's Postal Service.'

ME NAME'S BILLY, BILLY AGNEW, BUT NO ONE AROUND HERE calls me that. They call me Billy Quiz. Even me mam did sometimes. But only when she was getting a bit narky with me, like, which wasn't that often.

It was me dad who started it really. The Billy Quiz thing. There's a character in a comic called The Beano, I used to read when I was a little bairn. They called him Billy Whizz on account of his fast running. I can't run fast at all. I'm rubbish at sport. Always have been. One of them that was always last picked when they sorted out the footy teams at school.

But not with facts.

Facts is another matter.

There's lots of stuff inside me big, daft bonce you see. "A great wide universe of useless information," is what me dad says. I learnt most of it in an old red brick Victorian building, which is Walker District Library. I'm estimating there are about 12,000 books in there and I've probably read about 90% of them by now. Which isn't that impressive when you consider how many Saturdays and after-school nights I spend reading. Science books are me favourite but if I can't get me hands on something about Michael Faraday and electromagnetism, or Alessandro Volta and batteries, I read lots of other stuff. That's why I've read all the comics, periodicals and magazines in there, as well. Acquiring all them facts, over the years, is why I'm good at answering questions. And being good at answering questions is why me dad started calling me Billy Quiz.

That's all there is to it, really.

Except, maybe, for me and him and me mam – when she was still alive – being so different. There's an expression that people say a lot. A cliché is what you call it. This expression is rubbish from a science point of view. Makes no sense at all. It goes like this: "as like as two peas in a pod." Now when you first think about that saying you might feel like – no there's definitely something in it! I mean peas are all round and green and, when I've looked at them in a pod at the SPAR grocers on the Coast Road, I'd be the first to admit that they do look quite similar.

The thing is they're not.

And if you look a little closer you would see it. An Austrian bloke called Gregor Mendel discovered that in Victorian times.

He looked at lots of peas did Mr Mendel. 29,000 to be precise. And being arsed to look at that amount of vegetables – and let's be honest lots of people wouldn't be – he saw something. Observed it, like. Peas in a pod aren't alike. At least, not always. Five might well be a bit similar: perfectly round, perfectly green. Two more might be a little less symmetrical, a little less green. A bit rougher around the edges, like. And one might be all battered, almost square; hardly green at all.

It made me think about me and me mam and me dad on that day in the library when I first read about Gregor Mendel and all the years he spent observing Pisum sativum. Because, as a family, we're like that. I mean me mam was pretty and dark, all symmetrical, like me dad. And I'm all crooked-faced, spotty and me hair's ginger or, as I like to think of it, Martian red. I think that's why me mam bought me this telescope by the window. She understood that I was always going to be different to her and Dad but she really wanted me to know that she loved me just the same anyways.

I put me eye to the lens of me telescope and then twist the focus. I can still hear Dad whistling up a storm in front of the bathroom shaving mirror but now I've left him, the stab of first-day nerves in me belly, and everything else behind. I begin to peer back through time. Back through the darkness of space. Little dots of light are everywhere. Other stars. Other galaxies that may contain planets just like this one.

There's something else out there too – Viking 1.

The unmanned space probe is twelve months into its mission. Approximately 233 million miles from where I am sitting, and 35 days away from NASA's scheduled Mars landing. It will be the first U.S spaceship ever to get there. But, right now, it's just a small hunk of tin hurtling through space.

Chapter Three

This big, twenty-storey tower block that me and me dad are standing in front of is called Windsor Mansions and was built by the council about fifteen years ago on an estate called Faversham Hall. It looks like the handle of a big, concrete dagger, that's what I'm thinking. A great, big dagger that some passing giant has stuck right into the ground under the cover of darkness.

There's a sign that reads Windsor Mansions in gold plastic letters on a black plastic panel stuck near the doors of the building. It has some other writing, "PAKIS FUCKOFF HOME," spray-painted over it in white. You can see why even the people who live around here don't like walking around the estate too slowly. Especially at night.

Me dad leans over and slaps me on the back. It hurts a bit when he does that but I like that he does it. Because it's not a nasty slap but a nice one. The kind of slap that tells me he's watching out for me, like.

'There she blows, son, Windsor Mansions. Postman's hell.

Toe-rag's heaven. Twenty floors of pain. I've been walking them stairs for fourteen years.'

He gives me a second back-slap, just for good measure.

'Now, it's your turn.'

It's hot today. Very, very hot. The British Meteorological Office has made an announcement in the papers. They say the summer of 1976 is all set to be "The hottest summer since records began," and I believe them. I raise me armpit up and sniff. Uggh! Me pits are minging. Me right shoulder's already sore from the weight of a big, red canvass bag that holds loads of letters and parcels. I start walking towards Windsor Mansions with me dad. Then I stop.

I recognise the two skinheads straightaway.

One day in school, the teacher made us stand in front of all the others and talk about something you liked. The girls all said Donny Osmond and David Cassidy and daft pop stars like that. And the boys all said Malcolm McDonald, who was Newcastle's centre forward at the time, and Muhammad Ali. But not me. I said someone different. I mentioned Sir Isaac Newton's Second Law of Motion, instead. Everyone laughed and the teacher said I should watch out because I was in danger of getting ahead of meself. If he had understood anything about the Second Law of Motion, he would have realised that me "getting ahead of meself," was actually impossible. But I was too embarrassed to say anything. So, I just said nowt.

Things went really bad for me for a little while, after that. Some of the older lads heard about it and started calling me "Sir Isaac," all the time. Not because they had any respect for me knowing Sir Isaac's Laws of Motion you understand. But because they saw me as being a bit different. Not one of them.

I'd had that sort of thing a lot before – what with me spots and me hair being Martian red. But this time it got a lot worse.

These two – Blue Tear and Bino – the ones standing about 200 yards in front of me and dad now, grabbed me in the yard and took me up on top of the PE block. They said they were going to do an "experiment" with "gravity". But instead of an apple, like what the real Sir Isaac used, I could see they were going to use me instead. I didn't think I was going to die or anything. Well, not unless I landed on me head. I did a bit of quick calculation in me mind while they were dragging me up there and realised that since I only weighed five stone and the drop from the roof of the PE block was about fifteen feet that, according to the First Law of Motion, I would only be travelling at about seven miles an hour when I hit the ground and so was unlikely to hurt meself too bad, like. But the way they were with me then: all snarling and sniggering and bared teeth made the whole day one that I don't like to remember. Mr Roberts, the geography teacher, stopped them in the end. But, all in all, it wasn't very nice.

The two skinheads are standing next to an upturned packing case near a bairns' climbing frame that's close to the door of Windsor Mansions. They've already seen me. I turn back around.

'You're coming with me right, Dad? I mean I'm not supposed to do this on me own yet. That's what your gaffer at the depot said. And it's only me first day.'

Me dad takes out his comb and runs it through his quiff.

'Dad?'

He stops doing his hair and puts the comb back in his pocket.

'Yes, Billy Quiz. How can I help you?'

'The tower block, you're coming with me aren't you?'

'You're not scared are you, son?'

Me dad points at the two lads.

When me dad stops whistling so do I.

'Da-de-da-de-da-de-de,' Dad gives it one more go.

'Da-de-da-de-da-de-do.' I try and help him but it sounds a bit half-hearted.

Blue Tear smiles. He twists the dog's leash and his Alsatian snarls into life. I step back behind Dad because I've always been dead scared of animals. But, just as the dog starts barking, something happens. A curtain draws back at an open window on about the fourth floor of the tower block. Dad looks up. Blue Tear and Bino look up too. The woman at the window stares back down at us.

'It's her,' says Bino, his voice sounds a bit nervy, 'that old wife all the little bairns call the Windsor Witch.'

Dad looks across at me and nods at the door of the flats. Me and him start to walk towards them. Blue and Bino just keep staring up at the woman. As I'm walking away, I look back up at her over me shoulder. I sense it immediately and so, I can tell, do the other three. She is beautiful is this lady in the window. All perfect symmetry.

Chapter Four

I stare at the big, black clock in the main sorting room at the post office and feel a bit sick. It's still dead early.

Watergate, a mate of me dad's, sits down at the table with a bang. His tea slops over the edge of the metal mug he's holding. I look up at the ceiling to avoid his gaze and see a face staring down from it. I remember it quite well from the last time I was here. It's a dead large badly-painted, Greek god coming down to earth from a badly-drawn heaven. An old Victorian painting of Mount Olympus, to be precise. Mount Olympus was what the Greeks called heaven. The Victorians must have put him up there because of something called the Neo-Classical revival.

Watergate nods up at the painting.

'Anyone you know, Billy Quiz?'

I saw a documentary once on ITV about dogs that test cigarettes. The dogs were beagles and people lock them in cages and make them do lots of smoking. If those dogs could talk, I think they would make a sound like Watergate's voice, all harsh and dry and rasping. His face is a bit beagly as well.

The skin is sagging around his neck and mouth and he often looks dead sad and fed-up. It's his hair though that people talk about the most. He's in his fifties and there's not much left of it you see. Just three long strands of greasy grey hair flicked carefully across his bald white forehead and patted down on the other side. His hair is how he got the nickname – Watergate. It's after Richard Nixon, the American President, who sent burglars into the Watergate building to spy on the Democrats and then pretended that he hadn't. The blokes in the post office say Richard Nixon and Watergate have something in common – they both tried to organise "a badly botched cover-up."

Watergate's real name is Tommy Worrall.

'Sorry, Tommy?'

'Gaylord Fauntleroy up there on the ceiling. Is it any one you know?'

'I think so.'

'Think or know?'

'Hermes, it's Hermes.'

Watergate takes a swig of PG Tips from his mug. Finishes his tea. Smacks the cup back down on the table with a clang and then lets out a big burp. I know some facts about sound. That for instance the sound of a pin dropping is less than 10 decibels and that the noise the back of a refrigerator makes is about 35 decibels. Something louder, the Sony Music Centre that Dad bought Mam for her birthday a few years ago, might be about 80 decibels. Compared with those things, I estimate Watergate's burp is about 90 decibels. I should ring the brothers, Ross and Norris McWhirter, who own the Guinness Book of Records, and ask them to enter Watergate's burp into it. A bad stink comes out of his mouth that goes with the noise – the smell of Tudor pickled onion crisps.

'Who the shit is this Hermes when he's at home?' says Watergate.

'Hermes, the son of the Greek God Zeus, Hermes the messenger.'

Me dad says people need to be "patient" with Watergate on account of him seeing some nasty stuff at a camp in Germany called Bergen-Belsen, when he was in the army at the end of the war, but sometimes he makes it difficult.

Watergate puts both hands behind his head and then leans back in his chair and lets out the kind of 100 decibel burp that would offer Ross and Norris all the conclusive proof they needed. 'Oh, that Hermes. Hermes the messenger,' he says, as he gets up to go. 'I bollocking-well knew it.'

THIS JOB I'VE GOT WITH THE POST OFFICE IS PART OF WHAT they call a mentoring scheme. It's a new thing that they're only trying out in a few cities, like Newcastle, this summer, as part of a trial. Most places in the country you need to be eighteen to train to be a postman but in this new scheme you can be sixteen as long as you only go out and do an actual post-round with someone to look out for you, real proper, like, and show you the ropes. Like me dad, for instance.

Today's only me second morning in the depot and me eyes are still sore and red with little bits of sleep in them. It's going to take me a while to get used to all these early starts. We work three different shifts. There's Earlies, which is 6-1, Lates, which is 2-10, and Nights, which is 10-6, so that means there are people here grafting all the time. Me and me dad are working Earlies this week.

There's a big new post office opened in Orchard Street,

behind Newcastle's main Central Station, where most of the sorting of letters get done these days but we're in the old brick Victorian Head Post office on St Nicholas' Street, opposite the Cathedral. They still use this one for what's called "overflow" work but dad saysit's getting closed down for good.

I'm sixteen now so I should know better but everything seems scarier than the first time I was here with me dad; four years ago, on a special day when you could bring your bairns into work. It was a nice day that. Dad showed me round and lot of the blokes were dead kind. They gave me a load of little gifts like elastic bands and old stamps.

There are about forty booths that run down the central aisle of the sorting room. Each small cubicle is about five feet high and carved from the kind of dead old dark wood the Victorians seemed to like. The booths are all filled with middle-age blokes, mostly wearing the same grey uniform that I am. They are all working at a speedy pace, checking envelopes and directing mail into the boxes. Every inch of desk-space is covered by mountains and mountains of letters and parcels. When they get a parcel the blokes hoy that into one of a row of twenty hessian bags that are stuck to metal poles in the middle of the room, so the mouths of them sacks are always open.

Sometimes, the blokes start messing about; spinning parcels through the air, when they hoy them into the bag, and shouting daft stuff like: "How, Bobby, did you see that? They call me fucking Meadowlark Lemon!" Then they start whistling the theme tune from the Harlem Globetrotters cartoons, where there's this American basketball team who do mad tricks and crazy dribbling, and they all have dead glamorous names like Geese and Curly.

HERMES LOOKS PRETTY PLEASED WITH HIMSELF UP THERE ON the ceiling. That's probably because he's spent the morning flying about enjoying himself while I've been loading boxes of envelopes and lacky-bands into the big storeroom at the back of the main building where all the red post-vans are parked. Then I sorted letters for the last couple of hours.

There's been no sign of Watergate since I saw him earlier, which is a relief. Even if he did see some horrible stuff in the war, like me dad says, I'm not sure I like him very much, really. When the tea-trolley came around Phyllis who runs it asked where he was and couple of the lasses, who work behind the big wooden counters selling stamps, rolled their eyes at her. Phyllis shook her head and raised her hand to her lips like it was a glass. Then she said "Done a bunk has he? Old trouble again, I expect. Best not say owt to the gaffers, he'll get another warning."

I roll me sleeves up and look at the green metal box in front of me. This is a bit of post office work that I'm really looking forward to. It's going to be a bit like scientific research.

There are about twenty different letters and a couple of parcels in the box. All stuff that's been, what's called, "incorrectly addressed," so the postman hasn't been able to deliver them. Dad says there's usually about a hundred or so bits of mail like this that collects up each month. Some of them get sent straight back because the sender will have written their name on the back of the envelope or parcel.

The ones that don't get put in this green metal container, which is called the Returns Box. It's full of things where the sender has only written part of the address on, or just put a stamp on and no address, which happens quite a lot, apparently. Sometimes old ladies write on things like "57 Latimer

Avenue, or it could be 27 (the one with the yellow door near the iron mongers)," but then it turns out that Latimer Avenue is Latimer Lane or doesn't seem to exist at all. So, they've really just sent a letter to a house with a yellow door near an iron mongers somewhere in any place or city on planet Earth.

Even for the post office, that's hard to find.

In the course of the week, all that stuff gets put into this box and then someone has to steam open the letters and cut open the parcels, to see if they've got a sender's address anywhere inside. If they have, they get stamped RETURN TO SENDER and sent back to them.

There's a little metal machine called an AirSteam 750 with a flat base, so it stands upright on the desk, with a rubber strip at the top that's about the same size as an average letter edge. An old postypostie with a little brown moustache called Kenny "Kettles," because he's always making cups of tea, showed me how to use it. You press a red button on the base which lights up glowing red inside. Then you wait a couple of minutes for the water to heat inside the base. When it's ready, a little line of hot steam will come out of the rubber strip and you know the AirSteam is useable. If I can't be an astronaut when I get older, and, to be honest, I probably can't due to not being very good at sport, then I'd like to be the type of bloke who invents things like the AirSteam 750.

The red-light has been on for about two minutes now. I stare at the rubber strip. A thin line of wispy steam starts to float out of it. I pick up the first letter and start to open it. The edge of the envelope starts to blister, dampen and then dimple. I get a bit of a thrill when I see it do that. Even though I'm allowed, it still feels like I'm a kind of spy or something, a bit like James Bond, looking through people's private stuff. There's nothing exciting in this envelope though; just a card with a picture of a cartoon chicken blowing out candles on a cake and a message that says, "Happy Birthday, Karen, from Auntie Aggy." There's no return address on either, which is sad because that means that Karen will think her Auntie Aggy has forgotten her.

I open two more letters. One's got a five-pound postal order in it and no message and the other is a letter from a dad to his son, Robert, who's been sent away to some posh school somewhere asking him to "Try and fit in more, remember that your family name is Barrington."

That's got a sender's address on the inside, so I figure this Robert will get it eventually but I'm not sure that he will really want to.

There's a big parcel, wrapped up in brown paper, to unwrap next. I'm dead excited about that. I pick it up and hold it next to me head. Shake it in front of Hermes, up there on the ceiling; see if he can take a guess as to what's inside. His expression doesn't change much. I don't think he's got any more idea than I have. Still holding the parcel next to me head, and shaking it, I look down at the box. A funny-looking letter was hidden underneath it. The address says:

Rebecca.
Alter Strasse,
Bezirke Veindenburger
Wein.

I put the parcel down on the table and sit there staring at this odd letter. I read the address again.

Rebecca.
Alter Strasse,
Bezirke Veindenburger
Wein.

I've got a weird feeling in me belly now. There's something about this letter: the way it's just sitting there in the Returns Box. The way it was hidden under the parcel. It looks old, like it's from another time. But it wouldn't be in the box if it hadn't been posted in the last few days. I know it sounds mad but there's something about it that's making me think it's not for this Rebecca lass. I don't know why but it kind of feels like the person who's written it wants me to get it. And, once it's out from under the Airstream, I don't want anyone to see what's inside this Rebecca letter, except me.

I look around the room. Everyone's got their heads down working. That's good.

THE BOGS IN THE ST NICHOLAS' STREET POST OFFICE LOOK like they were designed by Isambard Kingdom Brunel, the Victorian bloke who wore very tall black hats and built that curvy metal suspension bridge in Bristol. There's big green metal pipes everywhere; stuck together with brackets and rivets and lots of dark wood. The radiators are huge and painted white but, despite them being massive, the blokes here say they never seem to work properly. Even though it's boiling hot outside it's brass monkeys down here, in the basement of the post office.

There are three cubicles built out of oak directly opposite the urinal. I'm sitting in the middle of the three with the seat down and me feet up, so no one can tell I'm here, staring down at the envelope that's resting on me knee. The writing on the front's been done with a fountain pen and the letters are all neat and precise. The ink is dark blue. The envelope paper is dead smooth. It's a posh sort called Basildon Bond, that you can only get from big department stores in Newcastle, like Binns or Fenwicks.

I take the letter out of the envelope and spread it out against me knee. The letter paper also looks pretty new. The handwriting is written in the same dark blue ink as the envelope.

Me hands are shaking a bit as I start to read it.

Dear Rebecca,

Ich sehe sie,

Even frightened you brought beauty to that place. Skin white as a winter moon; hands that trembled a hypnotic hopelessness. Your eyes pulled the darkness into them and walled it in. A firm, determined walk. Tiny steps like a geisha. An Alter Strasse geisha. Think of that. How does that happen?

You looked back. Realised everything. Walked forward. Towards the door. Through it.

Nothing trembles here.

Ich sehe sie, Rebecca

Yours

W. S

I can't understand much German but I know that Ich sehe sie means I see you because that was part of the really basic stuff we did in Mrs Chisum's class at school. That seems really odd for a start. Why would the person who wrote the letter write some of it in German and some of it in English? If you were writing to a German person, surely you would write to them in German, and if you were writing to an English person you'd write to them in English.

Loads of other questions jump into me mind and start me head fizzing. Why is this Rebecca lass frightened? What is on the other side of the door she goes through? But mainly, the thing I really can't get me head around with this letter is the stamp it's got on it. Most of the stamps people use at the post office have the Queen's head on them. The stamp on this W.S letter isn't like that. It's dead old and it's got a Nazi swastika and a picture of Adolf Hitler on it.

DAD SITS DOWN OPPOSITE ME WITH A PLATE OF SCRAN AND together we fill our faces. These dinner times are hard for me dad. I can always tell that because he stops smiling and whistling and all his daft chat. It's me mam he's thinking of. Sometimes I see him looking at the chair where she used to sit.

I don't really want to think about me mam's chair so I stare down at me scran instead. I've got one chip left on the end of me fork and just a big red pork rissole on me plate. That's why rissoles are called rissoles, in case you didn't know. Russeolus is a Latin word for reddish, that the Romans used way back in history. I'm staring down at me rissole and me last half-chip but I'm not thinking about scran any more. I'm thinking about space. I'm thinking that me rissole looks like Mars and the chip on the end of me fork looks like a small bit of tin blasting its way through space. "Nothing trembles here." Suddenly, that line from the W.S letter pops into me head.

AFTER ME SCRAN, I GO UP TO ME BEDROOM AND HAVE A GOOD deek under me bed. I pull out a box that says, 'Arrows of Tonto,' and put it on top of me Tin Tin duvet. I keep meaning to change me duvet covers because I'm too old for them now but I don't because Mam bought them for me. I open the box and pick up the white envelope, the one I've got from the post office, and, then, open it. Have a good look at it again. Same as I did as soon as I got back from work today.

I'll take it back tomorrow. Put it back in the mail. I mean I'm not going to steal it. That would be what me dad says is called interfering with the Queen's mail. No, I can't keep it. Even though, technically speaking, just by taking it home, I've already interfered with Her Majesty's mail a bit. But, like I say, there's definitely something about this envelope, even before I knew what it was, that made me think I was supposed to discover it.

The Queen seems dead nice on the telly when she does that speech every Christmas that comes on before the Two Ronnie's' Christmas Special. So, I reckon, as long as I take it back in a couple of days, she'll be alright about it. To be honest, even if I do take it back, they'll never find the person who wrote it because there's no return address.

When the Viking 1 lander gets to Mars, after travelling maybe 250 million miles through space, it's going to, what's called, deploy four completely automated biochemical laboratories, two cameras and an inorganic analysis chamber to look for signs of life. Imagine what it'll be like if they find some. Imagine being the bloke who's in charge of NASA, if they do that. It's not very scientific but that's how I feel about this envelope. Like I'm on Mars and I've just picked up a tiny signal that's being sent out by some, until now, unexplained kind of something, that humans haven't encountered before. First contact is what the blokes at NASA call that.

It's an odd sort of letter, alright. Especially the stamp. It's a real old one from the war. It's got some German-style writing on the bottom of it, that says DEUTSCHES REICH in big capital letters. Hitler's head is turned to the side and he's got a smart peaked cap on, a bit like the one Parker, Lady Penelope's chauffer off Thunderbirds, wears when he's picking her up to go and meet Scott and Virgil, for a big night out on Tracy Island.

They've got loads of Nazi stamps like this one in a case at the Hancock Museum in town; it's called the Motta Collection. They nearly all have pictures of Hitler on them, or SS storm-troopers standing next to very big swastikas. It's funny to think of people in Germany, when Hitler was around, sending out stuff like birthday cards and post-cards from their holidays saying daft things like "having a lovely time" and "wish you were here" and then putting stamps like these on them. Because there were lots of places in Hitler's Germany, like the camps Dad says Watergate saw at the end of the war, where even if they did let you send a postcard home to your mam and dad "wish you were here" isn't what you'd be writing.

I pick up the envelope and hold it in front of my eyes, so I can read the address again:

Rebecca,
Alter Strasse,
Bezirk Veiundzwanzig.
Wein.

I already knew Wein meant Vienna and I got out me old German dictionary from Mrs Chisum's class and looked up Bezirk Veiundzwanzig. District Twenty-Four is what that means. So, the address is:

Rebecca,
Alter Street,
District Twenty-Four,
Vienna.

What I need to do next, I reckon, is find out exactly where this District Twenty-Four is.

Chapter Five

I have these, what me mam called, Mucklestone Moments. When the Mucklestone Moments come everything gets difficult. The Mucklestone Moments are why I decided not to go back to school this September to take me A Levels. I had a really bad few weeks of them, a while back. And I couldn't do nothing except stare at me bedroom walls. I couldn't face going back because of them.

The reason Mam called them Mucklestone Moments is because of a big fair that comes to the Town Moor in Newcastle every year. It's called the Hoppings. Some people don't like it because they say its run by "Gypos" and "Pikeys" and, when they come to town, as well as selling dodgy toffee-apples and candy floss to all the little bairns, they nick stuff from people's houses, too. But me and Dad and Mam used to love it.

The Hoppings is massive. It can take you half an hour to walk from one end of it to the other and all the time you are walking you'll be passing dodgems and waltzers and hoop-la stalls, and that, with music playing dead loud and blokes shouting stuff like "Three balls to win a lovely coconut!"

Right near one of the main entrances are loads of gypsy caravans – they set up in the same place every year – where old women tell your fortune for a couple of quid. And next to them is a little tent with a few knackered old penny machines in it, that most people don't bother with.

One of them is an old-fashioned Victorian machine called Lord Mucklestone, The Fabled Visionary. If you roll ten pence down the slot, this Mucklestone will read your future. He's basically a big metal model of a head and shoulders who wears a purple-velvet suit, a monocle, and a turban. All encased in a big stand made of wood and glass. When you roll the ten pence brass band music begins to play and Lord Mucklestone's eyes roll back in his skull a few times. Then his monocle starts to move up and down three times and he talks in dead posh old-fashioned voice. "What! What! What!" he says. "Destiny calling!" After that, a little card will drop into a slot at the bottom of the machine. The card has stuff written on it like:

Future is: Most definitely delightful.
Or:
Future is: As rosy as the roses in Eden's garden.

When I was a bairn, I would stand in front of the Lord Mucklestone machine and I would ask it, in me head, if I'd be an astronaut or a famous scientist. One time, when I did that, the little card said Most certainly celestial and I got dead excited. But, another time, when I was about eight, the card said Perilous! All that you love must one day fade away, and, once I read it, I just started bubbling and holding on to me mam's hand. She said I was having a Mucklestone Moment and, after that, whenever I was dead sad or down in the dumps, she'd say that. So, in our family, Mucklestone Moments, as a name for me bad worrying days, just stuck.

Even little things like getting out of bed or brushing me teeth seem like great big giant tasks when the Mucklestone Moments come. Everything I think of seems like a really bad thing. Like each thought is a little stab inside me head. Like someone's come in the night and cut me brain out and put a giant pin cushion in there instead.

I think of me mam being dead and STAB goes a worry pain. I think of Dad trying to whistle on the morning of Mam's wake and not being able to do it and STAB another one slashes down at the little sad me that's hiding inside me Martian-red head.

I think of me and I feel like nothing.

I think of me and I feel all the pins in the giant pin cushion crushing down towards the centre of me brain. All I can see is me white skin and spotty face. All I can see is me standing up in class and the other kids all laughing. All I can see is Blue Tear and Bino dragging me up towards the edge of the PE block roof. And the thing is when the Mucklestone Moments are in me head I know they are right to do it. Because I didn't fit in with them and the other kids. That's why Blue Tear and Bino called me Sir Isaac.

I don't fit in at the post office either. Not really. I can feel some of the blokes on the sorting looking at me a bit funny, already. I didn't even fit in with me mam and me dad, though I know they loved me plenty. Sometimes, on the last two lots of Mucklestone Moments days, I just started walking; trying not to think about nasty stuff.

It doesn't work. I keep ending up here, in the same place I am now. Standing on the edge of the curb on Scrogg Road where me mam last stood, on the day she was run over. Why did she have to have the middle cheese plate? Why not the small plate? Why not the big 'un? And then I wonder where she is.

I know what science would say but on Mucklestone Moments days, like this one, I get sick of everything, even science. All I can think about is how much I want her to be somewhere. Then I think that, perhaps, if I step into the road in front of me, just like she did, it would be a kind of experiment. An experiment that would make some of the top names in science – people like Sir Isaac and Gregor Mendel – think I'd done them proud. I might get the Noble Prize for an experiment like that. But, the most important thing would be, if she is some place, I'd be able to go there and be with her.

"Nothing trembles here."

That line from the W.S letter comes into me head again. I don't know where they mean by "here," this W.S, but, wherever it is, I'd really like to go there.

NOTHING TAKES ME MIND OFF ME WORRIES ON THE Mucklestone Moments days more than book selection. Book selection is one of me favourite things ever. Some days, I can walk around the shelves in the library for hours before I find something that I haven't read already which really takes me fancy, like. But today is different. I knew exactly what book I wanted to have a look at before I came.

Now I've got me head full of the architecture of Wien. The architecture of Vienna, in fact, from a big green book called Vienna, History and Culture by G.F. Brookburn, which I've looked at a couple of times before, when I've been here, but never really read properly.

There's a big old church in Vienna, apparently, that's called the Ruprechtskirche. It's the oldest religious place there. There's a palace too, which looks dead grand called Schonbrunn which has something in it called a Tiergarten. When I look it up in the index at the back, this Tiergarten turns out to be a zoo. The oldest zoo in the world; built about 350 years ago. I really like that fact. The oldest zoo in the world! I'm not mad keen on animals but I like zoos. All the animals there are safe behind cages and you can get a good close look at what Charles Darwin called their evolutionary attributes.

Next to an old black-and-white picture of a sad-looking monkey in the Tiergarten is one of a grand building from the nineteenth century. The caption underneath it says Universitäts-Sternwarte Observatory completed in 1879. I'm dead excited when I see that picture because it's a place I've heard of before. The Observatory in Vienna is famous because it used to house the biggest refracting telescope in the world. A twenty-seven-inch lens made by the Grubb Telescope Company in Dublin. There's lots of better places now but once upon a time there's was no better place in the world to stare up at Mars than the Universitäts-Sternwarte Observatory.

I take the Rebecca envelope out of the pocket of me Levi's jacket and lay it on the page of the book; next to the picture of the observatory. I take the letter out of the envelope and put it, still half-folded, on the table next to the book.

I push me little finger under the corner of the page and lift it a little bit. I see a header on the page underneath that says Districts of Vienna. Perfect! I read the address on the letter for what must be the hundredth time:

Rebecca,
Alter Strasse,
Bezirk Veiundzwanzig.

Wein.

There's a whole chapter on these districts. Vienna is completely split into them, same as Newcastle's got different areas like Walker, Jesmond and Gosforth. These Vienna bezirke sound posher than places in Newcastle, though. They're all called exotic things like Neubau, Penzing and Simmering. But I notice something really odd straightaway – there are only twenty-three bezirke; twenty-three of these districts.

This G.F. Brookburn is dead clear about that.

There is no district twenty-four.

Me head's still spinning when I look up and see a fat middle-aged bloke talking to the librarian at the front desk.

It's Watergate.

To be honest, I'm surprised to see him. The only thing I've ever seen him read before is the racing tips in the Sporting Life, the Sun's page 3, or Modelling Monthly, a hobby magazine for people who like to build models in their spare time.

Watergate walks quickly down the aisle of the library and stops at one of the rows of book shelves near the B section, where I took the Brookburn book from about twenty minutes ago. He looks dead flustered. A bit upset, like. He bends down and starts running his hands through some of the books on the middle shelf. I'm thinking I should shout out to him but this is the library. "Quiet please" is the rules. So, I say nowt.

Then it hits me! Interfering with the Queen's mail! That's what I'm doing now. I mean, like I say, I'm going to take this letter back. I was going to do it the very next day, after I took it home. But, then, I just wanted to find out a bit more about it. I'll probably do it tomorrow now, or maybe Friday at the latest. Right now, technically though, I'm interfering with the

Queen's mail. I could get into real big trouble at the post office if Watergate sees me. I need to get out of here fast.

I stand up and slip me jacket back on. As I do, I let go of the page I'm holding and, because it's a big book, all the pages fall forward towards the front-cover. The book makes a flat thumping sound when it closes, which, because the library's dead quiet, sounds like an explosion.

I look up, expecting to see Watergate walking towards me. But, when I do, there's no one there.

I kneel down behind the library table, as if I'm picking a pencil up off the floor. Looking around very slowly, a bit like James Bond, I can just see the worn-out knees of Watergate's shiny suit pants through the gap.

Now's me chance!

I grab the half-folded letter off the table and leg it.

I walk dead fast down Scrogg Road, towards our house. I want to make sure I can get as much distance as I can between me and Watergate. I pat the pocket of me pants to make sure the W.S letter is in there. It is.

I feel a tight, sick, tug in me belly.

Bollocks!

I've left the envelope inside the Vienna book in the library.

Chapter Six

I stick out me hand and the yellow bus begins to slow down. It says Haymarket on the front of it but me and dad know it should say something else. Something in Latin, like Olympus Mons, because today the 72 bus from Scrogg Road to the Haymarket via Battle Hill has been changed into a Martian voyager. Them funny Latin words is what scientists use for naming the geography of Mars.

We go up top because me dad wants to light up a Benson and Hedges. He doesn't smoke much, does Dad, but he's always had one or two on Sundays; along with a few pints of Fed Special at the club. That's because Dad calls Sundays "Bob Bunion's day of rest." What he means by that is no post gets delivered on Sundays so he can put his feet up.

Me mam loved going places on the bus. She used to tap me on the shoulder all the time, and point at stuff out of the window. Like the massive pink-coloured metal cranes at Swan Hunter shipyards, she called them "Geordie Flamingos," or a field near the Coast Road where her and Annie, mam's best friend when she was a bairn, used to make necklaces out of daisies and write love notes to Clark Gable.

Dad shuffles up in his seat and starts doing what he always does – whistling the theme tune from Sportsnight as he reads the football bits of his News of the World – and I start doing what I always do – chewing on some treacle-toffee, and looking out of the window.

Like me and mam used to do.

Today, I can see little lads chasing each other on their Raleigh Chopper bikes and little lasses playing with clackers. There's a few teenage lasses, too; walking along in daft platform boots and tartan scarves and hats. These lasses are all fans of a Scottish band called the Bay City Rollers. They go to concerts and shout stuff like "Les, Les, marry me, Les," to the singer. Then scream so loud they can't hear him sing owt. Me Uncle Frank says, "That's probably for the best, anyways."

I take another sticky bit of treacle toffee out of the white paper bag and stuff it in me gob. Not far now.

The other thing I like doing, when I'm sitting on the bus, is thinking. And the only thing that's on me mind today is that envelope. I left it a couple of hours yesterday, just to be on the safe side, then I went back to the library. But I couldn't find it. I couldn't find the Vienna book either. Someone must have taken it out with the envelope still inside it.

Now, I really have interfered with the Queen's mail because I can't take that letter back to the post office in the same condition as what it was in when I found it. But, let's be honest, surely this W.S – the person who put it in the post-box – must have realised this Rebecca was never going to get it, unless this W.S is a bit doolally tap, or something.

I mean, with no street number on it and the name of a district that doesn't exist, they must have known it had no chance of ever getting there. They've got things at the post office to help with that sort of thing. Like if someone's got very bad handwriting, or they've missed the postcode off. But with just a name you've got no chance. There must be a whole lot of Rebeccas in the world. And that letter could be written to any single one of them.

AFTER ABOUT TEN MORE MINUTES, THE BUS PULLS UP AT THE top of the Haymarket next to a big metal statue of a woman with wings that's been put in front of the Civic Centre to make everyone remember all the blokes from Newcastle who got killed in the First World War. Me and me dad get off.

Next to the library, The Hancock Museum, on the other side of the road, is the place I like the best. Mam and Dad used to bring me here when I was a real little bairn to look at the stuffed animals and old birds' eggs. They did that for me, Mam and Dad, because they were never that interested in facts and museums, like what I am. It was the pictures and bingo and dancing that they always liked. Me dad did like one stuffed animal though. It was a big, moth-eaten, beardy old buffalo. He said it reminded him of me Uncle Frank's "extremely embarrassing nostril hair," and we all laughed about that together.

I did a trip here once with the school, when I was about eleven or twelve or something, and it was the best trip we ever did. Miss Jimson, the teacher, kept shouting out questions to the class as we went round – stuff like what's the Latin name for Ostrich – Stuthio Camelus, if you're interested – and what did the Egyptian's use to mummify bodies; which isn't bitumen, like a lot of people say, but palm oils and sawdust, and stuff like that.

Well, every question she asked I put me hand straight-up and got the answer right. For some of them, I could even tell her exactly what was on the little white card stuck on the case for that particular exhibit – word for word, like, because I'd been to the museum so many times before. When she asked about Bakt-hor-Nekht – the mummy on the second floor – I put me hand up and said, "Mummified body of female Egyptian from Old Period, discovered in the Nile Delta by Sir Aldred Philpott circa 1921." Exactly what was on the card.

I even told the class about a famous mummy in the British Museum that the dead posh archaeologists there had nicknamed Ginger because it's got red hair and everybody in the whole class laughed. Not in a bad way for a change. A good one.

There's loads of interesting stuff in the Hancock like exotic birds' eggs from all over the world, a giant stuffed Great White Shark that hangs in the Victorian hall stairway, and the Motta Collection of stamps.

I've got a special way that I usually do of walking around the museum starting with popping upstairs to say hello to Bakt-hor-Nekht and ending with the big shark. Once I've done that three or four times, I go for a Fairy Cake in the little café they've got here. Mostly Fairy Cakes, anyways, but occasionally I like to go mad and have something different. On them days, I have a Tunnock's teacake instead.

Dad usually just goes to the café straightway and reads his paper or, if he doesn't fancy that, he goes straight to the stuffed animals section and has good laugh at the buffalo.

Today's not a usual sort of day, though.

We're forgetting about Bakt-hor-Nekht and Fairy Cakes

thing. Doesn't even look like it's got decent spot welding on it. They'd be better off making it down the shipyards on the Tyne. Give some of them welders at Swan Hunter a job like that and they'd turn out a proper spaceship. That little thing looks like it would lift in a high wind; like the deckchairs at Whitley Bay when it's pissing down.'

Dad offers me his hand to shake.

'You're a week a postman already, Billy Quiz, so I'll bet you your first months' wages, son, that this bit of Alcan foil stuck together with candy-floss sticks never makes it.'

I don't take his hand.

'You're not betting against me, Dad. You're betting against science. The best science brains in the world are working on Viking 1. Blokes who know everything about gravity and relativity and stuff like that because they're spent their whole lives reading up on Sir Isaac Newton and Albert Einstein, just like I have.'

Dad turns starts walking a bit further down the tunnel. Then he turns around. I can see that he's laughing.

'Albert who? Billy Quiz. Sir Isaac, what? I've studied the classics meself – Elvis, Jean Vincent, Little Richard; you'll find them great sages all agree. Gravity and relativity aren't the things that the stick the universe together, son. It's love that does that.'

ME AND DAD HAVE BEEN IN THE PAPIER-MÂCHÉ TUNNEL FOR about twenty minutes now.

It's got ten countdown numbers on it. So, the model of the launch pad is number 1 and number 2 is the moon and number 3 is loads of information about our galaxy, The Milky Way, and it carries on like that. All these information stops come with models and pictures and bits of taped sound that are supposed to reflect points on the route, that Viking 1 must go along as it travels to Mars.

It doesn't make any scientific sense because obviously they only do the countdown when the rocket is taking off. When the real journey starts the countdown is finished. I think the people who have designed the exhibition are using something called artistic licence. What that basically means is that rather than concern themselves with the facts – like they should be doing – they have just decided to make stuff up because they think more people will come and see it.

The facts they are using are a bit rubbish as well. Just basic bits and pieces like Viking's average orbital speed is 1.002km and the longitude of its ascending node being one revolution every 18.6 km.

Basic stuff, I already knew.

Normally, even though I know lots of this stuff already, I would do each number one at a time; read everything and then move on. But, today, for what is definitely the only time in me life, I can't wait to get to the end of an exhibition.

I rush past Dad, who's reading the card for number 5, and walk quickly towards the end of the tunnel. I step out of the semi-darkness.

And there it is – the surface of Mars!

OK, it's only about twenty-foot by twenty-foot and has two red rocks and a small crater about the size of the sand-pits they have for the little bairns at school but the way they've done the lights and that – two big ones stuck on the ceiling, one on each side, with red filters on them that cast lots of spooky shadows, and with the music they've got playing that sounds a bit like the tunes they play on Dr Who just before a

Dalek is about to come around the corner...Well, to me, it's amazing.

I step a bit closer to the edge of the display. There's a big sign next to it that says PLEASE DO NOT STEP ON THE MARTIAN SURFACE. What I want to do, right now, more than anything else in the world, is exactly the opposite of that.

Stepping out onto the Martian surface is something I've wanted to do since I was a little bairn. It all comes from one day when me mam showed me some funny glasses that she kept in a drawer in her bedroom next to her hairclips and Elnett hairspray, after I'd been reading a big picture book me dad brought me from the library about Mars.

They were cardboard glasses with red plastic lenses that people in the 1950s used to watch 3D films with. I'd never seen anything like them. Her and Dad got them on their honeymoon when Mam's dad paid for them to go to London for a night, and stay in a dead posh hotel called the Holiday Inn. There was a pink ticket stub with them too. I can still see the writing on it. It said: Admit One Odeon Leicester Square, Grand Circle 1s 6d.

Mam sat on her bed and put one pair of the glasses on and then put the other pair on me.

"Here, our Billy," she said, "let's try these magic glasses and everything will look red, it'll feel just like we're looking through a spaceman's visor and walking around Mars, like the astronaut in that book you're reading."

I know it sounds daft now but I was only six and when I put them glasses on a big tingle went up me back, into me neck and all the way into me eyes and ears. Right away, everything in me mam and dad's bedroom went dead red. When that happened, just for a moment, I really felt like I'd stepped out amongst the stars. Stepped out on Mars.

Mam started laughing and came up close to me and pressed her nose next to mine and gave me a kiss, which felt weird, as she looked all red, and was wearing them glasses too.

It was dead funny seeing her like that. Because normally me mam was really nice looking. Everyone in Walker said that. Not just me and me dad. Some people used to call her "Lena Turner," after the blonde-haired film star Lana Turner. She really did look a canny bit like her.

In real life, she worked on the Pick 'n' Mix sweets counter in Woolworth's, and not many film stars do that, but she had the same thing film stars have got, I reckon. When she went places people – not just blokes, lasses as well – would turn their heads and look at her. Even when she was dead old, in her thirties and that.

She wasn't wearing any makeup on that day with the 3D glasses. She wasn't dressed up or owt. Her hair was up, in silver plastic rollers, and she had a plastic Larn Yersel' Geordie pinny on, but, now, when I think about me mam, which I do nearly every day, I always think about her sitting on that bed with them daft cardboard glasses on, laughing.

"You know what the best thing about these glasses is, our Billy?" she said. "They're what people call rose-tinted. Rose-tinted means when you put on glasses like these you don't see the world as it is anymore. No, when you're wearing rose-tinted glasses you see it how you want it to be. Just how you'd like it! When you're wearing them, you get to make not just the world, the whole universe if you fancy it, pet, be rose-tinted, so you can see it exactly how you'd like it to be..."

I STEP A LITTLE CLOSER TO THE MARTIAN SURFACE. THE model, even though it's full-size, is not much more sophisticated than the little one near the start of the tunnel, that Dad said was made out of Alcan foil and candy-floss sticks but in this red light and with the music, if I half close me eyes, it feels a bit like the real thing.

Like I'm actually standing next to it on the Martian surface.

I lean forward. I can just make out me face reflected in the foil on the side of the lander.

It looks ginger and spotty; same as it always does.

Then I see someone else reflected in the foil too. It's a Pakistani lass, about sixteen-years-old. She's plump with short purple spiky hair. She's got a big stud earring stuck through her nose and she's wearing leopard-skin pants with loads of holes in them. She's carrying a very large red papier-mâché rock. This lass steps straight over the guard rail and walks toward the Viking 1 lander leaving behind five Doc Marten boot prints in the fake Martian soil. She drops the rock next to the other two in the middle of the display, wipes some dust from her hands and then gives me a wide daft smile that's all white teeth and metal braces.

'Fecking Nora, it's Billy Quiz. How are you doing, donkey bollocks?'

Me dad steps out from end of the tunnel and looks at the weird lass standing on the Martian surface. He whistles a couple of lines from the Star Trek theme again.

'So, aliens do exist,' says me Dad.

'That's not an alien, Dad,' I say. 'That's Ninder Lally.'

42

I'VE NEVER BEEN THAT GOOD WITH FRIENDS AND THAT. MAM was me best one and she's dead. Ninder was me only real pal at school but we had a big falling out, about a dip-brained pseudo-hippy bloke called Afghan Larry. I haven't seen her since.

The other kids used to say Ninder was "bat-shit crazy." You can take it from me that there's no scientific evidence that conclusively proves the excrement of the mammal Chiroptera, your common bat, shows any particular signs of mental impairment when compared, in a controlled study, to any other form of shite. I'm fairly certain all your top psychiatrists, like Jung and Freud, will back me up on that one. All the kids meant, when they called her that, was that she's a bit of a one-off, I suppose.

We used to go to fireworks show on the fifth of November, up near Wallsend Sports Centre where one of the boiler-men from the shipyards would stick loads of Catherine Wheels up on a wooden fence with a nail-gun and then set them all off at the same time. That wall of Catherine Wheels used to remind me of the way Ninder Lally gassed on at the back of the class – lots of whizzing around in circles, loads of little colourful sparks and then a big explosion full of "feckings" and "bollocks" right at the end.

The first time I met her was in a chemistry lesson in school a couple of years ago when we were both in the third year. Her mam and dad had just moved across from Belfast, to be close to her Uncle Noor.

Mr Cartwright, the headmaster, a tall gangly bloke who most of the kids called LSP, which is short for lanky streak of piss, brought her in during the middle of the lesson and introduced her to Mr Tompkins, the chemistry teacher, right in front of the class. Mr Tompkins seemed a bit irritated at the time because he was holding some phosphorus in a jar that he was just about to expose to the air.

I liked her straightaway when I saw her. She had long dark hair, chubby arms and a pretty face. When LSP had gone, Mr Tompkins made a gesture for Ninder to take a seat. The only empty chair left was next to me. She came straight over and sat down.

'Budge up, donkey bollocks, or I won't be able to see nowt. This kid in front of me's got a heed the size of a mammoth's arsehole.'

I did as she said and budged up.

Mr Tomkins had been dead excited about doing experiments again that day because he'd only just had his chemistry supply cupboard restocked. It has been broken into a couple of months earlier and all his chemicals had been nicked. The teachers never found out who did it but all us kids knew it was Blue Tear and Bino.

He unscrewed the plastic top from a little glass container and emptied the phosphorus onto his gloved palm. It started smoking straight away. Then he dropped it onto his bench. It only took a couple of seconds before it began fizzing and popping.

The whole class were all oohing and ahhing and jumping back from the bench. They didn't understand, like I did, that phosphorus is very volatile and easily agitated, same as Italians can be sometimes over things like love and quarrels in the black-and-white films me mam used to watch.

Ninder didn't seem too impressed with it though. She dug me in the ribs with her ruler.

'What is it anyways?'

'Phosphorus, number 15 in the table of elements,' I whispered, 'it spontaneously combusts on contact with air.'

Ninder looked at me a bit funny when I said that. Then she grinned a gob full of braces at me.

'There's a word we did in Italian lessons at me last school in Bombay Street in Belfast. Word is simpatico. You heard of that?'

I nodded me head.

'Like minded, often together. It means that.'

She laughs.

'Course you have. "Number 15 in the fecking table of elements." Of course, you've heard of it.'

Mr Tompkins went back to the blackboard and started chalking up an equation to help explain. Ninder took out a book and pencil case that had a drawing of Bob Dylan on it and pulled out a couple of pens. I started making notes, too. Ninder wrote a word in biro on the cover of her chemistry text book. Then she showed me it:

Simpatico.

'I'm a lard-arse, half-Paki Paddy and you're a geeky ginger twat,' she whispered.

She stubbed a finger down on the word. I noticed the nails on one of her hands were painted green and on the other a very bright yellow. Then Ninder gave me a great big wink.

'Me and you kiddo – simpatico.'

Chapter Seven

Dad's gone off to the museum café because he's feeling hungry. Me and Ninder are sitting on a couple of orange plastic seats in front of the glass case that's got the buffalo in it. I was expecting her to be a bit funny with me, after last time, when we had that bust-up over Afghan Larry but as soon as me dad went she just started gassing-on at a million miles a minute, same as she always used to.

'Sorry, Ninder.'

'Sorry about what?'

'Your Uncle Noor. Him being dead and that. I read it in the paper, a while back. It was an accident, that's what The Chronicle said. An electrical fire, or something?'

Ninder shrugs.

'Nothing accidental about it. National Front, or some such toe-rags, them's the ones that did it, alright. I told everyone that. My mammy, my daddy, the coppers as well but not one of them wanted to listen. No one ever does listen to me. I always get the same: "Oh Ninder you're exaggerating. Oh, Ninder you're being a Drama Queen again."'

'You do exaggerate a bit, though. Remember when you thought you had cancer, because of that red mark on your neck, and it turned out to be a love bite you got from Davy Weavis?'

Ninder gets up from her seat. She walks up to the glass case and presses her nose against. I can see she's making daft faces at the buffalo.

'I might as well talk to this fecking hairy-arsed buffalo as talk to you, Billy Quiz,' she says. 'Because he knows what it's like to be persecuted. There used to be millions of them eating grass and that, all over the American plains. Now, most of them are stuck in glass cases in museums, like this poor bastard. I expect he's stinking in there too. It'll be years since they washed him. Bet all he dreams of every night is a big bottle of Silverkrin shampoo to give them tangled split-ends of his an almighty soaking. I'm not exaggerating this time, OK? Me and Mammy and Daddy stayed with Uncle Noor when we first moved here from Belfast, in the flat above his shop on Scrogg Road. It was a tight squeeze with the four of us, but he made it feel like a home, our home. One day, I was helping him in the shop. When it was time to put the metal shutter down outside, I could see he didn't want to do it in front of me. But, when he realised I wasn't going anywhere, he just shrugged and rolled it down. There was something sprayed on it.'

'What did it say?'

Ninder walks back across to where I am and sits down in the orange seat.

'"Pakis, fuck-off home!" That's what it said. Someone must have done it the night before. He'd seen it first thing in the morning, when he'd gone to roll the shutters up, but not said anything to the rest of us. There was other stuff too. One night, when I was behind the counter, a bloke in yellow riding boots, a sheepskin coat and a funny pork-pie hat, who'd had a few, came in and asked for to see my uncle. Noor wasn't in. So, I asked him what about and he said, "The usual, pet, tell him it's about the usual." But there was something about the way he said that made me think he was a piece of work, this fella.'

'What colour was his hat?'

She looks across at me and gives me the same kind of look she used to give the real thick kids at school when they didn't know any stuff about The Great Gatsby, or, To the Lighthouse, or any other of them, what she calls "proper books" that she reads a lot.

'Like I give a crap.'

'It wasn't purple, was it?'

'I can't remember.'

'It's just that there's a bloke called Jimmy Segs. Jimmy Knight is his real name but everyone calls him Jimmy Segs. He wears a hat like that, and it's usually purple. Me dad pointed him out to me in the Club, one time, and said he was "one to avoid." He runs a hot-dog van up at the Spanish City fun-fair, at the coast. He does the Hoppings as well, when it comes to the town moor. He's a real bad 'un, that's what me dad says.'

'He was a bit pissed, like I say. I didn't spend a lot of time chatting to him about what colour pork-pie hats were in fashion, down Scrogg Road, this season, or whether I fancied a hot-dog with onions. If that's alright with you?'

I look up at the buffalo again. Then back at Ninder.

'I know he's your uncle, Ninder, so you're bound to be upset and that, but I'm sure if Noor's fire was started on purpose that the coppers would have investigated it properly.'

'They didn't. As soon as they thought they could put it down to something electrical, they just did the paperwork, then and there, and pissed off. "Bigger fish to fry." That's what the sergeant said.'

'What about the insurance then? Didn't they have a proper look around?'

'There was a problem with the insurance.'

'A problem, how?'

Ninder looks down at her feet. Then turns back towards me.

'Turned out he didn't have any. He was in between companies or something.'

'In between companies, right.'

Ninder gets back out of her chair. She presses her face back against the glass of the case and pulls another couple of mad faces.

'You know what it's like, don't you, Buffalo? You know what it's like to be persecuted?'

From where I'm sitting, I can see most of her face reflected in the glass. Her expression changes. It becomes a bit more thoughtful, like.

She turns back around.

'I'm sorry too, Billy Quiz.'

'Sorry about what?' I say.

'About when we had that argument over that knob-head, Afghan Larry.'

I feel me cheeks go a bit red. I stand up and press me face to the glass of the case.

'So, you don't think I'm dead boring then? Always talking shite about science and that, like what you said?'

Ninder turns around so I can see her reflection in the glass again.

'You do talk shite about science and that. Always banging on about Boyle's Law and the Table of Elements, or whatever. I mean who gives a shit about all that bollocks, anyways?'

She taps on the glass of the case with her little finger, as if she thinks the buffalo is going to turn towards us.

'But Afghan Larry called you a loser and you're not that. I should have told him to feck-off when he said that and I didn't. That's what I'm sorry for. I'm sorry about that.'

I'M STANDING ON THE FIRST-FLOOR BALCONY WITH DAD AND Ninder staring at the big white shark. The three of us are all munching on a giant bag of Fairy Cakes that Dad has brought from the café.

The shark doesn't look as friendly as the buffalo. It's about fifteen-foot long, and hangs on chains from the roof of the main hall of the museum.

Me and Dad always like to stand at this particular spot because the shark has its mouth wide open with lots of sharp teeth on display and when I was a real little bairn me dad and mam would scream and shout and pretend that it was going to swallow the three of us together. It was scary but funny at the same time. If I shut me eyes, I can still see Mam's face all cracked and creased with laughing while we were doing it.

'Ponk rock?'

'Punk, it's punk, Mr Agnew. That's what the NME says anyways. It's a music revolution and I'm Newcastle's first revolutionary, if you like. A bit like Che Guevara, only with tits. Sorry, Mr Agnew, I mean boobs. Sex Pistols, The Clash, the Buzzcocks them's the bands for me these days.'

Me dad grabs a second Fairy Cake out of the bag and takes a small bite.

'The last time I saw you Ninder, pet, you had hair down to your arse; peace written on one arm and love on the other. It was only last year when I picked you and our Billy up from school.'

Ninder dips her fleshy brown arm into the bag and takes out a second cake, too.

'The way I see it is last year was last year and now is now, Mr A. I was all cheese-cloth shirts and Janis Joplin back in those days but after I read the NME, a few weeks ago, I decided that peace and hippies and all that was complete shite, so I went down to Flirt in the Handyside's Arcade and kitted meself out.'

Ninder steps back and give us a little twirl so we can get a better view of the holes she's ripped in the back of her leopard-skin trousers.

'I've given the cheese-cloth skirt to me mammy, so she can use it for dusters.'

Me dad doesn't look too impressed.

'I liked your hair the way it was, pet. I never even recognised you back there when we bumped into you on the Martian surface. How did you get a job here anyways?'

'Me mammy works here in the research department. They were late putting the Mars model up so she asked me to help out a bit over the summer. But I'm doing A Levels from September: English, Art and Sociology, at the big college on the Coast Road. I'm going to be a famous writer, or a famous rock star, or a famous journalist. Famous something, anyways. I can't quite decide which.'

Dad hands the bag of Fairy Cakes to Ninder. He always buys a big bag because he knows I like them so much and we usually take three or four home with us.

'You're already famous in Walker, Ninder, pet. Jesmond too, by now, I expect. There you go, help yourself.' He pats his stomach. 'Too much tea, I'm off for a slash.'

He heads in the direction of the Gents leaving me and Ninder and the great white shark alone together. Ninder nods in the direction of its huge gaping mouth lined with big sharp teeth.

'What's sharky eat?'

'Not much these days, I expect. He's been hanging there since 1958.'

Ninder smiles.

'Come on, brainbox, don't let me down?'

'Carcharodon Carcharias, the Great White Shark, feasts mainly on dolphins, porpoises and whales.'

Ninder delves her hand into the bottom of the paper bag and takes out two Fairy Cakes. She hands the bag to me, leans over the balcony and lobs one of the Fairy Cakes into the mouth of the shark.

Then she runs half-way down the stairs and lobs a second one. It bounces off the head of the shark and then drops twenty feet into the main hall of the museum. The red-lipped receptionist is walking through the passage carrying a tray with some tea-cups on it. A Fairy Cake falls from the sky and knocks her glasses off. She drops the tray. The teacups smash all over the place.

'I'm going straight to your mother, Ninder Lally,' shouts the receptionist.

Ninder flashes her a V sign, then sprints through the main

revolving door of the museum. A smaller door, right next to it, opens about ten seconds later.

Ninder sticks her head through it.

'Afghan Larry's an arse, Billy Quiz. A fecking hippy wombat.'

Chapter Eight

I rub some sleep out of me eyes and take another drink of PG Tips. I'm sitting with Dad in the main hall of the post office. It's four o'clock in the morning. Me and Dad are on Nights today. Which means I'm knackered.

Dad, Mrs Damoan, one of the supervisors, and a bunch of Facings women are all laughing and joking together about a Demis Roussos concert that's going to be on at the City Hall next week. Facings means they sort out all the letters into little piles with the addresses the right way up and then they hand them across to the proper sorters. The sorters use the addresses and a new thing, called a postcode, to put the mail in the right boxes. Then it gets sent out from the main post office to a local sub-post office for delivery. There's not many women who work at the main post office, either this one or Orchard Street. It's nearly all blokes. The women mostly do Facings, except a few who work behind the counters selling stuff like stamps and packets of lackey bands. Me dad says, that's the way it's always been at the Post office.

I see Watergate making his way towards me. This is the

first time I've seen him since that day in the library. He sits down and then points up at the picture of Hermes on the ceiling.

'You got me interested now, Billy Quiz. I was in Walker library last week, after visiting me sister. I hear you're a bit of a regular there yourself. Couldn't find the book I was looking for at first. So, I had a skim through an old encyclopaedia and looked your man up.'

There's something about Watergate's voice that's not nice when he says this. Like he's only pretending to be interested.

'He's playing with fire that's the way I see it. Your man Hermes is playing with fire.'

'That's Prometheus, Tommy. In the myths, Prometheus is the one who steals fire. It says so in this library book, Heroes of the Ancient World, that I read one day, when the one I wanted to get, about radio-active half-lives wasn't on the shel...'

Me voice trails off.

Watergate is staring really hard at me. Like he's trying to see right inside me, or something.He looks all around the main hall of the post office. Dad is still standing with the Facings' lasses. He's doing an impression of Demis Roussos for Mrs Damoan and they're all laughing.

Watergate leans in closer to me. I can smell his horrible breath. He's been eating Tudor pickled onion crisp again. But there's something else: a bit of whiskey stink, mixed in with the onions.

'He moved freely between the worlds of the mortal and the divine. That's what the encyclopaedia says. Not just a messenger but a conductor of souls into the afterlife. That's playing with fucking fire in my book. The way I see it, this

Hermes ought to learn to stop meddling and leave the afterlife to them that understand a bit more about it.'

Watergate reaches out slowly with his right hand and takes a hold of me arm. He fumbles around in one of the pockets of his grey postie's jacket with his left hand and then puts something on the table in front of me.

It's the empty envelope from the W.S letter.

'Lost something while you were there did you, Billy Quiz?' he says. 'I found that on the table you'd been sitting at. That's the Queen's mail, son. That's what that is. A person could go to prison for stealing that.'

I feel me face start to go dead red.

'I don't know what you mean, Tommy.'

Watergate's right hand squeezes a little harder. It's beginning to hurt. He takes the envelope back off the table with his left hand and stuffs it back in his pocket. Then he leans a little closer towards me so I get a proper blast of his pickled onion and whiskey stink-breath.

'See, son, what you don't understand is that letter was meant for me. I know there must be a letter. "Dear Rebecca, ich sehe sie," is how, I'm guessing, that letter started. So, here's what we're going to do. I'll give you a couple of days to get me back my letter, and if I don't get it I'm going straight to one of the top gaffers to tell them what I seen at the library.'

Dad sits down with a bang. He's got a big grin on his face. Watergate lets go of me wrist.

Dad starts whistling: Forever and Ever by Demis Roussos.

'Alright, Tommy lad,' says Dad to Watergate.

'Never better, Bobby son, never better. Me and your daft bollocks of a lad, here, were just discussing Greek mythology.'

Chapter Nine

I haven't been sleeping dead well for the last couple of nights since I talked to Watergate. I don't know why he wants this W.S letter, or how he knew that the start of it would say: Dear Rebecca, ich sehe sie, and that but I made up me mind last night that I wasn't going to give it to him. I mean, if I've interfered with the Queen's mail then so has he –by keeping a hold of that envelope and not handing it straight in to one of the gaffers. He mightn't get the sack but he'd definitely get into trouble about it. And I heard one of the lasses, who works in Facings, say the bosses were already fed up with him because of his drinking. Me and him, we might get booted out of the post office together.

Me alarm clock starts ringing. I told Ninder I'd meet her in the Handysides Arcade in town this morning because I've got a day off. I wish I hadn't now because I'm still knackered but she was dead insistent. Like she always is.

THE KARD BAR IN THE HANDYSIDES ARCADE IS A PLACE ALL the local kids love coming to. Especially on Saturday mornings, like today. This is where they get their posters of all the big pop-stars like Olivia Newton John, rock-bands like Hawkwind and Deep Purple, or movie stars like Clint Eastwood or Farah Fawcett Majors.

I don't really come here much meself. They do stock one poster of Albert Einstein; where he's got mad white hair and is sticking his tongue out, but that's about it as far as your great mathematicians and physicists are concerned.

I ignore the posters and push past a rack of Afghan coats so I can go right to the back of the shop. There's a wooden trestle-table there that has rows and rows of metal badges arranged in cardboard boxes on it. I pick up a yellow badge that reads I'M LIKE YOU, ONLY BETTER to have a good look at it. Then I feel a tap on me shoulder.

'Alright, Billy Quiz.'

I turn round so I can get a proper look at Ninder. She's wearing some weird lime green T shirt with loads of holes ripped in it, that's got a picture of some dark-haired, wasted-looking, lass on it with the name Patty Smith written underneath her, and a tartan kilt that's held together by an enormous safety pin. Her hair's not purple anymore though. Now it's orange. She's holding something in her right hand. It's a metal cage with a little brown furry thing running around inside it.

'A present.'

'For who?'

She shakes the cage up and down gently and then holds it out straight in front of me. The brown furry thing runs around and around at a scary pace.

'Who do you think, kiddo? I got it from the pet shop on the other side of the arcade.'

'Mam says I'm allergic to pets. She used to say that anyways.'

'It's a gerbil. Everyone likes gerbils.'

Ninder takes me hand and closes it around the metal handle of the cage. Then she walks up to a tall pretty lass in a yellow-and-white cheese-cloth shirt who's serving behind the counter. I just stare into the cage. The gerbil scurries into the corner and I can see its pink nose is twitching a lot. The pretty lass gives Ninder a real snotty look; right up and down, like.

'Can I help you, love?'

'I'm here for Johnny Rotten.'

'Johnny who?'

'Rotten.'

'Never heard of him. We've got a poster of Johnny Morris who presents Animal Magic on the BBC. Will that do.?'

Ninder turns around and points to the wall of the shop that has all the posters on it that the teenage lasses usually buy.

'You can't move in here for Donny Osmonds and David Cassidys and them Bay City nonces with their daft scarves and pointy haircuts, but not a single poster of the man who invented punk rock. That's complete shite.'

Ninder gives the posh lass a snotty look. Then she turns around and walks back towards me and points at the gerbil.

'He's for thinking.'

'Thinking?'

'Yeah, helping you think. You're a thinker, about science and that. I am too, but knowing stuff about Oscar Wilde and Albert Camus isn't going to be much help for the kind of thinking me and you need to do.'

'What do you mean, "me and you?"'

Ninder leans over to the tray of badges and picks up a little red and yellow one. The slogan on it says BOLLOCKS TO

EVERYTHING. She pins it on her lime-green T-shirt and admires herself in a standing mirror that's fixed to the wall.

'It's a concentration pet. So, obviously, soon as I saw it, I thought of you'

'A concentration pet?'

'That James Bond villain's got one. You know, what's his name? Blowhard.'

'Blofeld. His name's Blofeld.'

'Yeah, him. Well, he's got that concentration cat that he's always scratching and stroking when he's thinking about stuff. I thought you could do with one as well.'

'But this isn't a cat. It's a gerbil?'

Ninder takes the cage out of me hand and rests it on top of a wooden table. We both stare hard at the gerbil, who starts digging into the sawdust at the bottom of his cage near a little round wheel that's attached to the wall so he can run round and round and do exercises on it, and that.

'He's got fur. You can still stroke him, can't you?'

I press me face to the bars. When he sees me big spotty face this close up he runs straight across to the other side of his cage.

'What is it you want me to think about?'

Ninder takes me by the arm and leads me out of the shop back into the little street that curves around the Handysides Arcade. She's still wearing the BOLLOCKS TO EVERY-THING badge even though she hasn't paid for it.

'Same thing I've been thinking about for the last few days, Billy Quiz. Same thing me and you were talking about next to the Martian surface back at the museum – who the killed me Uncle Noor?'

I'M SITTING ON THE BUS GOING BACK TO WALKER WITH Ninder Lally and me new concentration gerbil. There's an old lady opposite us with blue-rinse hair and a white hat with a hat-pin on it who can't stop staring at Ninder's orange bonce, and Ninder's T-Shirt, and Ninder's badge that says BOLLOCKS TO EVERYTHING. I can feel I've gone all red in the face. Just being the person who's sitting next to Ninder Lally has made me do that.

The bus comes to a stop on the Coast Road near an old 1920s-style factory that isn't open anymore but where people used to make Wills Cigarettes. Ninder leans forward and taps an orange finger nail on the bars of the cage.

Then she points at the gerbil.

'Got it,' she says.

'Got what?'

'His name.'

'Look, Ninder, I don't like pets. I'm allergic to them like I told you. I don't care whether he's got a name or not. I don't want to take him home. I don't need to do any thinking anyway. I mean, I'm really sad about Uncle Noor but if the coppers think it was an electrical fault that caused the fire that killed him then they're probably right about that.'

'That's what I used to think.'

'Well, then.'

'For ten months I did think that but then, last week, I bumped into Mrs Hibbitt with the ear wax who used to go into Uncle Noor's shop most days for ten Players and a Daily Mirror.'

The bus starts up again and moves away from the stop. I can see the old lady staring hard at Ninder's badge.

I point at it.

'You should have paid for that.'

Ninder looks down at the badge and then back at me again.

'It says "bollocks to everything." The way I see it is if you're selling a badge that says that, one of the things people will be saying "bollocks" to is handing over twenty pence for a little tin-pot piece-of-shit badge.'

She opens the cage and takes out the gerbil. Then she leans forward and shows the little animal to the old lady with the white hat.

'Nazis killed me Uncle Noor,' she says to the lady. 'That's what Mrs Hibbitt with the ear wax says anyways and I believe her. She said she'd seen a couple of blokes hanging round the shop the week before it went up in flames. One of them had a tin of spray-paint. Same bastards who sprayed on me uncle's door, I reckon.'

The old lady takes a copy of the Daily Mail out of her handbag. Then she unfolds it big, in front of her face, so Ninder can't talk to her anymore.

Ninder sits back in her seat. She holds out her hands and offers the gerbil to me. I shake me head. The last thing I want to do is touch it.

'Archimedes, that's what I'm thinking,' says Ninder.

'Archimedes of Tyro? You want me to call a gerbil after the man who invented the screw and the floatation tank. No, I won't do it. It would be disrespectful to the whole of science calling a daft gerbil something like that.'

'Not him. What he said when he had that idea and jumped out the bath.'

'Eureka.'

'Yeah, that.'

The bus turns the corner and comes to another stop near the bottom of Scrogg Road. I get up and put the cage with the gerbil in it on the empty seat I've just got up from.

'I don't believe there are Nazis living in Walker. Not real ones. Not in 1976. If the police say it was an electrical fault, I mean they've got special teams, them and the fire department. Special teams of people whose job it is to work out stuff like that.'

Ninder looks down at the cage.

Then back up at me.

'I already told you they'd didn't do it properly didn't I? They didn't fetch any fecking special teams to me uncle's shop because they had "bigger fish to fry," that's what the sergeant said. I heard him tell me daddy that himself. Well, piss off then, Billy Quiz. I'll just have to do all the thinking myself.'

I go all red in the face again. Then I turn and start walking down the aisle of the bus. I have to wait for the old lady with the hat to get off in front of me. As I'm waiting, I can hear Ninder talking loudly into the cage on the seat beside her.

'Eureka, that's your name, isn't it? What better name could there be for a fecking concentration gerbil than that?'

Chapter Ten

Sometimes, I like me dad's whistling. Sometimes, he does it too much.

Tonight is one of the too-much nights.

He's been non-stop Demis Roussos songs ever since we got back from work. First, there was one called Far Away. Then, an hour or so of Auf Wiedersehen and, after that, for the last hour and a half, at least, one called Forever and Ever. It's doing me head in.

He keeps going into his room and putting a shirt on and then coming downstairs in just his underpants and the shirt and looking at himself from the front and side. Then he goes back upstairs and puts another shirt on. Comes back down and takes a look and then goes back up again. He's also spent about half an hour in the bathroom putting his hair a bit funny with a centre-parting, instead of a side one, by spraying loads of Cossack hair spray on it. The smell is really thick and keeps catching in me throat, when it comes down the stairs in wafts.

I can't understand why he's getting all excited about going to daft concert by an enormous fat Greek bloke who walks around in a giant white smock all the time – looking like he's just woken up on a camp site in the middle of the night and stuck his head through the top of his tent by accident.

He's never even been interested in Demis Roussos before. Him and Mam never liked stuff like that. But yesterday, he came back from an old record shop called Windows, near Grey's monument in the middle of town, with two Demis Roussos LPs in a brown paper bag. Then he stayed up late playing them over and over again.

I'm sitting in the living room watching Peter Woods read the BBC news on the telly. There's a lot of stuff about people in Poland maybe going on strike because the government's put up the price of sugar.

I hear Dad come down the stairs again. He comes into the living room and does a bit of twirl in front of me. This time, he's got his suit pants and jacket on. It's a new suit.

'What do you think?'

'It's purple velvet?'

'Purple velvet's in fashion, son. That's what Brenda says, anyways.'

'Brenda?'

Dad looks down at his feet.

'I've been meaning to say something, son.'

There's a ring on the door.

You can always tell our doorbell because Dad sent away to a place called Memphis in America for a funny one. It plays Blue Suede Shoes by Elvis Presley.

The bell goes again. Dad walks out of the living room.

Mrs Damoan, the supervisor from the post office, is standing on our front step. She's got a leopard-skin dress on, and red high heels. I can smell her perfume really strong; even from where I'm standing. She must have put half the bottle on.

'Brenda love, you look lovely,' says Dad.

I go back into the living room and slam the door behind me.

WHEN MRS DAMOAN AND ME DAD FINALLY GO, I GET UP AND turn off the telly. Then I walk through into the kitchen and sit down at the little wooden table.

Next to the Daddies sauce and Heinz Ketchup in the middle of it are two Fred and Wilma Flintstone salt and pepper pots. I won them for Mam at the Hoppings, one time. It was on a day when me dad came down the Helter-Skelter all the way from the top singing "It's now or never," by Elvis Presley and when he reached the bottom loads of people stood around and clapped. Mam told him he'd had "one too many bottles in the Comrades," but I could tell she liked it really.

Then Mam gave me five pounds because she'd been working overtime on the Pick 'n' Mix and let me go on all the stuff I liked. There were loads of exciting things you could see at the Hoppings.

Near where the Lord Mucklestone machine usually was, there were a few Hoop-La stands where you pay 20p and get three goes at hooping a prize with a white hoop. The prizes are all stuck to the top of big orange bricks or jars; things like Top Cat Alarm Clocks, strange Action Men that have been made in Hong Kong called names like Bobby Bullet and other littler stuff – jars of sweets or cans of cheap beer, called Double Diamond.

When we were passing one of the Hoop-La stands, I saw right in the middle of the stand, under a big orange spotlight, these Fred

Flintstone and Wilma salt and pepper pots. Dad always used to say that Mam used to a look a bit like Wilma because she had the same shape hair. Even though Mam's was blonde, like Lana Turner's, and Wilma's is red, like mine. So, when I saw the pots, I was mad keen to win them for her. I spent all me five pounds trying to get them but had no luck. Then Dad gave the bloke another 20p and, on me last go, I got the hook over Fred's big hair, which had been the really tricky part, and hooked him and his Mrs up.

I lean across the table and pick up the pepper-pot. It's a bit chipped now because it's five years ago since we got it. Wilma's ponytail has cracked off the back and one of her feet is missing. Her smile is still all nice and pretty though.

I put the pepper-pot in me pocket and walk upstairs.

I go into me bedroom and take out the box with Arrows of Tonto written on it. I put Wilma inside, next to some of me other precious things. Then I pick up the half-folded W.S letter, spread it out on me bed and start reading it again.

"Dear Rebecca, ich sehe sie," repeated twice. Could this Rebecca and this W.S be German? It would make sense but, in that case, why write the rest of the letter in English. Maybe the German bit is some sort of code? Maybe, Ninder was right about that daft stuff she said at about Nazis being in Walker after all, maybe it really does make sense.

There's a noise down stairs. Blue Suede Shoes is playing again. I go to me window and pull back the curtains. A man is standing next to our front door. He's got a can of Tartan Special in his right hand and is looking a bit unsteady on his feet. It's Watergate.

He bangs on our front door with his fists and then bends down and shouts through the letterbox.

'I want it, Billy Quiz. I know you've got me letter.'

I step right back from the curtain and let it fall back into place. There's no way I'm going to open our front door to him.

I stare down at the letter.

Dear Rebecca, Ich sehe sie.

I remember what Watergate said at the post office about how he knew that it would say that.

That's when I realise…

There must be other letters like this one. The only way that Watergate could have guessed this W.S letter starts, just like it does, saying: Dear Rebecca, Ich sehe sie, is if he's already seen another letter exactly like it.

Chapter Eleven

I didn't open the door for Watergate last night. I just lay on the floor of me bedroom where he couldn't see me, thinking about the red Hitler stamp on the letter and what Ninder said about Nazis. He kept ringing the doorbell, and knocking and shouting for about ten minutes but then he went away again.

It's hot today, same as yesterday. As I walk down Ninder's street, me face has gone all sweaty. Me Uncle Frank says there are two types of people who live in Jesmond, where she lives. Lentil eaters – teachers, social workers and students – is what he means by that. They live in normal terraced houses, same as the ones that are built in Walker and Wallsend. That's the first type.

Then, there's what Auntie Irene, Uncle Frank's wife, calls "all-fur-coat-and-no-knickers, sorts" – doctors, solicitors, people who own their own businesses. That's what she means by that. They live in dead posh streets with big houses on them.

This Lilly Avenue, Ninder's street, is kind of in the middle of them two types. The houses are quite big but not massive. They're been built with old grey bricks in the Edwardian days. Ninder and her mam and dad came here after they moved out of her Uncle Noor's flat on Scrogg Road, where they lived for a bit, after they first moved to Newcastle. Mr Lally, her dad, is a captain in the Pakistani merchant navy. That's how him and Mrs Lally met.

I pop me head over the gate at the side of Ninder's house and look into her garden. I see her straightaway. She's wearing her Dr Martens boots, a black bra and a big pair of white knickers which have the word Tuesday stitched on them in red. She's lying back in a purple kid's paddling pool which has Sploosh Family Robinson written on the side of it in luminous pink. Her left hand's holding a bottle of Mazola cooking oil and she's spreading lots of it on her chubby brown belly. In the hot June sunshine, her dark skin's gone all shiny, like the Saturday-morning fried eggs at the Top Notch Café down Worswick Street.

There is a blue-and-white striped deck-chair next to the paddling pool, on which she's put a red plastic transistor radio and a book that people were talking about in the papers a lot a few years ago – The Female Eunuch. It's written by a woman called Germaine Greer, who's what's called a feminist. These feminists have been on the telly a lot lately, they do stuff like burning their bras and not shaving their legs, so they go dead hairy. Auntie Irene doesn't like them. She keeps saying things, when they're on the ITV news, like "They wouldn't go burning no bras if they had tits like mine, these melons need proper structural support."

Ninder thinks she's one of these feminists. Every now and then, in between all them "fecks" and "bollocks" she uses, she'll drop in a few big words like "oppression" and "patriarchal structure." Mostly on days when some lad she fancies hasn't given her a ring. Yeah, Ninder's being saying she's one of these feminists for the last couple of years. One thing I've noticed though – she hasn't let her legs get hairy yet.

She sits up when she sees me. Then she puts down the Mazola and picks up a cocktail glass filled with yellow fizzy stuff that's on the grass near the paddling pool. She takes a sip.

'Me mammy's out at work so I've been making Snowballs with her advocaat, Billy Quiz. Snowballs in the sunshine. How are you liking that paradox?'

Ninder tips her head back and drains the glass. Then she throws it over her shoulder into the rose bed behind her, where it lands inside the wheelbarrow of one of Mr Lally's garden gnomes.

'Guess who I'm being?'

I walk over to her dad's garden hut and pick up another of the blue deckchairs and set it up a good ten feet away from the paddling pool before replying. Ninder's dad's away at sea again. I know she wouldn't be acting like this if he wasn't. Mr Lally's got a big soft spot for his daughter but he can also be a bit strict. Her mam's different. Her mam lets her get away with all sorts of stuff. And, because of her dad being away all the time, she's the one who brought Ninder up.

'I give up.'

'Him.'

'Him?'

'Archi-fecking-medes, you daft divot.'

'Archimedes was in a bath. That's a paddling pool with Sploosh Family Robinson written on the side of it.'

'Same difference. I've been thinking, that's all I'm saying. Thinking about me Uncle Noor and that fire, like you were supposed to do.'

I point at her big knickers which have gone a bit saggy from all the water and have a green grass stain on the back of them.

'Today's Thursday.'

Ninder leans forward and starts running the towel across her oddly-painted toenails.

'On the ball, same as ever, Billy Quiz.'

'Your pants say Tuesday.'

'I got them from a blinding knickers store at the quayside market called Franky's Hanky Panky. They're supposed to be Days of the Week under-crackers but their printer dropped a bollock and they all came out saying Tuesday. Right result that! I got twenty-one pair for £1.99.'

Ninder gets out of the pool and drops her towel on the grass. She picks up the gerbil cage and sits down on the towel. Eureka starts scampering around his the sawdust running from one set of little steel bars to the other. He looks like he's trying to run away from the big wet red T of Tuesday, which I can see poking through the bars just behind his nervously twitching furry brown head.

'I've decided to keep him myself but I was stroking the little bastard for two hours yesterday and I never come up with nothing on me Uncle Noor. As far as concentration gerbils go he's a disgrace.'

I reach into the top pocket of me denim jacket and take out the W.S letter. Then I get out of me deckchair and hand it to Ninder. I pull off me Polyveldts and argyle socks and roll the legs of me bell-bottom jeans up. I sit down on the edge of the paddling pool and dangle me feet in the water.

'Dear Rebecca, Ich sehe sie,' says Ninder; unfolding the letter and reading it

Ninder got an A in her German O Level, so she doesn't have any problems translating it.

'Dear Rebecca, I see you.'

She reads the rest of the letter. Then looks back up at me.

'Nice letter, that, a really nice letter, who wrote it?'

'I'm not sure but I think there's more of them,' I say. 'I think there might be a lot more. I've got a thesis. In science when we've got an idea about something we call that a thesis. I was thinking you and me might work on solving it together, like?'

Ninder looks uncertain.

'A thesis about what?'

'Nazis, Nazis living in Newcastle, or National Front, like you said. Maybe they did set fire to your uncle's shop, after all. There's a bloke called Watergate, who works at the post office. I think he might be one of them.'

'I'm not interested in your letters. I'm only interested in who killed Noor.'

'But they might be connected, that's all I'm saying. Finding out about one of them might help us find out about the other. Do you think your mam will let you go back to the museum yet, after what you did with them fairy cakes? Because I've got an idea.'

Ninder thinks for a moment. She still doesn't look too sure.

Then she nods her head.

'OK, I'm in.'

THE GREAT WHITE SHARK STANDS ON THE TIP OF ITS SNOUT IN A corner of the museum foyer. Two blokes from the council are standing next to it. One of them is giving it a good dust with a pink feather duster. The other is trying to wrap a leather harness around its middle, just under the end of its fin.

Ninder's mam comes out from her little office in the research department and walks towards us. She looks across at the shark and then gives her daughter a look. This is what Ninder calls her mam's "longsuffering face."

'Happy now, errant daughter?'

'It was just a cake. One little fairy cake. I don't see why they had to take the f...take it down.'

The receptionist with the red lips starts tidying up her desk and takes her handbag down from a wooden coatrack. She glowers at Ninder from behind her big glasses.

Mrs Lally waves at her. She doesn't wave back.

'Vermin, Glenda over there was worried about vermin. She rang the council and asked them to inspect it. You weren't the only one it seems. Those workmen found two sets of conkers, some false teeth, a cookbook by Fanny Cradock called Fabulous Fanny and a pickled egg that had turned dark green and gone as hard a snooker ball.'

Mrs Lally starts walking towards the main museum stairs. Me and Ninder follow her. She is really small. Ninder's only about 5ft 2ins but her mam is at least three inches littler than that with dark black hair, very white Irish skin and big brown eyes.

The three of us begin walking up the stairs. When we reach the half-way point I see the red glow from the Martian surface in the main auditorium and some of the silver foil on Viking 1's antenna for a small moment. It gives me a shiver just looking at and thinking about how close it really is to really being there. Then there's a clunk of a switch somewhere in the distance and someone, the security guard on the door I suppose, turns out the ground floor lights. We carry on up the main stairs and come out through a door onto the first-floor balcony.

Then we walk along the balcony past a couple of wooden cases with a glass panel door that are stuffed with displays of bird eggs and butterflies from all over the world. Once we've got past them, Mrs Lally stops and takes out a big bunch of keys.

'Twenty minutes only, I'll be downstairs in my office doing some paperwork. And remember, Ninder, I don't want you going near anything else in here.'

She taps one of the keys in the bunch with her thumb so we know that's the one. Then, as she hands the bunch to Ninder, she leans forward a little and does a spot-on whispered impression of Ninder's voice.

'Especially not that fecking shark.'

THE MOTTA COLLECTION IS IN A WOODEN CASE THAT'S covered by a sheet of glass. It's about six-feet long and four-feet wide and completely filled with loads of stamps. They're all laid out in neat little rows and resting on a faded bit of old green felt.

'Ahh, bollocks! There are hundreds of them.'

'Two-hundred-and-fifty-six actually,' I say, 'there's a section of a book they sell in the gift shop called History of the Hancock that talks about them. This bloke, Ernesto Motta, was a big collector of stamps in the 1930s and the 1940s. He was a doctor, who lived down south. When the war started the Government arrested him because they said he was a Fascist sympathiser and locked him up in a camp in Durham somewhere. He kept collecting all through the war and afterwards too, right through the fifties. When he died his wife, who was a dead strict Catholic, ended up giving them to the museum because she said she wanted to "atone" for this Ernesto Motta's sins. There's all sorts, even Penny Blacks and that, but these German ones were his favourites.'

Ninder takes the keys her mam gave her and slips one of them into the little brass lock of one of the cabinets – the one full of German stamps – and turns it. I slip me fingers under the edge of the case and push up. Then I rest the glass lid against the wall.

All the stamps have swastikas on them. There's all colours – orange, green, blue, red – and loads of others. About eighty percent of them have got Hitler's head on them, same as the one on the W.S envelope. There's just a few with storm-troopers or ones where Hitler's standing in front of a building waving, and a couple where there's him and Mussolini looking all dead pally together.

'The stamps look weird, don't they?' I say.

Ninder puts her hand into the case and picks up a blue stamp, which has Hitler's face on it.

'Weird, how? I don't get weird. They're Nazi stamps used by the Nazis to send Nazi mail. Whose face do you think they'd stick on them, Liberace's?'

'I just mean, like, all these little Hitler heads stuck in a case together; as if they were a collection of butterflies, or something.'

I try and remember exactly what the red stamp on the W.S envelope looked like.

Ninder puts the stamp she's holding back into the case and then points to a green stamp with Hitler's face on it, which has two swastikas, one on either side of it.

'That's the same words you told me about isn't it, Billy?'

She picks up the stamp.

'Deutsche Reich is German empire. Most of the rest have got that as well though.'

I shrug.

'Yeah, they are all pretty much the same. Not sure if your idea about coming here's going to help much, after all.'

I point to at an orange stamp in the bottom left-hand corner of the case.

'It would be better if me W.S stamp looked more like that one over there, because that one looks completely different to all the rest of them.'

Me and Ninder stare down at it.

Hitler's not on this one. There's this thin middle-aged bloke who's going a bit baldy, instead. He's a bit unusual this bloke, when you compare him to any of the other Nazis who are on the stamps in the case. He's not wearing an army uniform or anything. Just a normal, well normal for the 1940s, anyways, suit and tie.

We hear the clacking of some stiletto heels on the parquet floor. Me and Ninder turn around just as her mam comes through the door that leads from the main stairs. Mrs Lally comes across to the case and stands next to it.

'Any luck?'

Ninder shakes her head.

'No, the stamp Billy saw wasn't any different from most of these, looks like there's nothing special about it.'

Mrs Lally turns to me.

'You sure, William? Nothing at all?'

I start to shake me head. Then I get a flash in me mind of the envelope with the red stamp on it, when it was lying on me Tin Tin duvet cover at home.

'Maybe there is something,' I say. 'The watermark. It's got

a funny watermark. There's only a little bit of it on the stamp, just three letters, I think. One of them's a C, there's an S 'n' all. And the other one's...'

I close me eyes and try and remember.

Then I open them again.

'A V, I think, yes, a V.'

Ninder takes a step back from the case and readjusts a big safety pin, the kind they put in babies' nappies to fasten them up, that's clipped into her tartan mini-skirt. Then she looks at me.

'I'm no expert, you're the f...'

She glances across at her mam, then back at me.

'You're the postman, Billy Quiz, but won't that just be from the franking thingy at the post office.'

I shake me head.

'No, it isn't. That's the point. If it had been franked at the post office, them marks are big round circles with NEWCASTLE MAIN, printed inside them.'

Mrs Lally smiles.

'So, no V in them, then?'

'Yes, that's it!' I say. 'No V. But that's not the only thing that's funny about the stamp that was on the W.S letter.'

Ninder leans back against the wall and folds her arms.

'Go on then, genius.'

'There was a bit of watermark on the letter but none on the envelope.'

Ninder look across at her mam. Her mam shrugs. Ninder looks at me.

'So what?'

'If the envelope had got franked at the post office it would have had a big round NEWCASTLE MAIN mark on it, like I said, which obviously never happened because of the V. So, someone at the post office must have noticed it was a dead funny letter before it went through the franking machine and put it straight into the Returns Box, where I found it.'

'That makes sense,' says Mrs Lally.

A tuft of me ginger barnet flops in front of me face. I'm moving about a lot, getting excited talking about the W.S letter, hopping about a bit, jumping from one Polyveldt to the other.

I push the bit of hair out me eyes and smile at Ninder. I point at the other Nazi stamps in the case.

'Look at the watermarks on all them. Some of them have only got a small bit of watermark, like my letter, but other ones have got much more, so you can see how big and round the frank marks the Nazis used were.'

Ninder frowns.

'You've lost me, Billy Quiz.'

The untidy bit of me red hair flips down again. I push it back out of me eye line.

'There should have been a mark on the envelope. A frank mark. But there wasn't one. No mark at all on this W.S's envelope.'

Mrs Lally steps towards me and pushes me fringe back, so the bit of hair clears me eyes properly.

'And what's significant about that?'

'It means that letter and that stamp weren't franked together Mrs Lally. They couldn't have been or the frank mark would have been on the envelope as well as the stamp and it wasn't.'

Ninder sighs.

'So big deal, Billy. Who cares?'

I push me hands down into the pockets of me Levi's jackets and think for a moment.

'The stamp on the W.S letter was stuck to another letter before someone decided to use it again, that's what it means.'

'I'm still none the wiser.'

I sigh.

'Me neither, I suppose, I mean why would anyone send a letter to a district that doesn't exist and then, just to make doubly sure it doesn't get there, put an outdated German stamp on it that's already been used, either by them or somebody else?'

Ninder looks at her mam and then back at me.

Mrs Lally shrugs and then walks across to the glass cabinet so she can shut the lid. I step towards the cabinet and pick up the orange stamp with the baldy bloke with the suit on. I hold it out towards her.

'Who's that, Mrs Lally, the middle-aged bloke in the ordinary suit?'

Mrs Lally takes the stamp from me and holds it closer to her face. After a moment giving it a real good examination, she looks up again.

'His name is Speer, Albert Speer.'

I hold the orange stamp up close in front of me face so I can get a better look at this half-baldy Albert Speer bloke. Then I hand it across to Ninder. She puts it back in the case, locks it and then hands the bunch of keys to her mam.

'What was he mammy, Gestapo or something? Looks like it by the slimy hang of that suit of his.'

Mrs Lally smiles.

'No, Mr Speer's job was a lot less sinister that that, in fact.'

She puts the keys, with their silver roman-hat key fob, back into her pocket and then reaches across and switches out the light.

'Albert Speer was Hitler's architect.'

Tharsis.
Monday, June 21st 1976.
28 days until Viking 1 lands on Mars

Chapter Twelve

I nside Ninder's uncle's burnt-out shop, I can smell the mixture of dampness and charcoal. It feels really sad and strange to be here and see the way it is now. I can still remember it just as it was; all bright and cheerful with Uncle Noor behind the counter. He had very big teeth that were a bit odd and crooked at the front like a rabbit's. One of them, with a little broken bit out of it, was crossed over the other and his ears stuck out a quite lot. He had a nickname in Walker, when he first moved here. Because of the ear and teeth thing people used to call him Lugs Funny.

People use nicknames in different ways. Sometimes because they like you. Sometimes because of the opposite of that. Like with me, when they shout out "Alright, Billy Quiz" I know it's because they like me. And when they say "Sir Isaac" I know they don't. Well, most people around here called Uncle Noor Lugs Funny because they liked him and he liked them calling him that, too.

Ninder walks around the burnt shop floor and then bends down when she sees something on the floor. It's a picture of the Queen. Ninder holds it up to the sunlight that's shining through the gap between the corrugated iron she tore back and the door frame. The glass of the picture frame is smashed and the Queen's hair is a bit singed around the edges but she still looks all regal and unperturbed. Same as she does at Christmas on the telly.

'He loved the Queen and her empire. That's why he called his shop Mr Lally's Marvellous Emporium.'

Ninder takes a slightly crusty hanky out of the pocket of her leather bomber and begins to dab her right eye. It has a blonde-haired girl on it with pink ribbons in her plaits and pink letters which say, "What are little girls made of...?" It's one she got dead cheap from Franky's Hanky Panky, at the quayside market.

'According to The Female Eunuch,' says Ninder, 'me and Germaine Greer have always figured little girls are made of the exact same thing little boys are.'

Then she smiles at me.

Not a nice smile though.

A sarcastic one.

'That's a big dollop of spunk, in case you were wondering, Billy Quiz.'

'I wasn't.'

I feel me cheeks going red. She's only being so sarky to cover up how she's feeling. She's starting to bubble, crying on a bit, and I'm not sure what to do. I stand there like a complete lemon looking at the ground for a minute then I reach out and put me hand on her shoulder to make sure she's alright.

'He was a lovely bloke, your uncle.'

She stuffs the hanky back in her pocket. Then steps away from me and drops the picture of the Queen.

'It's just this new eyeliner. I must be allergic to it. Are you going to start looking, or what?'

THE WET ASH AND MUCK IN WHAT USED TO BE UNCLE NOOR'S storeroom has got right under me nails. I'm on me hands and knees crawling right through it. I can remember being in here once before when I was looking for a box of chocolates to give to Mam for her birthday. Noor showed me loads in the shop out front and none of them seemed quite right.

Me and him came back here into the stockroom and he found a great big box of Black Magic left over from the Easter before. I said I couldn't afford them but Noor said, "No problems, Billy kiddo, this Special Mammy Offer: any boy who loves his mother like you do, Uncle Noor's Marvellous Emporium lets them have big box of chocolates, very close to sell-by-date, for almost, nearly half price."

Back then, it had seemed really exciting to be in here. Kind of glamorous! The shelves had all been full with loads of boxes of Pek Ham and Heinz Tomato Soup. There were boxes of decorations, and fireworks left over from November, and an old poster from the 1970 world cup with a picture of Booby Moore, the England captain, on it saying OUR BOBBY AND TULIP HAM. A WINNING TEAM!

It's not like that now. Everything that's not been burnt in the fire has been nicked. The brick work around a small metal vent covered by bars in the back wall has been smashed and pulled away. The local kids have got it and nabbed anything that was worth having.

'I've asked around the doors, all the neighbours,' says Ninder, 'but no one seems to know anything. Found something?'

I turn around and stare at her. She's standing in the broken doorway to the storeroom with the picture of the Queen tucked under her arm. Rain starts spitting down through one of the holes in the roof. There's a crack of a bit of thunder.

Her dark eyeliner is still all smudged.

I shake me head.

'Nowt. Maybe there's nothing to find.'

'You sound like one of them, one of the piggy-wiggys. That's what they were supposed to do isn't it? Get blokes in white coats scrambling all over the area looking for clues. Fragments of stuff, hair, clothing and all that. Or, here's a thought – the remains of a box of matches.'

'Look, I said I'd help you find out about your uncle, if you'd help me with them letters. They might even be connected, like we said. But I can't find anything here, and ten months is a long time. I'm trying me best but everything is just ashes. He was in the flat upstairs and got killed by the smoke. That's what it said in the report from the Evening Chronicle you showed me. An electrical fault, most likely. Maybe you're right and they didn't do stuff like that because it seemed like such an obvious case to them. They're always talking about police budget cuts on the telly these days.'

'Budget cuts, my arse. The National Front is more like it. Or this Nazi, Watergate, and these coded letters you've been on about.'

The rain starts coming down proper fast, now. There's more thunder. This time a dead loud clap of it. Ninder holds Uncle Noor's picture of the Queen above her head and throws it down onto the floor of the storeroom floor. It smashes in two and all that glass that hadn't been broken already scatters amongst the ash and bits of burnt wet food cartons that are littered everywhere. Some of it just misses me face.

'Let's be honest, Billy Quiz, everyone knows the police are racist. They weren't interested in who killed me uncle because, to them, he was just a Paki.'

I stand up and wipe some of the dust and ash off me trousers.

A big bit of the broken glass has gone through a hole in the brickwork. It's sticking up at a funny angle on the concrete path outside the shop. I reach through the hole and pick it up. Don't want the local bairns falling down on top of that. It's standing up at a funny angle because one end of it is resting in a big dollop of dried-out dog turd, that must have been baked hard by the heat coming from inside, when the shop was on fire. There's a little bit of a pattern in the dog shit. What looks like the toe-print of a shoe. The print's got a couple of little marks in it.

There's a section in Fenwick's toy department in town where they sell plastic medieval knights. The knights have little plastic shields. These marks in the toe-print look like they were made by little shields, like that, pressing down into the dog crap. Next to the footprint is something else: a squeezed-out tube of UHU glue that's got a bit singed in the fire.

'The way science works, Ninder, is you have a thesis; an idea about how things might actually work but just you saying your thesis out loud and throwing pictures of the Queen around doesn't make it true,' I say. 'You have to have evidence to support it. Like in the middle-ages people used to think that the earth was flat but then Galileo and Copernicus came up with a thing called helliocentrism that said no, the earth is round and it spins around the sun. And they were right about that. But just them saying it was round didn't mean anything. They had to do experiments and stuff to prove it.'

I lay the glass down flat and point at the glue.

'Evidence, like that. Someone being here, just before the fire started, wearing funny shoes that have an odd pattern of little shields on the sole of them and carrying a tube of glue.'

Ninder walks over to where I'm standing and peers through the hole in the brick.

'They're from Blakeys, dingbat. Little bits of metal you put on the soles of leather shoes to make them last longer. That pattern's evidence of nothing at all. Half the blokes in Newcastle wear Blakeys in their shoes, like that! And that empty tube is probably from glue-sniffing kids. Noor told me he was thinking of not stocking glue anymore because some of the young 'uns around here had started sniffing it to get off their tits.'

The rain's really coming in through the roof now.

It's pissing down. I grab an old carrier bag off an upturned box and put the tube of UHU in it.

'Maybe you're right about the Blakeys but I'm not so sure about the glue.'

'Why not?'

'Uncle Frank bought me an Airfix model of Astronauts on the moon about six years ago, for Christmas. Me and him put it together on Boxing Day. You need special modelling glue to do that.'

I hold up the carrier bag.

'That's what this is. UHU modelling glue.'

Ninder shrugs.

'And?'

'Watergate, the bloke who might be a Nazi. I've seen him at the post office reading a hobby magazine called Modelling Monthly.'

WHEN I GOT BACK TO OURS IT WAS JUST AFTER SEVEN.

I'm standing in our bathroom scrubbing at me hands with a plastic nail brush, thinking about the shoeprints and the modelling glue me and Ninder found outside Uncle Noor's and trying to get out some of the muck and ash that's trapped under me nails. Ninder's right. Loads of blokes in Newcastle have Blakeys but I've never seen a pattern like them knight's shields before.

There's a noise next to an alley at the back of our house where there are three lock-up garages; two with green doors and our one with a yellow door. There's a bit of graffiti on them that the local lads have done that says GEORDIE AGGRO.

I look out of the window and see me dad, next to the garage with grafffiti sprayed on it. He's picking up a rubbish bin that he's knocked over. He picks up an egg carton and a squash bottle and puts them back in. Then he does something odd. He looks all along the alleyway to the left, and all along the alleyway to the right, to see if anyone has heard the noise.

The way he's standing now looks funny to me, sort of sneaky. Me dad takes a key out of his pocket. He undoes the padlock on our garage and opens it. Dad looks around one more time. Then he goes in.

THERE'S SOMETHING ABOUT A CLOCK IN A LIBRARY THAT SEEMS to work the opposite to the way most clocks do. Most clocks make you feel like – TICK, TICK, TICK – time is racing by but a clock in a library makes me feel the opposite of that; like time is slowing down. Like it'll go so slow that I'll be stuck in here forever. Taking a million years, or something like that, just to turn over one page. So, maybe, if I stay in the library, I really will get a million years to think about this one thing I am thinking about now which is: maybe there's no District 24 in Vienna but there could be an Alter Strasse. I mean perhaps the letter isn't such a big mystery after all and this W.S just made a mistake and Alter Strasse is in District 22 or District 23 instead. In which case, even though it's a funny address, what W.S has written might make sense to this Rebecca, who lives there and even though there's no street number on it, it's possible some Austrian postie might just be able to deliver it.

I stick me hand in me pocket and take out a wine gum – one of the black ones, they're me favourites – and pop it in me gob. I open the G.F Brookburn architecture book up, go to the index at the back and start running me finger down the A section. It doesn't take me long to discover that there is no street in Vienna called Alter Strasse.

I sigh and sit back in me chair. I'm no further forward.

Then something catches me eye

A pink slip stuck just inside the flyleaf. It says Walker Public Libraries on it. The pink slip is what the librarian stamps when you take a book out. Each stamp represents someone who reads the book. The stamps make a list of all the people who've taken out the book in the last few years. Each number is linked to a little box of red cards they keep at the library.

There's loads of times, in the past, when I've taken out a book, that I've looked at these pink slips and thought about all the different people who've taken out that book as well. Like who they are and where they live. And do they like other things, the same as me, like watching Tomorrow's World, on the telly, wearing Polyester tank-tops, from Farnon's in town, and eating Birds Eye Rissoles.

I stare down at the numbers on the pink slip in the Vienna book and notice something straightaway. Most books you take out will have lots of different numbers on them. Some will have a bit of repetition where a person has liked the book a lot but this one's different. One of the numbers: 375682, has been repeated over and over again.

This 375682 must have taken the Vienna book out about fifty times since 1953, when the library first stocked it. Of the last ten people to take out the book, nine of them are this 375682. In fact, there's only one other number that I can see recently and that's two stamps back. Whoever this 375682 is they are obsessed with Vienna and this G.F. Brookburn book, same as I am.

A bit of the black wine gun has got stuck on me back teeth.

I push the tip of me tongue towards it making a bit of a slurping noise as I do. The woman librarian, sitting underneath the clock at the desk, has a red cardie on, a little string of pearls and funny pointy specs, a bit like Thelma wears on Scooby Doo.

She takes the specs off and stares across at me.

I stick another wine gum in me mouth, pick up the Vienna book and jump up out of me seat. I walk quickly up to the desk at the front. The one the librarian's sitting behind. She takes a rubber stamp, and me little green library card with me name and address details written on it, and stamps both of them. She hands me back the book. Then she points at a big sign that's screwed to the wall behind her desk.

It says NO EATING IN THE LIBRARY.

Chapter Thirteen

Me favourite science fiction book is The Invisible Man by an old Victorian bloke called H.G. Wells. There was lots of times at school when the other kids were after me that I used to wish I could be like Griffin, the man in that book, and make meself invisible. This plan I've come up with is like the opposite of that, though.

I think I'm going to call it The Very Visible Woman.

I'm on Nights tonight, so I've got the afternoon to meself. It's two o'clock and about seventy-five degrees outside so there's nobody else in the library. Everyone's outside playing football, or sitting drinking beer in the park, or swimming at the beach up at Whitley Bay. I'm sitting by a big window with some old stained-glass pictures of ships in it that have been built at the shipyards down by the river. It's near the M-section shelves. Ninder's sitting at the table that I usually sit at. The sour-faced librarian with the same glasses as Thelma from Scooby Do is sitting at her desk working away at some paper-work, just like she always does. I look over towards the main doors to make sure that nobody else is coming in.

Then I nod at Ninder.

She leans under the table and takes something out of her duffle-bag. It's a cardboard box from Carricks, the bakers. She puts it on the desk next to the book she's reading – The Carpet-baggers by Harold Robbins. Ninder takes out a mint éclair.

She smacks her lips dead loudly. The librarian looks up. Ninder begins to eat the éclair. She stuffs the whole thing into her gob, at one go, and then makes a couple of loud chomping noises.

The librarian gives Ninder a hard stare. She points up at the sign that says NO EATING IN THE LIBRARY. Then she puts her head down and goes back to her paperwork.

Ninder swallows the rest of the éclair. She puts her hand into the Carricks' box and rustles around amongst the paper cake containers inside it. She takes out a cream horn. I feel a little stab of nerves in me gut.

That's me signal.

The librarian looks up at Ninder's chomping face and pushes her glasses towards the end of her nose. She points at the sign again.

'Can't you read?'

Ninder wipes a bit of cream off the end of her nose and then takes a huge bite of sticky pastry. I get up from me desk and start walking around the back of the M-section. Ninder chews a couple of times and then let's out a burp so loud it echoes right around the library.

'Not much point in me coming to the library if I can't is there? There's a book by Germaine Greer called The Female Eunuch, she says all women – you and me as well, she means – we've lost touch with our libidos. We need to fight back, get in touch with our bodies, taste our own menstrual blood. I haven't tried that yet but these mint éclairs taste so fecking horrible, I reckon Germaine would say "fair does, that's close enough, pet." There's a sexual revolution going on, that's what I'm saying. Why don't you join it?'

The librarian gets up from her desk and starts walking towards Ninder. I tip-toe to the end of the M-section and stand next to a big section of books by a bloke called Alistair Maclean. They're all called things like Ice Station Zebra and The Guns of Navarone. I peep out from the end of the shelf.

The librarian is standing right in front of Ninder's desk staring down at her. Ninder is staring back. She's chewing really slowly, on purpose, and bits of pastry crumbs are dropping out of her mouth and landing on her copy of The Carpetbaggers.

I duck back behind the Alistair MacLean's and reach into the pocket of me Levi's jacket. I take out a piece of paper on which I've wrote down the reader number of the person who'd taken out the G.F. Brookburn Vienna book out so many times. This 375682.

Ninder pushes the last bit of cream horn into her mouth and smacks her lips together dead loudly as she swallows it.

'I'm going to have to ask you to leave the library!'

The librarian's voice sounds so mad it feels like she might have a heart attack, or something. Ninder looks past her and moves her head a little bit. She's telling me to get on with it.

The librarian's head whips around. I jump back in behind the shelves and peer at her over a little gap in between the top of the next shelf and Ice Station Zebra. She turns back around. Ninder takes a strawberry tart out of the cardboard box and makes little num, num, num noises.

'Put that back,' shouts the librarian.

I step out from behind the shelves and go straight to the metal filing box, filled with little red records cards, that sits on the librarian's desk. The cards are all in numerical order with big brown dividers in them that say things like Above 200000. They don't have names on like your personal library card does but they do have addresses. I flick through the cards in the Above 375000 section, find card number 375682 and stuff it into the top pocket of me jacket.

Ninder sees me do it and stands up.

She starts licking the strawberry on top of her strawberry tart. She dips her middle finger in the cream and holds it up to the librarian. The librarian grabs The Carpetbaggers from the desk and starts to shake the pastry crumbs out of it. Then she turns around towards me.

I step out of the end of the M-section and stand flicking through the pages of book called Where Eagles Dare. Ninder begins to walk toward the main door of the library. I slip the Alistair Maclean back into its correct place on the shelf – I hate people who put them back in the wrong one – then I start to walk out with her.

The librarian follows us towards the main door. Her face has gone beetroot red and she's got a big spot of strawberry jam on her white sleeve.

'You're barred, pet,' she shouts after us. 'You and this Germaine Greer. Not the gormless ginger one though, he's harmless.'

Ninder doesn't stop walking but turns her head back to shout at the librarian.

'Piss off, Mrs, I know your sort, ice-cubes for nipples and a Brillo Pad where your fanny's supposed to be.'

The librarian stops walking. Then she lifts a middle-finger and points it straight at me.

'OK, him as well.'

I TIGHTEN THE STAND ON ME TELESCOPE ONE LAST TIME AND then stick the end out of a gap between the branches of the bush. I point it towards three small houses that are about two-hundred feet away from us. Me and Ninder are sitting inside a small circle of bushes on top of a little grass hill that has a couple of big electric pylons on top it. Every now and then, electricity runs through the cables above our heads and gives a dead loud snaky buzz.

'Are you ready?'

'Nearly, I just need to calibrate the lens a bit.'

'Ah, jeez with your nearly, it'll be dark in half an hour. The curtains will close. Then we won't be able to see nothing.'

It's baking hot again, same as it has been nearly every day this summer but there's a bit of a breeze. Inside the bushes, a couple of old empty beer cans keep catching in the wind and rattling around our feet. In me pocket is the little card that me and Ninder stole from the library. The address on it says: 15, Larkspur Avenue, Chapel Park Estate, Newcastle upon Tyne. It's the address of the person who's been taking that G.F. Brookburn Vienna book out of the library.

Chapel Park is a dead big new estate on the west side of Newcastle, miles away from Walker. I've had to get two buses just to get here. Every house is made from brown bricks and each one looks pretty much the same as the next one. Seems odd this person would even have been a member of our library, in the first place, but maybe it's because a lot of these new estates don't have their own libraries built on them yet. Some of the people who moved here maybe just kept going to the library they used to be in when they were a kid.

Ninder takes a stick of pink bubble gum out of her skirt

pocket and unwraps it. Then sticks it in her mouth. She smoothes out the wrapper on the palm of her left-hand.

'Bazooka Joe,' she says, pointing to a little cartoon kid wearing a black baseball cap and an eye patch on the front of the wrapper. 'He was my heartthrob when I was about six. I even wrote to the bubble-gum company to ask if I could be his girlfriend.'

I'm kneeling down behind the telescope. Looking down the hill without using it I can see that two of the houses in front of me look neat and tidy with freshly dug flower beds full of roses but the garden of the third one looks all unkempt and overgrown. It has a greenhouse at the side with a couple of smashed glass panes in it and an old Ford Anglia parked on the drive.

I rest me eye behind the viewfinder.

'Did he write back?'

Ninder opens her palm up and lets the breeze catch the Bazooka Joe wrapper. It flies up through a gap in the branches and blows away.

'Course he didn't write back, Billy Quiz. He's a cartoon fecking character. He doesn't exist. Same as this District 24 W.S is writing to. But they did send me twelve packs of bubbler instead. Wrote back two more times under other names after that. Got meself thirty-six packs of bubbler in all. Bargain!'

She watches the wrapper drift away past a white cloud up towards the sun.

Ninder gives me one of her looks; the sort she does when I tell her facts about the Dynamical Theory of the Electromagnetic Field, or this cat that a bloke called Erwin Schrodinger put in a box and then decided he wasn't sure if it actually existed, or not. Stuff she can't be arsed with me banging on about.

'You sure doing this makes sense? I mean you sure it's going to help us find out about me Uncle Noor?'

I shrug.

'You've got your theory about Nazi's living in Newcastle, that's all I know. That letter means something funny is going on. That's for sure. But we need a lot more evidence to prove that the two things might be connected.'

I begin to focus the telescope on the bay window of the house with the untidy garden. It's still a bit blurred and fuzzy. I can't quite get it right. I lick me lips to concentrate and then make two more tiny twists on the black-metal knob. Bingo! I've got full focus. The curtains are orange and brown, with a funny pattern on them made up of illustrated different sorts of cats. An evil-looking marmalade-coloured moggy stares right back at me. Maybe it's the one Erwin Schrodinger's being looking for? Best thing, though, is they are drawn right back which means, with just a tiny twist on the dial, I can see inside the living room.

There's a bloke sitting at a dining table, reading the Vienna book. He's got a half-full glass in one hand and a bottle of Whyte and Mackay's whiskey in the other. It's Watergate.

Chapter Fourteen

I'm standing at the front of the door to Windsor Mansions near the kids' climbing frame where me and me dad first saw Blue Tear and Bino. I lick me lips. They taste all salty.

Blue Tear and Bino aren't here today. But neither is me dad, either. When I got to work this morning one of the top gaffers who's got an odd-looking face with a lot of pock-marks on it, a bit like the little dents you get on potatoes, who all the sorters just call King Edward, or Ugly Ted, said Watergate, called in sick again. He's probably got another hangover, I expect, from all that whiskey he was drinking when he was reading the G.F Brookburn book. I'd love to know why he's so interested in it.

I'm not supposed to go out on me own, at my age, but Dad's had to cover for Watergate and they're short-staffed at our depot today because there's a one-day strike on at Orchard Street. So, Ugly Ted, said I'd just have to do it on me own today.

There's two ways to deliver the post to big tower blocks

like Windsor Mansions: top-down or bottom-up. If I go top-down, I'll get the lift all the way to the twentieth-floor start delivering there and use the stairs to come down a floor at a time. If I go bottom up, I'll start on the first floor and make me way up, using the lift one floor at a time.

On the one hand, top-down is the route me dad usually takes as he thinks it's quicker. On the other hand, there's always the risk that I'll step out of the lift on the top floor and straight into Blue Tear and Bino.

I stand for about a minute trying to make me mind up, like, but nowt happens. I think about going back to the depot and saying I feel sick. But then I think about Dad and how proud he is about me being a postman – carrying the Queen's mail and all that – and I think no, I've got to go through with it.

I try and whistle but nowt comes out.

Then I hitch up me bag on me shoulder and walk through the door of the tower block. I go straight to the lifts and press the button that says "Twenty." I don't even know if Blue Tear and Bino are in Windsor Mansions but now it feels as if I've made a big-plate, middle-plate, small-plate decision just like me mam did.

I've made an eeny, miny, mo.

THE LIFT NIFFS OF PISS AND SPEW. IT'S GOT WRITING ON IT, all over like. Words, like Packi and Slag, in red and black biro. I keep thinking about the doors opening at the top and coming face to face with them two skinheads.

"Think of nice things instead." That's what Mam used to say to me whenever she could see one of me Mucklestone Moments on the horizon. Or, she'd take them red Mars specs of hers out. Put hers on first and then give me mine, and say "There you go, our Billy, now just imagine that everything is as nice as licking a sugar cone on Whitley Bay beach, that everything's exactly how me and you like it."

So, I try that now. I close me eyes and think a bit rose-tinted, pretend I'm wearing me mam's red Mars specs. I think of the lift in Binn's department store, in town, that Mam used to take me in, when I was just six or seven. It was all posh with dark wood and shiny mirrors. When the doors closed, I would pretend it was a space lift. A lift that was going to take me and me mam to the top of one of the Apollo spaceships.

Just the two of us, going on a crazy cosmic adventure.

There's a big PING sound. I open me eyes. The lift doors shoot open and a green electric sign shows the number twenty. There's no Apollo spaceship here.

But no Blue Tear and Bino, either.

ME SHIRT IS SOAKING WET WITH SWEAT AND I FEEL REALLY knackered. I've done sixteen floors but there are still four left to do. I can see why me dad and the other postmen all hate Windsor Mansions. Most massive tower blocks like this one have metal boxes at the bottom which the postmen and the people who live there can use for letters and parcels but whoever designed the flats on the Faversham Estate must have forgot about that; same as they forgot about putting in some nice streets for people to walk down, or nice fields for bairns to play in as well.

I STEP OUT OF THE STAIRWELL ONTO THE FOURTH FLOOR AND look around. There's no one about. The corridor is dead long and dark and empty like the other ones I've been in. The only people that I've set me eyes on in the last hour and a half are an old lady bringing shopping back from Prestos supermarket and a couple of little bairns playing football in the stairwell. The walls are all white with a thick red strip down the middle of them, and most of the doors are red too. Some of them are different colours; ones that've been changed by the owners from the red the council put on in the first place, even though they're not supposed to do that. A couple of doors have door-mats outside them and one, at the end, even has a basket hanging over it with a plant pot that has white flowers in it.

I turn to the first letterbox and pop a couple of letters through it.

I'M REALLY GETTING INTO THE RHYTHM OF THIS BEING A postman lark now. I push a small parcel covered in brown paper through the letterbox on Flat 4F and start whistling.

I turn round and stand in front of another door.

This one isn't red. It's yellow. It's flat 4G. With the basket of white flowers hanging in front of it. There's big bit of black spray-paint graffiti on the wall next to the door. It says, "Watch out for the Witch!"

Me hand goes into the postbag and I pull out another bundle of letters. As well as the letters, there's a small parcel covered in brown paper and tied together with string. The parcel's got no name on it, just an address: Flat 4G, Windsor Mansions. This is the one, alright.

A big fat SLAP slaps on me back.

I look around but I don't really need to. I can feel it's them before I even see their faces.

With that tear tattooed on his cheek and a smile on his face Blue Tear looks all happy and sad at the same time. Like he can't make up his mind whether to kiss or kick me. Bino's face is a bit easier to read. He looks like a vulture who's just got an invitation for a slap-up plate of scran. He stretches out his too-white hand and takes the parcel from me. Reads the front of it – I'm a canny bit impressed that he can read – and then hands it to Blue Tear.

'This is nice like isn't it, Blue? Sir Isaac's come to see us all on his own-some.'

Blue Tear takes the parcel. Has a right good deek at the front of it. Then has a little think before he asks me a question. Albert Einstein did some sums and that; which proved that, out in space, time can be bent and seem longer or shorter depending on where you happen to be standing. From where I'm standing now, a minute feels like a couple of weeks.

'Not whistling anymore eh, Sir Isaac?'

He runs a finger over the back of the parcel and then loosens the string and begins to take it out of the brown paper that's covering it. I'm speaking before I even realise I'm saying owt. It's thinking of me dad that makes me do it. He would never put up with mail tampering or nothing like that, would me dad.

'That's the Queen's that is,' I hear meself say. 'It belongs to Her Majesty the Queen does mail. You can't open that. No one can.'

'Can't?'

Blue Tear says the word in an odd way. Like it's the first time he's ever heard it. Like it was a foreign word. Something a Klingon might use, if they were trying to speak English, in an episode of Star Trek.

'Can't??'

He says it again. But louder. His voice goes a bit more to the sad side of sad-happy. He pushes his face close to mine. A sneer-smile spreads across it as he goes from happy-sad to sad-happy once again. His voice is all whispering like when he was speaking to me on the PE hut roof.

'See Bino here, Sir Isaac. I mean people divn't like him and them pink eyes of his since he was a little bairn. Call him ghost-boy, shite like that.'

Blue Tear pulls away from me a bit. I look down the corridor towards the stairs but I know it's useless. He sees me look and goes all sad-happy, happy-sad again. Raises his voice a bit.

'Me point is this, Sir Isaac. He's hard as fuck is me mate Bino. All them twattings he had from various bastards on the grounds of him being a bit on the far side of whiteness, will get you that way.'

Blue Tear's face comes so close to me I can smell the Thunderbird wine on his breath. His voice goes all low and whispery again. It sounds a bit like the voices that come into me head and say nasty stuff to me, when I'm having me Mucklestone Moments.

'Yes, he's hard as fuck is me mate Bino. But he don't get to say "Can't" to me around here. No bastard does. Not you, you snivelling ginger twat or Her Majesty, the fucking Queen!'

Blue Tear steps back and shakes the parcel. He rips the rest of the brown paper off it. There's a green cardboard box inside. The box has got gold letters printed on it that say: Café Wagner.

Blue Tear looks at it for a moment and then reads out the

words that's on it in a nasty voice which is all full of exaggerations and loads of sneeryness.

'Café Wagner…'

Bino starts to snigger.

'Wagner, that's Kraut talk that is, Blue. Here, giz a deek.'

He grabs for the parcel but Blue Tear steps back. Holds it up in the air and waves it about. Taunts him with it. He looks all funny and uncomfortable does Bino when Blue Tear does that. He's gone a bit red.

He reaches his hand out towards the parcel and Blue Tear's face goes straight from happy-sad to happy-happy. He jumps back again all gleeful and smiling at his mate. For a moment, a really tiny moment, like, I think Bino is going to lamp him one. Suddenly there's a scraping sound. A key turning in a lock.

The yellow door of Flat 4G opens. A woman is standing in the doorway. She is beautiful this woman.

All perfect symmetry.

ME AND BLUE AND BINO AND THE WINDSOR WITCH ARE ALL standing saying nowt. Maybe a minute's gone by. One of them long ones Albert Einstein talks about. Like she really has cast a spell over us. Finally, she lowers her head. Her hand stretches out.

'My parcel please. I would like you special gentlemen to please give me my parcel.'

She doesn't sound like a witch. Her voice is dead soft with a funny sort of accent. Like a German in the films, but not exactly the same, no, it's mixed with something else I can't put me finger on.

Blue's stares down at the parcel in his right hand. He looks all confused. Like her using that word "special" has made him feel some sort of something he doesn't quite understand. Then he reaches out with his free hand and ruffles me hair. Pretending like he's me mate.

'Later, eh, Billy Quiz? Me and Bino will see you around again soon.'

Then, without looking at her again, he hands the woman the parcel and starts to walk away down the corridor. After a couple of seconds, Bino follows him.

She looks down at her parcel. Then back up at me. She doesn't say anything. I want to ask her about it. Of course, I do. But when I look at her face nowt comes out. It's not because I'm scared of her.

She doesn't look like the kind of witches you see in the films, this lady. One with loads of warts and a big hooky nose and that. No, the opposite, in fact. She's dead pretty. Like one of them film actresses on the telly: Sophia Lauren or Alexandria Bastedo from The Champions TV series that me dad likes.

Don't get me wrong. She isn't a young lass. Old in fact. Older than me mam was when she was hit by Mr Pontefract's Hillman Imp. But, even though she must be forty or maybe even fifty years old, as old as that, and there's wrinkles on her skin and bits of grey in her hair, looking at her it feels like when I look at the stars in me telescope.

You're not seeing how beautiful they are now, them stars, because the light takes so many years to travel across space towards us. No, you're seeing how beautiful they were then. Back in time. In a moment that's long past from maybe a few billion years ago. That's all you're seeing when you look at a star. Just one brief billion-year-old twinkle. This lady's face is like that. When you look at it you can feel all them moments from long ago. All them blokes that must have stared at her.

She smiles at me. Then, still holding her parcel, steps back inside her hall and shuts her door.

After that, I just stand there staring at the yellow door, for maybe a minute or more. Thinking about all them stares.

All them men and lads, like me, who really wanted to but couldn't say owt to her. All them long ago, far away twinkles.

Chapter Fifteen

Mrs Damon leans across me and picks up a postal order from the pile of blank ones on the old teak desk. I get a blast of her perfume. It's not like the ones me mam used to wear which were soft in the air and smelled a bit like the flowers in the park near Leazes' boat lake. It's all strong and harsh. Being this close to her, in the hot front-room of the main post office, makes me feel a little sick. Her perfume must be full of something called musk which is taken from deer glands and makes the base of lots of scents. Musk is a word that comes from a really old Indian language called Sanskrit and means testicles. I expect if lots of woman knew that they were spraying something called testicles all over themselves every time they used a bottle of Charlie or Smitty they might think twice about it.

The big booth me and Mrs Damoan are in has got two glass windows set into a wooden front about twelve-feet wide, where people queue. Sometimes they just want to buy stamps or postal orders but lots of times they hand over a little red chitty the postman has left for them, and me or Mrs Damoan go out back to get parcels for them that couldn't be delivered. The two queues never ever seem to go down. No matter how many people we serve, there's always at least four or five of them standing in front of each window.

She licks her lips and digs around in a green leather handbag she always carries with her that's got lots of gold studs stuck on it and a line of black leather tassels on each side. Finally, she takes out a pound note and offers it to me.

'Do you fancy nipping to the corner shop for a couple of ice lollies, Billy, pet? Bill Giles, on the weather, says it's going to be eighty degrees.'

This is not a specific post-office-related question so I do what I've been doing for the last couple of hours when she tries to make chit-chat, and that. I say nowt. Mrs Damoan sighs and puts the pound note back her handbag. Then, she turns to a bloke with grey coat and a pipe in the queue in front of her glass window, and stamps his postal order so loud the noise makes him blink.

THE CLOCK NEXT TO THE SECURITY MIRROR SAYS TWENTY TO four. Now there's only one person left in me queue. Mrs Damoan gives her last customer their parcel and then turns over a card that's hanging on the glass in front of her booth from OPEN to CLOSED.

'I'm off for a cuppa, want one, Billy, love?'

I just keep filling in the form I've started. Mrs Damoan picks up her handbag and walks around the back of me chair. I can smell her perfume again; sharp and sticky in the hot air. It catches in the back of me throat.

'Be kind to your dad,' she whispers as she passes behind me. 'The heart has its needs, pet.'

She walks past me chair and then takes a packet of tabs out of her pocket. Then she walks out of the door at the back of the office. I turn back to the man I'm serving and hand him his parcel. He gives me a big wink.

'Make any man happy them jiggles would.'

'I'm a man of science.'

'And?'

'We're immune, like.'

'To what?'

'Jiggles.'

'You must be the first, son. That's all I can say.'

He tucks his parcel under his arm and heads for the door. When he reaches it he turns around again and, laughing, shouts back to me.

'You must be the bleeding first.'

I'M JUST ABOUT TO FLIP OVER THE SIGN ON ME BOOTH FROM OPEN to CLOSED when I notice there's still one customer left. She's sitting on an old bench at the back of the front room underneath a big cork board that's filled with notices. Things like posters of the panto at the Theatre Royal and little card notices for lost dogs and cats that people have put up there. The woman is staring hard at a poster on the board. It's one that's got a picture of Viking 1 on it; advertising the Destination Mars Exhibition at the museum.

There's something about the way she's sitting there that makes me feel like she's been there for a canny while, like. I just haven't been able to see her because of the queue of people standing in front of me.

I lean down and shout through a little hole in the glass we use to talk to customers.

'Can I help you, Mrs?'

The woman has short dark hair and is wearing a long dark dress and, even though it's so hot, a thin black jumper, with long sleeves that cover her arms. Her shoes are very flat and also black; a bit like the ones you see nuns wearing. She just keeps staring at the poster and does not turn around.

I try again. This time I shout louder.

'Are you waiting for a letter or a parcel? We're just about to close.'

She turns her head towards me. I recognise her straight-away. The beautiful witch-woman from Windsor Gardens gets up and walks towards me.

She stands close to the protective glass in front of me. She twists a couple of times at a little white bead that's tied to the chain around her neck. This close, I can see her eyes are the same colour green as the trees in a forest picture me mam showed me once at the Laing Art Gallery in town.

'Kaiserschamm.'

'Sorry?'

'Cake, I'm here for my cake if you please.'

She seems a little different than when I last saw her; when she was all calm in front of Blue Tear and Bino. She has this very far away look now. Like part of her is here and part of her is somewhere else. It almost feels like she might disappear right in front of me. Just flicker and go, like they do on Star Trek, when Captain Kirk and that crew member you've never met before, so you know they're going to die anyways, get beamed down onto the surface of some dead sinister planet.

'We don't sell cakes. You need a bakers for stuff like that.'

She thinks about this for a moment. Then she smiles. When she does that it's like she flickers back into who she was when I first met her. All calm and composed.

'Postman!'

She stretches out her hand and draws a perfect circle around the glass screen in front of me with the middle finger of her right hand. It roughly matches the shape of me head.

'You're not whistling today, Postman, I like your whistle. I remember your whistle. From my window, I see you do that.'

'Me dad's the whistler; he does most of the whistling. Except for "Dark side of the Moon," I'm quite good at that.'

She puts two fingers together and then presses them where the middle of the circle she just drew on the glass would be. I'm wondering if it's some kind of spell she's doing.

'Eeeny, meeny, miny, mo. That's what it was. That's what I recognised. Please do, Postman, for me, whistle that.'

I shake me head.

'I have another parcel, Postman – cake, Kaiserschmarrn, I think, a great delicacy. Most days now, I get some cake.'

I remember the little green box that I delivered for her from this café with the German name – Café Wagner. Now, I understand.

'Once upon a time, Postman, I was in a place where every night I would be dreaming of Kaiserschmarrn and a little cream.'

'You need a chitty.'

She stares at me.

'Kaiserschmarrn, Postman. You are looking please?'

'If you're out and they can't drop off they leave a chitty, a red chitty. Have you got a chitty?'

'Every week for many months now some persons of great mystery sends me this cake. Then, on Saturday, no such lucks.'

I pick up a blank chitty from the desk in front of me and show her it.

'One of these.'

She smiles.

'An admirer admires me, Postman. I had many when I was young. And now, another. He sends me Kaiserschmarrn this figure of mystery. A token, perhaps, of his lasting esteem?'

I don't answer her. I don't know how to. Her lips shut flat and go dead still. After a few moments, the rest of her seems to go all stiff too. Like someone's pressed a button on her back and switched her off. Same as happens to Lord Mucklestone's mechanical monocle on his machine at the Hoppings, when your 10ps run out.

'There are lots of parcels back there. The storeroom's really packed. It will take ages without a chitty. Unless you've got your chitty we're supposed to say no,' I say.

She shrugs. Then holds out her hands to show me they're empty. Her fingers are long and dead beautiful but the nails are bitten right down into the tips of her fingers.

'No such lucks, Postman. But, perhaps, just for me, you will look?'

THERE WAS A WOMAN AT MAM'S CHURCH SOME PEOPLE CALLED Little Laura, on account of there being two Lauras who went there and the other one – who they called Big Laura – was a fat lass. Well, everyone felt dead sorry for Little Laura because, when her husband ran off with a nurse he met at the bingo, she tried to top herself by jumping off the Tyne Bridge. A copper got her before she could do it. After that, she was, what they call, "sectioned" and sent to the loony bin in Gosforth, where they gave her loads of drugs. When she got out, Len Gossop, who takes the collection plate around at church, started calling her "Weather Head," because her moods would change so fast. One minute happy. The next all sad. "You can't never tell if it's going to be sunny or showers, in Little Laura's head," is what Len Gossop said.

Talking to this witch-woman from Windsor Mansions today feels a bit like the way talking to this Little Laura would do sometimes. Like I don't know where I stand. Like I need to be dead careful what sort of things I say to her, in case big dark clouds of funny Cirrus and Nimbostratus start forming inside her head.

The wooden clock next to the security mirror says twenty to five. I've been looking in the parcel storeroom for about twenty minutes but there's no green boxes in there, tied with brown paper and string.

When I come back through into the main office it's empty. There's no sign of the woman from Windsor Mansions.

Chapter Sixteen

I've been watching The Sky at Night on the telly since I was a real little bairn. The presenter, Patrick Moore, is probably the only person in the country who's as excited about Viking 1 landing on Mars as I am. He's wriggling in his seat and spluttering and slobbering his words and keeps saying things like "Only days to go, just days before the Viking lander touches down on the Martian surface; this is tremendously exciting!"

Then he gets out a little diagram of the orbiter and shows how, when Viking 1 reaches Mars and starts its orbit, the lander will break-away and then float gently down to the surface of the planet.

I sit down in the armchair in our living room and spread meself out a bit, take a drink of tea and a bite of Jaffa Cake and stare down at the W.S letter. I lie back in the chair and scratch me head. I still haven't a clue who this W.S is, or why Watergate likes that Vienna book so much, or why he wanted the letter so badly. I still seem to know next to nowt.

Blue Suede Shoes starts up. I put me me Esso mug down

on the table and get up. Then I walk down the hall and open our front door.

Watergate is red in the face and swaying a bit. The wispy bit of his comb-over is lifting in the breeze. There's a bottle of whiskey stuck into the jacket pocket of his shiny brown suit. He's wearing scruffy black boots on his feet. He sticks the right one across the sill of the door so I can't close it.

'I don't know what you're playing at, son, but now's the time to stop.'

He's slurring his words but I can see he's not completely hammered.

Now I'm pretty certain Watergate's a Nazi; he looks all different to me. His eyebrows seem more bushy and shifty, his fat nose looks more sneaky and twitchy and his hair; well, I suppose, his hair always did look a bit like something you'd spot on top of a bloke singing the Horst Wessel; moving up and down, the way it does – like a mini conductor's baton – to the music. I can't understand why I never spotted it before.

'At work, they said you were ill.'

Watergate leans further into the doorway and holds his chubby hand out.

'Let's be having it. You shouldn't have nicked it in the first place. I would have gone straight to your dad but he's had a belly-full the last year or two with your mam's accident and that, so I figured I'd just sort it meself.'

He seems real mad. Dead scary.

Me dad's at the club. He won't be back for hours. I've got no choice. I turn around and go back to the table in the living room. Then come back out again. I hand the W.S letter to Watergate.

He grabs it.

Unfolds it, then turns it upside down and the right way up again, as if he's looking for something.

'Where is it?'

'Where's what?'

'The drawing, the little drawing of the building. The drawings are what I like the best. Most of the other ones have them in, you sure you haven't got one?'

'Other ones? What other ones?'

Watergate steps forward and grabs me by the collar of me shirt. He pushes his face close to mine. All I can smell is whiskey and pickled onion crisps.

'Listen, you little shite, I've had enough of your fun and games. Where's me drawing?'

'I don't know what you mean, Mr Worrel, honest, I don't.'

Watergate looks me right in me eyes. A proper hard stare. I can feel him deciding whether he's going to believe me or not. His hand loosens a bit on me collar. He turns around and starts walking down our little path. When he gets to the pavement he turns back and gives me another look.

'Any more of them letters turn up, son, you to bring them straight to me. They're mine, no one else's, is that understood?'

I nod me head. Then watch as Watergate, still swaying a bit, walks away down our street.

Chapter Seventeen

I sit down on the back of the nineteen bus and take the Vienna book out of me haversack. I got it from the library this morning. Thanks to Ninder mouthing off, I'm banned now. Banned from doing me most favourite thing. But it's me day off today and I remembered that the librarian, who looks a bit like Thelma from Scooby Do, doesn't work on Tuesdays, so I sneaked in, on the off chance the Vienna book would be back on the shelves.

It really does look like a lovely place this Vienna, with all wide boulevards and grand old theatres and hotels and opera houses. There's lots of pictures in the book of girls and women wearing massive floaty old dresses that the Victorians wore, crinolines they call them, and carrying, what's called, parasols which is a posh word for umbrellas. They are all walking around a big street called the Ringstrasse in the days just after the First World War.

The bus rolls to a stop and starts to shudder a bit as the engine keeps running. It only stays at the stop for a moment or two. Then it starts to move forward again. I turn a page and see the black-and-white picture of the observatory again. I shut me eyes and think about how amazing it would be just to be able to go to this Vienna and look at the stars through a telescope as big as that; staring up and out way past Mars and Viking 1 even, until all you could see is the tiniest pin pricks of light scattered all over an inky black nothingness.

Then I open them again. The bus lurches around a corner near Fat Pete's Fish and Chip shop on Heaton Road and the jerky movement flips most of the pages over.

'Leave that alone.'

I look up from the book.

A big lad with a dead white face is standing in front of a woman with grey hair. He's holding her red Salvation Army collecting tin in his hand and is shaking it next to his ear.

'Leave that alone, young man.'

This time she raises her voice. The woman looks really scared. There's a bloke with a haversack reading the Sun but he has his head down. He seems to be really concentrating on a story about Garry Glitter. The lad holding the collection tin looks up and sees me. He smiles and hands the tin back to the woman.

'No harm done, Mrs, just messing with you a bit. Having a laugh, like.'

Bino starts walking straight down the aisle towards me.

THE LITTLE METAL SIGN THAT SAYS WINDSOR PARK GARDENS is all cracked and peeling. Someone has written Linz is a Fat Slag on it with a black marker pen. There are empty fag packets and smashed beer bottles scattered all across the grass and one of the swings has no swing left on it anymore. The metal frame stands empty. In the middle of the park is a bit of tarmac, and in the middle of the tarmac is a big rocking horse. No one calls this place Windsor Park Gardens around here. Everyone just says Rocky Horse Park.

Bino gives me another boot up the arse with his Dr Marten. Seeing all the pain they've caused runts like me down the years it seems a bit weird that they ended up calling every skinhead's favourite weapon after a doctor.

It's about the sixth time he's kicked me since he dragged me off the bus by me ear which is all red, sore and throbbing. He's wearing white Stay Press trousers, hitched high above his boots, a white Fred Perry shirt and crimson braces with little golliwogs on them. I think you could get them novelty braces free with a special offer that Robertson's Thick Cut Marmalade ran last year.

I feel Bino's boot slap into me arse again.

'Ahh!'

I push me free hand, the one that's not holding the Vienna book, back to cover me bum cheeks, and look over me shoulder at him. His nose always twitches a bit when he grins. It's twitching a lot now.

'Pissed your pants yet, Sir Isaac? Don't worry if you do, son. In this heat we'll have you all dried up in no time.'

He boots me again and I stumble towards a massive see-saw with two horse's heads stuck to each end of it that kids use for seats. Mam used to bring me here sometimes when I was little and let me play on it. It looks a lot worse for wear than the last time I saw it. The red paint that covers the two horse heads is all popped and blistered. You can see the knots and lines in the wood underneath it. Each head used to have a big yellow and white marble for an eye but only one of them has one now. The other one, the one on the right-hand side, has had its eye gouged out.

Blue Tear is sitting on it.

BLUE TAKES A PACKET OF TABS OUT OF HIS POCKET AND LIGHTS one up.

In the distance, I can see some little kids playing football on the green grass and a black dog chasing the orange ball around with them. There's an ice-cream van parked at the opposite gate of the park with a row of people standing next to it. Even if I shouted out for help, they'd be too far away to hear me.

The highest thing in the park is an old climbing frame. It's only about five-feet tall, though. I feel meself calm down a bit. Even I can survive being thrown off that. Blue Tear takes a long draw on his tab and then lets the white smoke float up into the light blue of the sky.

He smiles his sneer-smile.

Bino reaches forward and grabs the Vienna book from me. He starts to flick through the pages. Then he gives me another boot in the arse, and pushes me towards his mate.

'A present for you, Blue.'

Blue Tear stares back down at the tarmac. He's got an empty marmalade jar at his feet. One of the ones Robertson's make, with little golliwogs drawn on the front. It matches Bino's braces. There's a crawling mass of something inside the jar. He picks it up and shows it to me and Bino.

'You got a favourite uncle, Sir Isaac?'

In the Commando comics I used to read, when I was a little bairn, there's lots of times when the hero has to walk across a minefield. This is one of them.

Hoping it's the right answer, I nod me head.

Bino puts the book down on the ground next to the peeling red paint of the blind horse's head that Blue Tear is sitting on. He leans across and takes the jar from his mate. Then he holds it up above his head. Bees, they're bees. A yellow-and-black mass is squashed into every corner of jar. They're crawling all over each other trying to get close to the metal lid.

'Me Uncle Ossie, Ossie Mingle, he's mine,' says Blue Tear. 'Me mam used to like a lot of Smirnoff and not much orange in her vodka and oranges, when I was bairn, so I had lot of uncles. Just about any arsehole who talked to her in the toon, when she was on the lash, was me uncle at some point. But they'd all fuck off, sharpish. Not Ossie, though. He likes collecting things does me uncle. War stuff, guns and uniforms mostly, these days, but when I was a little kid, of eight or nine, me and him, we used to come here, to this park, sit on this wonky fucking rocky horse and I'd bring a jar like this one. A marmalade jar with a picture of a daft grinning golliwog stuck to the label. Then, me and him, we'd start collecting ourselves some of these busy fucking bees.'

A little bit of hot breeze blows across the park. In the distance, I can hear the flat, stretched tinkling of the ice-cream van's knackered old bell, getting further away.

Bino hands the jar back to Blue-Tear. He takes it and kneels down on the tarmac. Then he puts the marmalade jar on top of a flat bit on the rocking horse's head. Bino grabs a hold of me arm and forces me to kneel down next to Blue Tear.

Then he kneels down beside me.

No one says nowt. We just stare down at the bees in the jar. They're starting to move a lot more slowly now. Bees don't have lungs. They breathe through little tracheas in their bodies that let in air. In a sealed jam jar like that, all crammed together, they won't last long.

Blue Tear takes something shiny out his pocket. A sharpened screwdriver with a plastic handle.

'I told Bino to keep a look out for you.'

Bino grins, goes all sheepish, when Blue Tear mentions his name. His white, white cheeks go tinged with a little bit of red.

'I seen him on the bus, Blue. I seen him on the bus and I knew you were after him.'

Blue Tear hasn't stopped staring at the bees in the jar. They're nearly all still now. Only a couple of them are moving.

'We used to do this. Me and me uncle. Come here and do our collecting together. High times and that, when he'd let me go out and do this collecting with him. We'd watch the jar and watch and watch and wait and wait and wait. Same as we're doing now. Until none of them fucking bees were moving.'

Blue Tear pushes the sharpened screwdriver down into the lid with a sharp twist of his hand.

'He's been like a proper old man to me has me uncle. Lives down south he does, near the Big Smoke. He still likes collecting things. All sorts he goes after, war stuff mostly because he's ex-army but other stuff too, like stamps and posters. And that got me to thinking after me and Bino bumped into you the other day – me old unky might just like to collect someone like you, Billy Quiz. You and that Paki-slag school mate of yours, Ninder Lally.'

I shake me head.

'I haven't seen her for ages, Blue,' I say, not wanting to tell him anything about Ninder.

Blue stares hard into me eyes.

'Pity that, because I give me uncle a ring last week and told him all about you and young Ninder. Then I mentioned how her mam works at that museum in town. He got all excited when I said that. Now, he's come up special to see you. Tonight's good for him, I expect, Billy Quiz, how about you?'

One of the bees at the top of the pile starts to move a little as the air reaches it. A couple of others begin stir a bit too. All slow and dopey, like they're waking up out of a bad dream. Like they've escaped it. Then a small white flame sparks up in the bottom of the jar. I recognise what it is straightaway. The white lump of phosphorus begins to burn more and more brightly as the air flows into the jar. There are little fizzes and pops as the bees begin to fry.

Blue Tear stares down at the white flame that's burning through all the little bodies inside the jam-jar. Then he looks back up at me.

'I'm not sure I can make tonight, Blue,' I say.

'An experiment, Billy Quiz, you like them, don't you? Me and Bino done the chemistry lab at school before we left and nicked a load of gear, including this phosphorus. Know what I like about this experiment, of mine, the best?'

I shake me head.

'No.'

Blue Tear stares back down at the burning bees and smiles.

'They need the air to breathe. Them bees,' he says. 'But when I punch the holes and let air in it sparks the phosphorus and, well, it's the thing they need the most that kills them.'

Ossie Mingle doesn't have whites in his eyes. He has yellows.

Up close, like this, they look the same colour as the frothy dregs you get in the bottom of the pissers at the club on Saturday nights. His pupils are light blue. Same colour as the little cubes they drop down them bogs to try and disinfect them. He talks really low. Almost in a whisper. When he does, sharp, pointy teeth peep out from behind his lips. The skin which covers his face is all creased and wrinkled and matches the colour of them eyes.

He tries to slap a little colour into his cheeks. 'Caught malaria out in Malaya, serving our gracious majesty in the Medical Corp, young William. Nurse, I was, a good 'un too. Healed the sick and made a tidy something or other by purloining the occasional ampoule of morphia to administer to them squaddies who, thanks to our somewhat challenging jungle habitat, were just plain fucking sick of living.'

He holds the palms of his hands out in front of me.

'These are healing hands, son. But I went out to fight the yellow man, came back fucking yellow meself. Jaundice they call it. Yellow jaundice. Comes and goes though. Today it's back. Maybe something's not agreeing with me? Haven't been sleeping too well, lately. Restless I am. Up and down, pacing our front-room. I mean banana-fucking yellow ain't a comfortable colour for a good honest English man to be these days, if you catch my drift?'

The walls in the British Legion are stained with browny-yellow marks from all the tabs the old Fusiliers and Paras have been smoking down the years. There's a big snooker table just behind us and Bino is playing on it. There are a couple of blokes playing dominoes near the bar, and an old fella, with some sort of military blazer on, banging 10ps into a fruit machine.

Me, Ossie and Blue Tear are sitting in a corner of the Legion's lounge. Blue and Bino rang him from a phone-box near the Rocky Horse Park. Then brought me straight here.

There was nowt I could do about it.

Ossie takes a sip from his glass of bitter-lemon.

'I'm a collector you see, young William. I likes to get my hands on a little bit of this and that. Campaign memorabilia mostly. Cap badges, old uniforms, weapons from the wars. Anything with a story is what I like most.'

He looks at Blue Tear and then across at Bino, who's leaning over the snooker table lining up on a red.

'Why do you have to bring fucking OMO over there with you?' he says to Blue. 'How does that slogan go: "Only OMO gives guaranteed extra whiteness?"'

Blue grins. Then he slips his right hand under the table and brings something out of the side of his black Dr Marten and puts it on the table. It's a really long knife with a big metal handle.

Ossie picks it up.

'Stories, young William, that's what I like, for instance, what we have here is a Fairburn-Styles fighting knife designed before the war by another William, Mr William Ewart Fairburn, and his mate, Mr Eric Anthony Sykes. A couple of ex-Brit coppers in the Shanghai police. Standard issue out in Malaya, where I was. So, not so valuable then, you might think, to a collector, like me, as every fucking square-basher had one of these? But that's where you would be wrong.'

Ossie's sits back in his chair and hitches his pants up. He's wearing purple leather crepe-soled shoes.

Blue Tear's face cracks into one of them sneer-smiles that

he does. He picks up the knife with his right hand and presses the tip of it into the palm of his left. A little pin-prick of blood begins to ooze to the surface. Ossie just carries on talking.

'Something nasty happened out there in the jungle. A massacre, they said. Little kids and that. Throats cut, body parts missing. Yellow ears, yellow fingers, yellow toes. Maybe one of them homesick squaddies had an ampoule of morphia too many, and went a little crazed in the sun? It can be that way with them ampoules. A man can dream so sweet with them, young William. Golden slumbers, if you like. But, take my word for it, them dreams can turn to darkness faster than a cloud running in front of the sun.'

Ossie takes the knife back from Blue.

'There's nothing I hate more than that, son, a sweet dream that curdles. A sweet dream that turns sour. Can't abide them. Sour dreams like that, some men they can't shake 'em. Dreams like that, they can cover a man whole, drown him slowly from the inside, begin to suffocate all his days and nights. In the end, hold him as tight as a stillborn in a grieving mother's arms.'

He runs his little finger across the blade of this Fairburn-Styles knife.

'But maybe I'm letting my imagination run a little wild, a little fanciful. It was trophy hunters more like, eh, young William? That's what I expect. Looking for something interesting to take back to Blighty. A little bit of lobe or pinky finger. Precious memories, same as you and your little pal, Ninder, might bring a couple of Polaroids back from Benidorm or…Bangalore.'

When I hear Ossie say Ninder's name I try and look as if nowt's the matter.

'I've never been to Benidorm, Mr Mingle. Or...to either of

them places. And, like I said to Blue, I haven't seen her for ages and ages.'

There's a crackle of static. A bloke who's standing on the stage does a couple more taps on the mic. Blue-Tear reaches up with his little finger and touches the tear that's tattooed on his face. Then he leans in over the table and sort of squeezes me cheeks and rubs me chin a bit, like a mam would with a new baby.

'Found this knife on the jungle floor they did, Sir Isaac,' says Ossie. 'Because it's nipped off all them ears, toes and fingers – because it's got a story – that means a lot to blokes who collect stuff. A story like that is something people will pay for.'

Ossie puts the knife back down on the table and leans back in his seat. He rests his feet up on a bar stool. Me dad used to have a pair of shoes with crepe-soles like that. He used to wear them to take me mam dancing to the Oxford Ballrooms in town.

'Like the clip of them soles, young William? Brothel creepers is what people used to call shoes like this, back in the day. I mean, the way I see it, a man like me's got no call to be creeping about in no brothel. But, if you want to call them synagogue creepers, call them mosque creepers, call them jungle creepers, well, then maybe.'

Blue Tear starts to snigger.

Ossie stares across at him.

'What you fucking laughing at, son? Did I invite you to interrupt my conversation?'

Blue stares back but says nowt.

Ossie turns to me again.

'I need your help, young William. That's the long and short of it. That's why, as soon as I heard Blue, here, talk about you and your mate, Ninder, and her mum's job at the museum, I hotfooted it all the way up here. There's something I'd like you to help me add to my collection.'

The best thing, I'm thinking, is just to agree with anything now. Then try and work out what I'm going to do once I get outside the Legion. I nod me head.

'Whatever you say, Mr Mingle.'

'Good. That's good,' says Ossie.

He leans forward and drums his fingers on the flat blade that's lying on the table. Then he puts the middle finger of his right hand up to his lips.

'Silence is what I expect from you now, son. Keep schtum and say nowt.'

ME DAD CUTS ANOTHER BIT OF SELLOTAPE FROM THE ROLL AND sticks it on to the slightly worn blue Formica that covers the top of our kitchen bench. He pulls up the edges of some sparkly wrapping paper and covers the top of the brown perfume box. Then he uses the piece of Sellotape he's just cut to keep it in place.

I get up from the kitchen table and use me knife to scrape me chips and rissoles into the little Pedalo bin that we keep near the sink.

Dad looks over at me.

'You alright, son?'

'Fine.'

It's the first thing I've said since I got back from the Legion.

I don't feel like I can talk to me dad these days. So, I can't tell him about Watergate acting all funny. Or Blue Tear and this

Ossie Mingle and what they said at the Legion. No, I can't talk to me dad about important stuff anymore. Not now he's decided to betray me mam with this Mrs Damoan.

'You've gone a bit peaky. And you've hardly touched your rissoles. Have you got something on your mind?'

'Not hungry.'

Dad walks over to the fridge and opens it. He pulls out a blue-and-white striped bowl and holds it out towards me.

'What about Angel Delight? It's strawberry flavour. Your favourite.'

'I'm fine.'

I start running some hot water into the washing up bowl in the sink and stare out of the kitchen window. Dad steps up beside me and picks up a yellow tea towel that's got a picture of the singer Frank Sinatra on it and some white type that says CROONER. LEGEND.

'You wash, I'll dry eh? We'll make a proper team, like Starsky and Hutch.'

He starts whistling.

'It's for her, isn't it?'

'Her?'

'Mrs Damoan.'

Dad stops whistling, puts the towel down and goes back to the box and picks it up. He takes his car keys off the kitchen table and puts them in the pocket of his jeans.

'It's called Tweed Parfum de Toilette spray. I saw an ad about it on the telly.'

I stop the hot tap and then put some Fairy liquid in the bowl. Dad walks across the lino and then shuts the kitchen door behind him. I hear the knob turn. He opens it again and pops his head around the door.

'Wilma's gone.'

'What?'

'The Wilma Flintstone pepper-pot is missing.'

I don't turn around. I just keep washing me plate.

'Put it back will you, our Billy,' says Dad. 'Fred's all by himself on the table over there; if you ask me, he's looking a bit lonely.'

Chapter Eighteen

Ninder takes a pink "What are little girls made of?" hanky out of her pocket and unfolds it on top of me Tin Tin duvet cover

I've been feeling like I should tell her about Blue Tear and his uncle and how they know her name and everything. But I know I won't do that. She acts dead tough on the outside Ninder but she knows Blue Tear from school. She'd be scared about him coming to find her. Maybe they won't get back in touch. Maybe it will just be like it used to be at school with Blue and Bino; him and his uncle will just get bored and drift off, when they find someone else to pick on.

Eureka gobbles up the cucumber. His little nose moves up and down all quick and quivering as he does it; like a tiny spot of pink jelly on a dead small furry plate.

'Gerbils are just supposed to eat hamster food. Cut up veg like that is only recommended as a treat. I read a pamphlet in the pet shop in the Handyside Arcade that explained all about it.'

'I thought you didn't like pets?'

'Uncle Frank took me there once. We were looking for a sunken shipwreck for his guppy tank.'

Ninder takes another bit of cucumber from the hanky and holds it just above the bars of Eureka's cage. She's fed him about seven bits already.

Eureka stands up on his back legs and holds onto the bars of the cage with his front ones.

'I've stroked this little fella loads. But I'm no further forward thinking about Noor's death. So, I thought I'd bring him around here and try him on you again.'

I reach across to me bedside table and pick up a piece of scrap paper. I've written down as much of the W.S letter that Watergate took back as I can remember on it. I start reading it out to her again.

Ninder reaches across and grabs it.

'I'm not seeing how all this stuff about these letters is helping me. They're helping you, yes. Because that's what you were interested in the first place! But not me, the only thing we've got that seems relevant to me uncle's death is a dried-up bit of dog shit with some funny patterns made by Blakeys in it, and a tube of glue. I mean, even if he is a Nazi, how do we know this Watergate's really got anything to do with me Uncle Noor's death anyways?'

I try and grab the scrap paper back off her.

'We know he's took that Vienna book out all them times though, Ninder, so we know he's interested in Vienna, same as the writer of the letter is. And that he's taken other letters from the post office, same as this one you've copied out. Maybe there's two of them? Someone who writes to Watergate and he writes to them back. There are definitely more letters, anyways. That's what he said to me when he came around out house: "The other ones." He was dead clear about that. And he mentioned that these other ones had drawings in them, as well. They might be drawings of targets, or something. Buildings these Nazis, or National Front, whatever you want to call them, are planning to attack. Same as they might have done, I suppose, to Uncle Noor's shop. But I agree with you we still don't know for certain that someone started the fire that killed your uncle on purpose. You haven't got any evidence to prove that. In science, you need evidence. That letter is evidence. The way Watergate's been behaving, all odd, staying off work loads, threatening me, and taking that G.F. Brookburn book out of the library all the time, is evidence. The fact that the glue we found at Noor's was modelling glue is evidence.'

Ninder crumples up the scrap paper dead slowly and lobs it into me metal bin with prehistoric cave paintings on it that Mam got for free with two packets of Daz washingup powder.

'I've got all the evidence I need. It's called gut instinct, boffin-brain. This letter thing of yours is a blind alley. I'm as certain as this twitching fecking gerbil here likes cucumber! Those coppers just decided, straight off the bat, Uncle Noor's death was an accident. I don't believe it. When he moved here, he had that place completely rewired. The police weren't interested. You'd better help me find who did it or I'm not helping you out with this W.S letters donkey bollocks anymore. And make sure you have a proper look this time...'

'I'm not a trained forensic scientist; just a kid who likes science. And you were there too, remember?'

Ninder undoes the little cage and takes out Eureka. Then she holds him out to me.

'Go on, stroke him. I know you don't like animals but something will come to you. Trust me.'

I really don't want to take a hold of him but, in this mood, Ninder won't take no for an answer. As I start to stroke him, he makes a funny coughing noise. Then his whole body shakes up and down a couple of times.

'What the matter with him?' says Ninder.

Me and her stare down at me Tin Tin duvet. A little pool of bright green gerbil sick is covering Professor Calculus's face.

UNCLE NOOR'S EMPORIUM SEEMS EVEN MORE KNACKERED AND vandalised than the last time I was here – just to keep Ninder happy, I said I'd have one more look, like.

I've been searching around the floor, on me hands and knees, for about twenty minutes now. I'm just about to get up and go home when I spot something half-hidden, under a bit of burnt floorboard. It's near the hole in the brickwork that I found the baked dog-crap, with the Blakey pattern in it, and the tube of glue.

Me fingers stretch down to it but I can't get a proper hold.

I try a couple of more times. Finally, just as I think I'm not going to be able to reach properly, I feel me fingers grip right around a tiny piece of melted something. I'd probably have found it last time I was here if it hadn't started pissing down. It's a burnt blob of black plastic. All round and knobbly. A couple of centimetres thick. I twist it around between me fingers. There are a couple of letters printed on the other side, in the only bit of the plastic that hasn't melted. A letter U and a letter S. US. It says: Us…

Like whoever torched Uncle Noor's shop has left this here as a kind of confession.

Chapter Nineteen

Ninder looks down at the bit of black plastic in her hand.

'Us?'

I point at the two partially-melted letters,

'Yes, us; a U and an S.'

She hands the lump of plastic back to me.

'So, now we know it was us, that's what you're saying? Us could be anybody. Nice one, Billy Quiz, you've narrowed down the list of suspects, for setting fire to me uncle's shop, to the entire population of the world. That's not evidence, I should never have said I'd come back here to Chapel Park with you.'

'It's melted; it must have been melted by the fire, being melted means it was there before the fire started. I've never seen a top like that on any of the sauce or pop bottles your uncle stocked. Maybe the people who started the fire brought it with them? It's evidence, alright.'

Ninder squats down next to me and me telescope. I budge

up a bit. We're kneeling inside the clump of bushes, on the hill, next to Watergate's house.

'Evidence of you being a prize wombat, yes, maybe.'

I put me eye back to the viewfinder of me telescope.

'Is he in there?'

'No, he must be in the kitchen, or something.'

'What can you see?'

'Same as last time. It's just a front room like anyone else's. He's got an empty mug on the arm of a chair that's in front of his telly. There's a dirty blue-and-white plate on the floor that was there the last time; with two more next to it now. Some beer cans and a whiskey bottle on a table at the back, and an old green shoebox, with some papers in it.'

Ninder kneels down next to me.

'Let me have a gander.'

Still on me knees, I shuffle to the side.

She puts her eye to the telescope and starts blowing a small pink Bazooka Joe bubble out of her mouth as she does. She keeps blowing and the bubble gets bigger and bigger. Then it pops over her chin. She leans right back from the telescope and uses her hands to push the remains of the gum back into her mouth.

'I can't see nothing, Billy.'

'Nothing? I can see Mars with that telescope and Mars is millions of miles away.'

'Nothing about Nazis, that's what I mean. I thought he'd have posters up or something. Or a flag. Or, I don't know – a pair of jackboots hanging on a shoe-tree that's been carved to look like Hermann Goering's bum-hole, but there's nothing. It just looks like anybody's living room only a bit more untidy than most.'

Ninder sits down on the ground next to the telescope. She

starts chewing on the gum again. I put me eye back to the viewfinder and stare dead hard. There's a picture of an orange cat on the wall behind the dining table which matches the ones on his curtains. I don't know if that cat Schrodinger was thinking of was a ginger one. I hope it was. It would be really nice to think me and Erwin Schrodinger's cat had the same colour hair.

The ginger cat picture is resting on a mantelpiece with a couple of ornaments on it. Two odd-looking brass dogs and photo of a woman in a frame. I focus on the photograph and recalibrate the lens so I can see as much as I can possibly get it of it. The woman in the photo is wearing a red dress and has a nice smile. Dad told me Watergate was married once. It must be his ex-wife. I move me telescope down and to the right slightly, so I can see what's in the green box on the table.

I can see the edges of a few bits of paper straightaway. Maybe it's some more letters. Just as the viewfinder centres on the box, Watergate steps into view and I lose sight of it. He's wearing a white string vest and the kind of khaki shorts held up with a black belt that blokes wear in the army. I can see that he's looking at himself in the mirror above the mantelpiece. Suddenly, he snaps to attention and gives an army salute. Then he turns around and goes towards his window. He pulls the curtains shut. Now, all I can see is the orange cat pattern again.

I sit up.

'He just did a salute, an army salute.'

Ninder grabs the telescope off me and pushes her eye up close to the lens.

'Was it a Sieg Heil?'

I shake me head.

She presses her eye closer to the lens.

After a moment, she sighs and blows out another big pink bubble. Then she pops it.

'He's shut the curtains now. We'll have to come back tonight,' says Ninder.

'It's a telescope, not an X Ray machine. It can't see through curtains.'

Ninder's voice goes dead mischievous.

'Of course not, Billy Quiz. That's why, tonight, me and you are going in.'

NINDER PUTS HER HAND INSIDE THE POCKET OF HER LEATHER donkey jacket and takes out a half brick. She nods to the frosted glass panel in the back of Watergate's kitchen door. Then she holds her arm back ready to smash it.

I grab a hold of her.

'Muffled,' I whisper. 'You'll need to wrap it in cloth, or something, to muffle the sound. It's eleven o'clock at night. You'll wake the whole street up.'

Ninder looks around in the darkness. There's nothing to see in Watergate's garden except a smashed green house and little red gnome's hat surrounded by tall grass. It must be a long time since Watergate got his mower out. The tip of the red hat looks dead weird. Like it's a little temple, or something, that's being slowly covered by the surrounding jungle.

'You're the science brain, Billy Quiz, think of something.'

'Maybe we should just go home?'

She gives me one of her looks.

I lean a bit closer to her so I can whisper even lower.

'You're into women's lib, and that. You think of something. What would this Germaine Greer do?'

Ninder looks around the garden again. Her nose scrunches up a bit at the end, as she's thinking.

'Here, hold this.'

She hands me the brick and then leans down and reaches under her skirt. She does a little up-and-down movement with her legs. Something falls around her Dr Marten's. She steps forward and out of her knickers. Then she takes the brick back off me and wraps it in them. As she pulls her arm all the way back again, I can just make out the T of Tuesday in the moonlight.

I LOOK AT THE PICTURE OF THE FAT ORANGE CAT IN Watergate's living room. It looks a lot different now I'm not staring at it from the lens of me telescope. It's got a real sly expression. Like it was hoping me and Ninder would turn up.

'What if Watergate comes back?' I whisper.

'He's playing darts with your dad, over Durham way. They won't get back until well after twelve. That's what you said.'

'Yes, but what happens if he comes back early?'

Ninder is standing in the middle of the living room. She's got a small pocket torch in her hand. She turns around. The light from the torch shines right in me eyes. I start blinking.

'This Watergate's a Nazi. That's why there was a swastika stamp on that letter he's been after. He knows other Nazis is what I'm thinking, and one of them could have been involved in killing me Uncle Noor. If he shows up, I'm going to batter him on the bonce with a half-brick covered in me Days of the Week under-crackers. That's what's going to happen if he comes back.'

There's not much in Watergate's living room. A sofa and an

armchair. His telly. The ginger cat picture. An old dining table with a Formica top on it that is patterned black and white like a zebra skin. On top of that, there's the green shoebox I could see earlier through the telescope, and a couple of other things too: a half-empty bottle of whiskey and a cardboard box full of bits of plastic and little tins of Hummel model paints. I take a couple of steps towards the table and pick up one of the bits of plastic. I hold it up to the moonlight coming through the bay window.

Then I freeze.

Through the glass of the window, I can see an old bloke standing on the pavement outside. He's staring directly at me and Ninder. She turns around towards me.

'What the feck you doing now, Billy?'

I put me finger to me lips. Nod me head in the direction of the old fella outside the window. Ninder stops dead still. The bloke keeps staring straight at us. He doesn't say nowt.

Me heart is beating like it's going to burst right out of me chest. 'Smokey? Is that you, Smokey?' shouts the bloke. 'I've got your favourite; it's Whiskers.'

A black cat slinks out from under the bay window and walks towards him. The old bloke picks it up and starts to carry it down the street.

I let out a big sigh. So does Ninder.

'The daft old git didn't see us,' she says.

I pull out a chair from Watergate's dining table and sit down on it. I rest me hands on the table. I can feel meself calming down a little bit. I loosen the fingers of me right hand and stare down at the little plastic figure I'm holding in it. Its head is shaven so it looks a bit like a little skinhead. A midget Blue Tear. A tiny Bino. Except this skinhead is wearing blue-and-white striped pyjamas. Its face is still white, plasticky and unpainted. Ninder is rooting through some paperwork that's stacked on the mantelpiece behind me. I grab a hold of the green box.

That's when I see them. White envelopes. Lots of them. Some of them with swastika stamps on. But some with ordinary stamps on, too. They are all filled with letters.

Ninder stops in front of a door. She turns the knob and opens it. Then she shines her little torch inside.

'Bloody hell, Billy, have you seen this?'

I jump up from the table and stand right next to her. Me and her stare into the darkness of the little room together. The thin beam of her torch travels slowly across the model that fills the entire room, as if it's a searchlight. I follow it as she picks out the little huts, guards towers, and hundreds of thin figures wearing the same blue-and-white striped pyjamas as the one I've got in me pocket.

The little beam runs across the whole compound until it reaches a building surrounded by rows of neat flower-beds which has very big chimney stuck to the top of it. Ninder switches her torch off and the chimney disappears.

'Jezuz, Billy. Fecking Jezuz!'

There's a noise in the street outside.

I turn around and look out of the big bay window. The old bloke is back but he hasn't brought his cat with him this time. He's brought a policeman instead.

Ninder turns and sees him too.

'Let's leg it!'

She runs through the door that leads to Watergate's kitchen. I follow her. We peg it through the kitchen door and out into the overgrown garden. Ninder knocks over Watergate's garden gnome as she clambers over his fence. I put me Polyveldt through one of the greenhouse's broken glass panels but then I'm over the fence and running.

Me breath's coming in short, sharp bursts. Beads of sweat are dripping down me head and neck but we've made it to the top of the hill. I turn back and look down past the two big electricity pylons and the little clump of bushes where we hid the telescope this morning.

The copper is still chasing us. Ninder runs by me.

'Keep running you daft fecker.'

I turn away from him and start running again.

Just as Ninder reaches the line of trees at the top of the hill I catch up with her and we dive into the wood together. We keep running for another minute or two and then, when we're right in the middle of it, we stop. I sit down on the trunk of a big fallen tree and try to catch me breath.

Ninder sits down next to me.

I put me hand into the back pocket of me cords and take something out.

'Auschwitz,' I say. 'I've seen it before on the World at War on the telly.'

I lay out three letters I took from the green box, and the little model of the woman in the blue-and-white striped pyjamas, on the trunk of the tree in front of her.

'He's building a model of Auschwitz.'

Chapter Twenty

This Nimble bread, that Dad's started buying, is something to do with Mrs Damoan. I'm sitting on me Tin Tin duvet cover drinking tea from me Esso mug and taking small bites from a PEK sandwich. I'm only taking small bites because this Nimble bread tastes all dry; like eating cardboard. It's some new stuff for slimmers. Mam would never have bought bread like this. She always got Hovis.

Me and Ninder had to hide in the wood for about an hour until the police went. They didn't go up the hill to look for us, or anything. One of them went around the back of Watergate's house with a torch and mooched about for a bit. Then him and the other one, a WPC, just sat on the bonnet of their Panda car for about ten minutes and smoked a couple of tabs.

I've got the three letters we took from the house spread out on top of me duvet. The first thing I can tell about them is that they are all written by the same person who wrote the one to Rebecca, about the door and her not trembling. The person who wrote that Rebecca letter and Watergate's envelope wrote these new ones, alright.

The handwriting's exactly the same.

The first one says:

Ari,

Alter Strasse,

Bezirke Veindenburger,

Wein.

The other two have exactly the same street bit, and are sent to this Bezirke Veindenburger, District 24, that I already know doesn't exist. The names on them are Adina and Benjamin.

I pick up the Ari one and take it out of the envelope. I unfold the letter, which is on the same old-style paper as all the ones I've seen, and spread it flat on the duvet cover.

I stare down at the spidery blue writing that covers the page.

Dear Ari,

Ich Sehe Sie,

You were such a gentleman, Ari, such a fine old gentleman, with your full lips and well-cut grey hair. You leaned down, so politely, and helped me take off your patent-leather shoes.

I have had those shoes buffed and polished for you.

You were a strong one, Ari, a strong one; when you leaned down so courteously and helped me slip off those fine shoes you already understood that your journey was ending there.

Ich Sehe Sie, Ari

Your

W. S

I'm not sure what all this stuff about this Ari bloke and his patent-leather shoes is about. I mean, why would he give this W.S his shoes in the first place? Especially, if they were really expensive ones like he, or she, says they are. And why would

W.S polish them up and keep them for him in this place they're on about that I know, for certain, doesn't actually exist?

There's a cough and a snort from the room next door as me dad turns over in his sleep and starts snoring. I take another bite out of me PEK and Nimble sandwich. I pick up the second envelope, the one addressed to Adina, and take out the letter inside it. I put that one down on me bed-spread and begin to read it.

Dear Adina,

Ich Sehe Sie,

I saw you once before then, I think.

I saw you waiting under the Hubersturwarte in the Lainzer Tiergarten for some recalcitrant lover.

You wore the most delicious pink cloche hat.

Are they here too, Adina? Is that what you are wondering?

Have they also been brought to that unimaginable place?

No, I will not allow it.

I have built a Tiergarten, too.

He looks for you there, Adina; under das Huberstuwarte, the watchtower.

He, like me, will never stop watching.

He, like me, waits for you still.

Ich Sehe Sie,

Adina

Your

W.S

There they go again, this W.S, going on about building stuff.

I hear another noise from the room next door.

Me dad's stopped snoring. I see a light appear under me door as Dad steps out of his own room and heads towards the bog. I grab a hold of the three letters, turn off me side-light, jump under me duvet and stick the envelopes under me pillow. Then I roll over and try to get some sleep.

It's only a few more hours before me shift starts because I'm on Earlies, but it doesn't matter. I can't sleep anyway. Every time I close me eyes all I can see is the same thing. Which is the model in Watergate's house; with its little guard towers and trees and tiny figures dressed in blue-and-white stripes.

Chapter Twenty-One

Ninder takes a good deek around the little side street in the centre of town. It has a couple of travel agents and a record shop in it. A dead old-fashioned street sign says Ridley Place.

'Why the feck are we here?'

I walk a little further down the street. She walks with me

'I've been thinking about the letters me and you took from Watergate's house,' I say, 'and this W.S, who's writing the letters. That him, or her, might be some sort of builder, or an architect maybe. And about why he, or she, would be building an observatory, when I know from the Vienna book that Vienna's already got one. And the same thing goes for a Huberstuwarte, a watchtower, because it's already got one of them, too.'

I stop in front of a small café with a green-and-gold painted door. I look through the window of the shop at all the nice cakes and biscuits it's got on display in silver-tiered cake stands with white paper doilies on them. Ninder's eyes light up a bit when she sees them cakes.

'Mostly, I'm thinking about the green box on Watergate's table. The one that he was keeping the letters in. Because it wasn't a shoe box after all. It had a little gold coffee cup drawn on the side of it…'

I point up at the green and gold sign that's hanging above our heads.

'…a gold coffee cup that looks exactly like that one.'

A little bell tinkles as me and Ninder step inside the Café Wagner.

I LOOK DOWN AT THE BOX I'M HOLDING. A GREEN BOX WITH A gold drawing of a coffee cup on the side, tied up with gold-coloured string. It seems funny to be standing here in Windsor Mansions without me postman's uniform on; just me ordinary clothes, and no post-bag but still holding a parcel at the same time. I stare at the black door bell that's stuck to the yellow door. I've been here for five minutes already but I still can't bring meself to push it. Even if the beautiful witch-woman behind the yellow door isn't a Nazi, or a witch, just the fact of her being dead pretty makes it difficult for me to talk to her in the first place. I stretch out a finger towards the doorbell.

I still can't make meself push.

Let's examine the facts:

1. Someone sends her parcels from this Austrian Café Wagner in town.

2. Watergate must go to the same café as he's got a box from it inside his house filled with odd letters. Letters that are maybe written in some sort of code. It could be Watergate that's sending her the parcels.

3. Watergate must be a Nazi of sorts; he is building a model of Auschwitz in his bedroom.

She's got to be in the middle of this somehow.

I pull me finger away from the door bell.

If Watergate's a Nazi then so, most likely, is she. There could be loads of them, like a secret cell, all using this café to exchange these letters which have been written in code. I lean down and gently place the parcel on the doorstep. I think I'll just leave it there for her. Maybe I'll come back tomorrow with Ninder. She's better at confrontations than me. Me and her can confront this Nazi-witch-woman together.

I look up. The door begins to open.

The beautiful woman stands there with a small green watering can in one hand. She's twisting with her fingers at the little white bit of jewellery that hangs around her neck, like she did the last time I saw her. I just stare up at her. I can't bring meself to say nowt. She looks down at the green cake box I've placed on her step. There's a tiny popping sound. The white bead falls in front of me and rolls across to the wall with some new graffiti on it that says "The Windsor witch lives here." It looks kind of funny. Like whoever painted the graffiti had put it there on purpose. As though it was a tiny white full-stop at the end of their dead badly-sprayed-on sentence.

I drop down low and then crawl over on me hands and knees and pick it up. I turn back around and show it to her. Her face goes all still. A bit like she's having one of them "Weather Head" moments Little Laura, from me mam's church gets.

Then she smiles that smile she does. The one that makes me think of them faraway twinkles. She leans down and picks up the green cake box I've brought with me. She stands up again.

This time she holds the yellow door wide open.

Ausonia.
Monday, 12th July 1976.
9 days before Viking 1 lands on Mars

Chapter Twenty-Two

This Nizanna – the witch-woman says her name is Nizanna – looks like she owns her own library, or something. She's sitting at a little table in her living room, sewing the clasp of the white bead back onto her neck-chain. There's books all over the place. I don't know what I was expecting a Nazi's house to look like but this isn't it. Some of the books are in German but most of them are in English. Not the kind me mam and dad like – your Mills & Boon romances, or James Herbert thrillers – but proper writers like Charles Dickens, and that.

She's got one of Dickens' lying open and half-read next to a purple, velvet-covered, sewing box on top of the little table she's sewing at. There are two old black-and-white photographs standing on the mantelpiece above the fire: one shows her, as little bairn, maybe ten years old, with what must be her mam and dad standing behind her.

Her dad is dead old for a dad; he must be at least fifty, with a big grey beard and white whiskers. He looks a bit like a thin version of the Santa Claus who comes to Santa's Grotto at the

Co-op, every year. But, he's got an old-style suit on that looks like it must be made of tweed, and his eyes are all deep and staring, and brainy looking; like he must be a professor. This Nizanna's mam is younger looking than him; maybe thirty, I reckon. She's dead pretty with dark hair, like her daughter.

The photograph next to it is a black-and-white one of a house. It's difficult to say how old the house is because although the photograph, itself, looks old the house looks new. I've never seen anything like it. Not around Walker way, anyways. It's all square with white walls and big stairs going up to it out of a nice garden. It's a posh house, alright, because I can see a bit of the place next door in the corner of the photo, and it looks massive with loads of chimneys and big windows. But the main house in the photograph is more like a big white square box with lots of glass cut through it all over the place. Them big windows are the sort you could stare out at the night sky forever. I'd love to be able to keep me telescope inside a house like that.

Nizanna finishes sewing and puts down the needle. She moves her head from side to side, so her dark hair shakes about a bit and catches some of the sun that's shining from a little window behind her. She slips the little silver chain and white glass bead back over her neck. Then she takes the bead between two fingers again and twists it slowly from side to side, just like she did before.

Nizanna pats the necklace flat against her black blouse.

'There, there, Postman, all back together again. Now, everything is exactly as it was.'

She smiles and gets up from her chair.

'Coffee for you and I, Postman. Coffee I think, and cake.'

I nod me head.

'Thank you.'

I've been here ten minutes already but it's the first thing I've managed to make meself say to her. I've felt too nervous with her maybe, being a Nazi spy and that. When I speak, Nizanna smiles. Then she walks into her kitchen and shuts the door behind her.

I can't believe she's a Nazi. Not with that smile. Me mam had a friend called Shirley Cowan who she used to drink with in the Comrades. Mrs Cowan was always talking about what's called "Past lives," where people think they've lived before and been someone else. When this Nizanna smiles at me, she makes me feel a bit like that. That me and her have met before some place. That we're old friends, already. I hope she stays like this. I don't feel dead comfortable with her when her "Weather Head" comes on.

I'M SITTING ON AN OLD-STYLE SOFA IN NIZANNA'S LIVING room, which is covered in red velvet and has two big purple cushions propped up, one on each side of it. There's a little wooden table and chair next to it. That's where Nizanna's sitting. On the wooden table is the green cake box that me and Ninder bought at the Café Wagner.

Nizanna's cut the big piece of Kaiserschmarrn that was inside the box into two pieces and put each piece on a small white plate with a thin gold band around the edge of it. There's what's called a cafetière on the table too. It's made of silver and glass. Nizanna's poured me and her a cup of black coffee each. It looks dead nice; that dark thick liquid against the white and gold of china cups and plates.

Nizanna leans forward and puts a bit of cream into each cup. I really like the way she does that. She turns the silver spoon she has in her hand right over and pours cream from a little gold-and-white jug over the back of it. Then there's a little pause before the cream seems to reappear from nowhere and float up into the middle of the cup; turning the coffee brown.

'An Obermeier, this is called an Obermeier, a special kind of coffee. I make an Obermeier in your honour, Postman. It is so lovely that we have it with Kaiserschmarrn. Once upon a time in my life, as I tell you, I was in a dark place where every night I would be dreaming of Kaiserschmarrn and a little cream.'

I lean forward and take a bite of me cake. I can see why this Nizanna likes it so much now. It tastes really sticky and sweet, like it comes straight from Willy Wonka's factory.

Normally, if you don't know someone well and you're in a little room with them, like a lift or something, and they don't say nowt and you don't say nowt it makes me feels all awkward. Most times like that, I just go red. But I don't feel the way I usually do eating cake with this Nizanna. She just looks over at me every now and then takes a sip of coffee and smiles. When she does that I feel a bit odd and strange. Like there's some sort of secret between us. Like it's me who's maybe the spy, not her.

She points at me plate.

'You, like your Kaiserschmarrn?'

I nod me head.

'Tastes like the apple crumble me mam used to make. We didn't have proper cream, like this, just Carnation milk out of a tin, but it was still dead tasty, like.'

'Thank you, thank you, Postman, for bringing it to me.'

'It's instead of the one you lost.'

'Lost?'

'The one you were looking for at the post office.'

Nizanna starts twisting at the little white jewel that hangs around her neck. She stands up, walks across to the mantelpiece, and straightens the picture of her and her dad that I was looking at before.

Then she starts to clear the plates away.

'He who is my admirer, I believe this person has sent me that.'

I pop the last lump of Kaiserschmarrn into me mouth, and pick me plate and cup up. I follow Nizanna through the white door into her little kitchen and put them down on her sink drainer.

She puts a little black plug into the sink and runs the hot-tap. I drop the plate and cup I'm holding into the water. I look around and pick up a little red tea towel from a silver rail that stuck behind the door. She doesn't ask me to do it. I just do it. I want to. It's making me feel really nice inside; me and this Nizanna standing next to the sink together. It feels a bit like when me and me mam used to do the dishes together. When I think about that it makes me say something. I just can't help meself.

'Me friend, Ninder, thinks you're a spy. You and this bloke called Watergate, who works at the post office. That you've not just been exchanging cakes but messages and secrets and that. I did too, but I'm not so sure now. I mean I was scared of you a bit, before I came in here, dead scared – because I thought you might be a Nazi, and that. But now I've sat down with you and had a bit of that apple cake I don't feel that like that anymore.'

Nizanna takes a bottle of Fairy Liquid from the window sill and squirts some of it into the sink. Little bubbles of soap begin to float up onto the surface of the water. First one pops, then another.

'A spy?'

'A Nazi spy. I thought so too, like I say, but now I'm not so sure.'

She turns off the tap and the hot water stops running.

'A Nazi spy with a secret code of Kaiserschmarrn. This is who you think I am, Postman? This is why you come here?'

She stares at me hard. I can feel me cheeks going redder and redder. Then her shoulders begin to shake. She's laughing now. Laughing loads. Really chuckling, like she's going to wet herself. After a moment, or two, I start laughing meself. I can't help it. Me and this Nizanna wifey just stand there at her little metal sink, watching the soap bubbles pop, and cracking up laughing together.

Chapter Twenty-Three

Afghan Larry pushes a bit of blonde hair out of his eyes. He sways his head to the right; like he's in one of them slow-motion bits on the shampoo ads on the telly. He leans across the table in the Man in the Moon pub and puts an arm around Ninder. The plectrum he's got tied to a bit of leather string around his neck – the plectrum he always tells lasses was found clutched in "The dead hand of Jimmy Hendrix at the Samarkand Hotel" – dips in to the top of his pint of lager. I don't like it when he grabs a hold of Ninder like that. Afghan Larry always has his hands all over the lasses.

Don't get me wrong, there's never been any sex stuff between me and Ninder. I generally try and avoid embarrassing situations like that. I've found that lasses generally try and avoid embarrassing situations like me, too, so that means everybody's happy. When I first started getting what Uncle Frank used to call "Hair on your sprouts," I had some funny thoughts after we all watched a film called Some Like it Hot one Christmas. There's a bit in that where Marylyn Monroe walks down a railway platform in very high heels and her bum starts wiggling like Birds Angel Delight on a space hopper. Once I'd watched it, I couldn't stop thinking about her bum for hours. So, I went upstairs to our bog and thought about it some more, and after a couple of minutes I had what Charles Darwin might have called a biological effusion. So, that's what I do now when it comes to sex stuff – pop upstairs to our bog, have a quick biological effusion and then think about something sensible like Newton's Second Law of Motion, or Boyle's really interesting law about the inversely proportional relationship between volume and pressure, instead.

Ninder takes a swig of her lager and lime. Then she puts her glass back down on the table.

'Jewish?'

'Nizanna Aisha Oz. That's her name. It's a Jewish name, she says.'

I do me best to do an impression of Nizanna's accent.

'"Tell your friend it's unlikely I am Nazi spy on account of me being Jewish," that's what she said.'

It's not a very good accent. I sound a bit like Mike Yarwood – who does impressions on the telly – doing that famous Swedish actress – Greta Garbo.

'Not a Nazi, then?' says Afghan Larry.

I take another drink of me orange cordial and say nowt. Ninder gives him one of her looks.

'In general, Larry, you'll find your Jewish Nazis are a bit thin on the ground.'

Larry shrugs, gets up and goes to the jukebox in the corner of the room. Even though it's another boiling hot summer day he's still wearing an Afghan coat like he, pretty much, always does; which is how he gets his nickname: Afghan Larry. He'll probably come back in a minute and tell me and Ninder that he's a currently a roadie for whatever band he puts on the jukebox, even though he's really a Sociology student at Newcastle Poly, with a Saturday job in Clarks shoes, in the Bigg Market. I saw him there once. He works on the Polyveldts' counter.

As Larry puts some money in the jukebox and presses a button, Smoke on the Water by Deep Purple begins to play.

LARRY MUST HAVE GONE TO THE BOG. HE'S BEEN AWAY FOR A good bit now. Me and Ninder have been gassing on about this and that.

The Man in the Moon is a big underground pub that's been built in a square shopping centre next to the Central Library in town. It's one of the places in Newcastle where all the hippies hang out. Ninder isn't fitting in well. She's wearing a short spangly cropped top with loads of holes ripped in it and a skirt she's made for herself out of a couple of old bin bags. Two Hell's Angels standing near the bar drinking pints of lager, are giving me and her funny looks. Every now and then one of them whispers into the ear of the other one and they both start laughing and nudging each other.

Larry comes back into the room and starts putting some more 10ps into the jukebox.

'You said you didn't see Afghan Larry anymore. That you weren't going to? He calls you fat-arse Lally, behind your back and Lallytanic, stuff like that.'

Ninder picks up her glass and has a drink. She looks across at Larry by the jukebox.

'He is dead fit, though. So, when he came around ours last night, I thought, why not go out. Just one drink. Where's the harm in that?'

'That plectrum has got nothing to do with Jimmy Hendrix.'

'You said that last time, when we had that bust-up.'

'He wasn't even playing his guitar when he died. I looked it up.'

Ninder sits forward in her chair and starts rolling a fag on the little plastic table in front of her. I take another sip of me orange.

'Do you think we should go to the coppers? I mean, maybe we should.'

She stops spreading the tobacco on her Rizzla paper and looks back at me.

'About what, exactly?'

'About Watergate.'

Ninder lifts her right eyebrow a bit. It looks quite hard to do. There's a big gold stud stuck through it, that looks like, in theory, it should be able to keep her eyebrow stuck in the same place forever.

'Don't be stupid, Billy. What do you think we'd tell them? Oh, I say, officer, my friend and I had broken into the house of one his colleagues to steal some letters, when we happened to stumble across a model of the death camps at Auschwitz which confirmed to us what we already suspected...that he was the leader of a Nazi spy ring who was communicating with a woman who lives at Windsor Mansions. But then, when we went all Poirot and Miss Marple on her case, and actually fecking talked to her, she didn't turn out to be a Nazi at all.'

Ninder leans across the table and slaps a sloppy wet kiss on the end of me nose.

'You're a complete idiot sometimes, do you know that, Billy Quiz? In spite of all them facts you know.'

She's right. The coppers would be just as likely to arrest me and her, as sit down and listen to us.

I sit back in me chair and look around the room. Through

the clear Perspex top of the jukebox, I see a metal bar lifting up one of the records and sticking it down on the turntable. A little fizz of static electricity crackles through the big black speakers stuck on top of the silver-and-purple plastic bar counter. Afghan Larry's next choice begins to play: All Along the Watchtower by Jimmy Hendrix.

The two Hell's Angels are still sniggering at the bar. Ninder sticks two fingers up at them. They start laughing even more. One of them shouts over at us.

'Made your knickers out of bin bags as well have you, pet?'

Afghan Larry comes back across the room and sits back down next to Ninder. He nods over at the two blokes.

'Moroccan black, Nepalese temple balls, those two can get you anything you want. Want someone doing over they can help out there as well, babe. Guy who works behind the bar at the City Hall, told me that there was a bloke who pissed in his pint one time when he went to the bog and then laughed in his face when he drank some of it. He pointed him out to them two. Then he slipped them five quid and two tickets to a Mott the Hoople concert.'

Ninder hands a rolled-up tab to Afghan Larry and then picks one up herself. She takes a little lighter out of her handbag and lights them both up. Another song comes on the juke box. It's by Jimmy Hendrix, too: Third Stone from the Sun. Larry sits back and puts his arm around Ninder; waves his Jimmy Hendrix plectrum in time to the music.

'Six months in hospital he was, babe, this bloke was six whole months in the RVI.'

Ninder sits back in the chair and takes a draw on her tab. She's lets out a big blue ring of smoke, which seems to kind of dance in front of her to the music, and stares hard through it at them two Hell's Angels.

I push me chair back and get up from the table.

'It's not right, not without proper evidence, not even with it.'

She looks up at me.

'What's not?'

'What you're thinking about.'

I point me finger at Afghan Larry.

'Larry will have to help you then, Ninder, because I'm not going to do it.'

I PUT ME KEY IN THE DOOR AND TURN IT.

It's dark inside our hallway. Dead dark. If he's in, me dad usually leaves the light on next to the hat-stand he and me mam got given as a wedding present by Grandma Brenda, who died of pleurisy; although Uncle Frank always says it was tabs and cheap brandy from the offy that did for her really. Not tonight, though.

I haven't had any proper scran meself since lunchtime. I'm so hungry I could eat a scabby cat. I walk straight down the hall and into our kitchen. Me heart nearly stops when I see him.

There's a bloke sitting in the pitch darkness at our table. I stretch out me arm and flick the light switch. Dad's sitting in his usual seat but he's not smiling or whistling or owt like that. His face is all red and flushed.

He's got some stuff lined-up on the red and white checked tablecloth in front of him. There's the two envelopes me and

Ninder got from Watergate's house and the Wilma Flintstone pepper-pot.

'I saw Watergate today, son. He told me some stuff.'

I walk across to the table and sit down at me usual place.

'They're not his. Them letters aren't his. Not really.'

'He says you stole them from his house and he's going to the coppers in the morning, if he's doesn't get them back.'

'He didn't write them, that's not his handwriting and they're not addressed to him. They're not his.'

'There's always been kinks in your thinking, son, and never more than when that that crazy Ninder's about. Fucking hell, Billy, lad, you can't just break into people's houses. He's a bit funny, I know, is Tommy, but, basically, he's a mate. If he wasn't, he would have gone to the coppers straightaway and where would you be then. He said as much himself.'

Dad puts his hand on the top of the pepper-pot and turns Wilma's head to face me.

'I mean what do you think your mam would have made of all this if she was still here? You know what she was like about right and wrong.'

Dad gets up from the table and goes to the sink. He pours himself a glass of water from the tap. Then he sits back down again. I reach across and pull the pepper-pot to me own side of the table. I turn Wilma's face away from me dad, so only I can see her.

'You're trying me patience, Billy, son.'

'Mam wouldn't like Mrs Damoan, I don't.'

Dad reaches across and takes hold of Wilma's head. I grab a hold of her body.

Dad tightens his grip. I tighten mine.

'You're shagging her aren't you? That's what everyone at

work says. How can you do that when me mam's only just gone?'

I feel me dad's grip loosen a bit.

'It's been nearly two years, son. I'm lonely that's all. People get lonely.'

'Slag.'

At first, it comes out as a bit of a whisper.

'Slag!'

The second time I shout it.

'All blonde hair and big tits and that. She's a fucking slag!'

Me dad lets go of the pepper-pot. He stands up slowly. His breathing's gone all fast and heavy. Then he stretches out his hand and hits me smack in the face. I drop Wilma. She lands on the kitchen floor and smashes. Dad sits back down again on his side of the table. Big plopping tears start rolling down his face. It's the first time I've ever seen him bubble. He didn't even let me see that when me mam died, although I heard him do it. I put a hand to me face and feel me hot red cheek.

'That's what they do,' I say. 'Blue Tear and Bino and them, at school they used to belt me like that.'

For a moment, I think I'm going to tell him about Ossie Mingle and Blue Tear and Bino and what they've been doing to me and how me and Ninder think there's a Nazi spy ring, somewhere in Newcastle, and the weird witch-woman, who lives at Windsor Mansions, who we thought was in it, but now we know isn't. Let it all burst out...

But then, I can't help meself, I start bubbling too. Me and me dad sit at the table and look at the little pieces of knackered crockery on the kitchen lino – sit there saying nowt – just staring down at the broken bits of me mam's Wilma Flintstone pepper-pot.

Chapter Twenty-Four

Dad parks his blue Ford Escort next to a red phone box on Watergate's street and cuts the engine. He looks across at me. I don't look back. I stare down at the little pile of letters and the key that I'm holding in me hands. Dad gives out a big sigh and gets out of the car. He starts walking across the street to Watergate's house.

I jump out of the Escort and start running after me dad.

'Auschwitz,' I shout.

Dad shrugs his shoulders. Then he turns back towards me.

'What is it now, son?'

'He's making a model of Auschwitz, Dad. The death camp where they killed all them Jews.'

'That's right, son, Tommy likes making models. That's why, when he sits down at the table with us at work, he's usually reading Model Maker magazine, or something like it. He's very good at it. So good, in fact, that, from time to time, he's even made them for special exhibitions at the Hancock Museum. They did one on the Holocaust, about five years ago. Since Tommy makes models, and had also visited some of the camps themselves at the end of the war, they asked him to make one of Auschwitz. That will be what you saw, I expect, when you took it upon yourself to break into his house.'

Dad sighs.

'If your mate Sherlock Lally had bothered to ask her mam, who actually works at the bleeding museum in the first place, she could have told her that for nowt.'

I stand at the end of Watergate's garden path feeling all daft and stupid. Dad rings the bell. When the door opens I can just make out a woman's eyes and a bit of her nose behind the gap between the security chain and the doorpost.

'Our Tommy's not here,' says the woman. 'I'm house-sitting for him.'

I feel meself relax a bit when she says that.

'Will he be back, later?' asks Dad.

The woman takes the chain off the door and opens it fully. When she does that we can see she's a bit plump with grey hair and is about sixty, I reckon. Her eye make-up is all smeared. It looks like she's been bubbling.

'You're Bobby, aren't you, Bobby Agnew, I recognise you from the club. I'm Alice, Tommy's sister.'

'You alright, Alice, love?' says Dad.

She nods and wipes her eyes with the corner of a big pink pinny she's wearing.

'I'm fine, Bobby, pet. Nice as nine-pence. Our Tommy's not, though. Coppers rang this morning; a couple of blokes jumped him when he got out of his car last night. Kicked him black and blue, they did.'

WHEN ME MAM DIED SHE DIDN'T GO STRAIGHTAWAY. SHE HIT her head on a pavement slab that some workman had left on Scrogg Road. If it wasn't for that slab, the doctor said afterwards, she might have been alright. Mr Pontefract, the insurance salesman, wasn't driving that fast, when he had his heart-attack. I mean she still would have had some bumps and bruises and stuff. Maybe some broken bones too, but she would have made it.

They brought her here, to the Royal Victoria Infirmary, when it happened. A really big hospital near Newcastle's football ground. I can still see me and Uncle Frank sitting in a little room near the emergency department. They'd given us both cups of tea in small green cups and pink wafer biscuits, which matched the hospital walls, to go with them.

Me and Uncle Frank waited ages watching the tea go cold in the green cups and not touching the biscuits while me dad went to see the main doctor.

Then Dad came back into the room. He didn't come over to us. He just sat down on a green canvass chair, near a little teak coffee table that was covered with magazines called things like Tit Bits and Chit Chat. One of them had a picture of a comedian off the telly, Bernard Manning, on the front. He was wearing a red bow-tie and all grinning and smiling next to a headline that said STARKERS NUN READS ZODIAC TO PRAYING VICAR. Dad picked it up and started to read it but he was just turning the pages really. His hands were shaking. We knew then, me and Uncle Frank. Dad didn't have to say nowt.

I don't know what they were thinking when we were all in there, together. But, what I was thinking about was a little bit of disagreement me and me mam had, that morning. She'd wanted me to go to church with her. Dad never bothered with all that daft mumbo-jumbo stuff but Mam did. There was one on the corner near us called St Jude's. When I was small I used to go with her but then, when I was about twelve or thirteen, I told her I didn't want to go anymore. That morning, I' told her believing in a supreme creator was disproved by a book Charles Darwin wrote called On the Origin of Species by Means of Natural Selection, or the Preservation of Favoured Races in the Struggle for Life, and made about as much sense as the dinosaurs believing in Father Christmas. Me mam wasn't very pleased about that. She looked dead sad when she left for church. That was the last time I saw her.

'ME DAD SAYS THEY USED TO CALL YOU RED TOMMY.'

Watergate pushes himself up in bed and straightens his green hospital pillow with his good arm. His face is all bruised and swollen and he's got a big cut above his right eye, which is purple and knotted and bloody because they've had to put six stitches in it.

'They did, son, yes, when I was your age, all through me twenties too.'

The ward is quite small with only six beds in it. There are three other patients in here besides Watergate. One bloke's asleep with loads of plastic pipes and stuff stuck in him, the other two, a bloke in his twenties with a broken leg in plaster and a middle-aged man with his head in bandages are sitting up in their beds playing cards on the other side of the room.

'Do you mind if I ask you something, Tommy?'

He shakes his head.

'What sort of glue do you use for your models and that, is it UHU?'

Watergate smiles.

'Don't be daft, Billy Quiz. Humbrol, only ever Humbrol. No proper model-maker would ever use anything else.'

I smile back and reach across to push a bowl of fruit a little closer towards him, like.

'Have some of your fruit, Tommy.'

Watergate uses his good arm to push the bowl away.

'They're Cape grapes, son, our Alice brought them in. She doesn't know any better. You won't get me touching stuff like that; farmed by white farmers using the sweat and labour of black South Africans and benefiting a racist Apartheid regime.'

He lets out a massive belch.

'I could eat an elephant's arse, though. Getting the fuck kicked out of you always makes me ravenous. It happened a few times in the war.'

I reach down into the haversack I've brought with me. I take out a bag of Tudor pickled onion crisps, and hand it to Watergate.

'Maybe these, then.'

Watergate's eyes light up when he sees them.

'Champion, Billy Quiz. I can't see Tudor oppressing any of them potato farmers out in Northumberland, can you?'

Watergate holds the bag between his good arm and the fingers peeping out of the top of his crepe bandage on his bad one. He tries a couple of times to pull the bag open but he can't get a good enough grip.

'Bastard's only sprained the doctor says, but it hurts like bollocks in a vice.'

I take it from him, open the bag, and then offer him the crisps.

'It was me, Water...Tommy, who broke into your house.

I'm really sorry, like. Me and Ninder thought you were a Nazi spy. If you want to tell the coppers about it, Dad says I had to tell you he'd understand.'

Watergate dips the hand of his good arm into the bag takes a big handful of crisps.

'I knew it was you, son. Of course, I did.'

I take out the two letters from me haversack and then lay them on the blanket next to him.

'That's never a full house, you cheating bastard,' shouts one of the blokes, playing cards.

I get up and draw the green curtain around Watergate's cubicle.

He stares down at the letters.

'We called her the Letter Lady. She wrote them for fifteen years,' he says. 'Ever since I first met her. Then she stopped. The one you found in the library is different to the other ones I've got though.'

'Different how?'

'It's brand new, the paper is new. Basildon Bond I think they call it. As soon as I saw it, I knew that could only mean one thing.'

'Mean what, Tommy?'

'She's started again, Billy Quiz. The Letter Lady is back writing.'

Chapter Twenty-Five

Me and Watergate can hear Black Knight by Deep Purple blasting out from the basement bar of The Man in the Moon pub. We're standing about twenty-feet up on a big concrete walkway, that turns back around Newcastle's main library, looking down onto the square, where the pub is.

His face still looks a bit puffed up and there's dried-up blood clotted above his right eye, where they took his stitches out. He's got a white crepe bandage tied around his wrist. They only let him out of the RVI this morning.

It's half past eleven; nearly chucking out time, even for bars with late licences like The Man in the Moon. We've been standing here for about ten minutes already. The music gets a bit louder, as the door of the pub opens. It's the Rolling Stones now, Satisfaction. Three hippy blokes come out into the square. They all walk off towards Northumberland Street laughing.

Watergate turns towards me.

'You've had me all wrong, son. But I'll forgive you for that. Them letters can get you that way. Not thinking straight. Not seeing things how they really are, maybe. That's what they done to me anyway. And you are just a young 'un. You want to know more about them letters, of course, you do. I get that. I could tell you. But showing's better. There's a place we need to go to then, you and me, out near Wallington Hall, in Northumberland. If I take you there, that will explain a lot about the Letter Lady.'

'What sort of place?'

Watergate smiles.

'Scary to some, I'd say. But not to me, son. To me it's a place away from the rest of the world. A place where sometimes, even without a bottle of whiskey inside me, I've been close to forgetting me and my troubles.'

The music gets louder again as the door of the Man in Moon opens up again. It's Jimmy Hendrix: Third Rock from the Sun, again. Three blokes and a lass come outside and stand, talking and laughing, in the doorway of a shoe shop.

Watergate points down at them.

'You were right, Billy Quiz, the two big lads, they were the ones who done me. Who's the other one, the nonce with tart's hair?'

I stare down at the two Hell's angels in the square and the blonde-haired bloke wearing an Afghan coat who's handing them a brown envelope.

'They call him Afghan Larry.'

'And the weird looking lass, wearing what looks like a bin-liner?'

'Are you going to the coppers?'

'Not sure what I'm going to do yet, son'

I shake me head.
'I don't know her.'

THE RED POST VAN TURNS LEFT ONTO ANOTHER COUNTRY ROAD
and passes a stone wall and an old broken tree.

She's a big county, is Northumberland. Dad and Mam used
to bring me out on the bus to this Wallington Hall for picnics
and that years ago. It would take ages. Me and Watergate
passed the turn off for it about ten minutes ago.

Watergate's got one of his brown slip-ons stuck on top of
the accelerator pedal. They're imitation crocodile skin. Me dad
bought some too last year in a sale at Marks & Spencer but he
doesn't wear them much because he said they made his feet
stink like a skunk's arsehole. Watergate's foot is pressed right
down to the floor. He winces every now and then. They let him
take his sling off at the hospital but his arm must still be
tender.

The van shoots over the brow of a hill and from here, in the
bit of valley below us – even with the sunshine beginning to go
because it's nearly twenty to ten – we can see flat green fields
and big clumps of darker green and brown. The woods around
here seem to go on forever.

I lean forward, so I'm not so hunched in me seat.

'Why does this Letter Lady write a bit in German and a bit
in English, Tommy? I've never been able to get that bit.'

Watergate turns his head a bit towards me.

'It took me a while to get me head around that n'all, son.
There was a doc at this place, where we're going now, who
reckoned that German bit in the letters, ich sehe sie, it was
significant, meant something to her, something important.

That's why she would always say it twice, and always in German.'

'But the envelopes are in German too?'

Watergate shrugs.

'I can't see the logic in that either but, then again, writing them letters in the first place isn't exactly the sort of thing a logical mind would do, is it?'

He nods in the direction of a grey stone building that is standing by a stream near the top of a hill up to our left. It still must be half a mile away and surrounded by trees but there's some sort of chimney, stuck on the right-hand corner of it, that's peeping right up through the tree tops.

'There it is, Billy Quiz, there's Ravenswood Lodge.'

A GIANT HEINZ TOMATO SOUP SUNSET IS TURNING LOADS OF the sky red behind a clump of dark black trees towards the back of the building. In the middle of the trees stands the big chimney me and Watergate could see from the road. It must be about a hundred-foot-tall and at least twenty feet wide at the base. This close up, I can see it's not a chimney after all. It looks older than that. The grey stones are all rough, but cut quite even, two-foot-wide and two-foot-high most of them; more like boulders, really.

The post-office van makes a crunching sound as it rolls across the gravel forecourt. Watergate stops the engine, and puts the hand-brake on. He opens his glove compartment and scrambles around for a bit to find his torch. Then he opens the driver's door and gets out.

I open the door on me own side and do the same.

Some of the sky behind the trees is a darker red than the

rest; it matches the cuts and bruises and the bits of black clotted scar on the right side of Watergate's head, near where his comb-over starts to sweep back. He rests his right hand on his fat belly and lets out a big burp. A couple of ravens fly up from the branches above our heads.

Watergate watches them go.

'They're not supposed to be here, Billy Quiz, them birds. There's an old wife's tale about this place. A witch got burned inside the tower, hundreds of years ago. Screamed so loud, she did, they reckon, that all the birds around here disappeared. Never came back. Only thing they left behind was them empty nests and the sound they used to make – their caw.'

He nods towards a sign that's resting on the ground beside two metal poles; shines his torch at it and picks out some words: NHS Mental Health Care, Northern Area, Ravenswood Lodge. Then everything goes dead black as the last red bits of the sun drop down behind the horizon.

ME AND WATERGATE ARE STANDING RIGHT IN FRONT THE MAIN buildings now. I can just make out the black shapes of three of them next to the tower. One of them is old, from Victorian times. It's got a wooden door with carvings of insects on it and some arched windows cut into its stone walls. It looks like the kind of old church they have on the Songs of Praise TV show that Mam used to watch on a Sunday.

The other two, from the little I can see of them, have much flatter roofs. They look like the kind of prefab houses that were built after the second world war, in the streets, down by the Tyne.

Watergate goes to an arch-shaped window that's next to

the big wooden door with the insects on it. One of its glass
panes is knackered. He pushes at the frame and the widow
swings inwards. He shines his torch beam through it. I can
see a couple of medical supplies boxes, with the words
SANIJAB SYRINGES written on them. They are standing,
one on top of the other, beneath the window. I jump up, onto
the stone window frame, step down onto the boxes and
I'm in.

A SMALL QUARTER OF MOON, THAT LOOKS A BIT LIKE A SLICE
of old toe nail I saw once on Uncle Frank's bathroom lino,
shines some light through a skylight. Watergate's breathing a
bit heavy now. Me and him are walking down a long corridor.
There's different windows set into the walls of it. Lots of them
are still in once piece but some of them have got knackered
panes of glass. The first bit of the corridor is Victorian with
bits of oak panels and carved decoration and that. Now it's
changed. The walls are plain and flat. We must have crossed
over into a bit of the mental hospital that was extended forty,
or fifty. years ago.

It's spooky in here. I keep thinking we're going to come
around a corner and see Shaggy and Scooby Doo, doing that
real slow cartoon running they do when they're trying to get
away from a headless horseman.

Watergate stops walking and gives a big burp. Me nose
wrinkles up a bit from the stink. He reaches into his pocket and
takes out a couple of Rennies indigestion tablets.

'A bottle of Whyte and MacKay's for breakfast each
morning obviously isn't the miracle cure for heartburn that I'd
convinced meself, that it might be.'

I look around the corridor. It's got a couple of doors, one on either side.

'How much further, Tommy?'

Watergate shoves the indigestion tablets in his mouth. He burps again. Then shines the torch onto a sign that says Community Room, that's stuck to a red door just to our right.

'We're here, Billy Quiz, we're here.'

WATERGATE RUNS HIS TORCH AROUND THE WALLS OF THE Community Room. It's pretty big; about a hundred-feet square, with a load of old tables and chairs gathered in a circle around a big old telly with a knackered screen.

'See them?' whispers Watergate. 'Can you see them?'

At first, I can't see nowt.

I blink a couple of times and try and focus a bit harder.

Then I do.

Letters.

Hundreds, no, thousands, of letters.

I STAND IN THE MIDDLE OF THE ROOM AND TURN AROUND AND around.

The letters have been taken out of their envelopes and pinned up on almost every inch of the walls. All four walls, doors, windows everything, apart from the odd patch of peeling yellow paint, have been covered with the same thing. The torch picks them out slowly; one after another. They're stuck so close together on the walls that it feels – in the darkness – like we've discovered a colony of bats hiding in here. And that, at any minute, they might all fly up into the air.

Watergate walks across to the wall behind me. He picks one of them off and hands it to me. Then he turns the torch beam on it.

It's by W.S.

'I was caretaker here at Ravenswood. She came in '48, she did, after her husband died, a Geordie captain in the Guards. McNeil, his name was – she met him just after the war. He never stopped a bullet in five years, then, just back from the war, died of cancer. She never spoke in all that time. Not once in fifteen years she was here. No words. No spoken words ever. But writing, writing. Always writing. Sometimes ten, fifteen, twenty of these letters in a single day.'

He moves the torch along the wall. And finds another letter, and another and another.

'Everyone would pretend to post them. Play along, like. Bring in stamps and stick them on the envelopes, put them in the internal mail, then take them out again later when she wasn't looking. I even managed to get me hands on loads of stamps that some other squaddies had collected when they were overseas during the war, and bring them in for her.'

I go to the wall opposite and pick one off. Bring it back so Watergate can shine the torch on it.

The paper has got a little drawing stuck to it. A bit like an architect's drawing of a house. A blue-print is what architects call something like that.

'It looks like the houses in the Vienna book, Tommy.'

Watergate shines his torch around the walls again; picking out letter, after letter, after letter.

'Lots of them have got drawings stuck inside them like that: houses schools, cafés...There's even a library; a lovely library, Billy Quiz, with carved wooden shelves, just waiting to be filled with all them books you love so much, son.'

Watergate walks over to one of the upturned chairs. He picks it up and stands it upright.

'I loved to read them. The way she writes, it's beautiful. I started to collect them. Sometimes it felt like she could read me mind. Like she must have been writing to me, instead of them names she put on the envelopes. Otherwise, how could she know I was feeling like that? Kept them upstairs here in a storeroom, I did. So I could read them again, and again, and again. Over, and over, and over. Only a few at first, but, by the time I left, I had thousands of them.'

He sits down in the chair.

'Other people loved them too. Had them pinned up in their own offices. Some of the patients even had them stuck up by their beds. At nights, doing the rounds, I'd catch them reading them over, and over, just like I did. As if it was a kind of therapy. That's why we called her the Letter Lady. When I worked here in the fifties, everyone called her that.'

Watergate gets up again and stands in the middle of the room. He turns a full circle, taking in all the letters on the walls as he does.

'When she had been writing for a few years, it was like she'd cast a spell over the whole place. They'd get anxious, the other patients. The Letter Lady would scribble for days: drawing her pictures, writing her letters, and then she'd stop for day or two. I don't know why, maybe she was just knackered, or, perhaps, she felt, just for a moment, she simply couldn't carry on imagining things anymore. Her stopping would get the other patients – nut-jobs and basket-cases is what the world would call them – right on edge. You could feel it here, at nights when you walked around Ravenswood, feel them all waiting for her to start again. But a couple of days was the most she ever stopped for. As soon as she started again, they were happier – calmer. They believed again. Believed in them letters, same as she did.'

'But how, Tommy? I mean this Alter Strasse doesn't exist. None of them letters have ever arrived anywhere.'

Watergate turns towards me.

His cheeks flush a little. Like he's a bit angry.

'They felt real to them, Billy Quiz. That's all I know.'

I step a little closer towards him.

'So, in their minds, by the end of her writing all these letters, Alter Strasse was a place that they felt actually existed?'

Watergate steps towards the wall and unpins one of the letters that's stuck to it. He folds the letter back in two and then slips it back into its envelope.

'Yes, in the end, I think her, me and almost everyone here thought of Alter Strasse as a place that actually existed. A place we could escape to.'

'Escape from what?'

A strange look comes into Watergate's eyes. Like he's having to remember something that he's put a few too many of them Whyte and MacKay's, into forgetting.

'I was in the Durham Fusiliers in the war, then I got transferred to the 11th Armoured, because they were short of drivers, so that's how I ended up there.'

'Ended up where?'

'Everyone knows the name. The name's the scariest bit about it all. Because, if you say the name enough times, it makes what they done there seem...well, almost normal.'

'That was the camp you saw at the end of the war? Me dad told me about it.'

Tommy nods.

'We liberated it with a load of Canadian lads in April of '45.'

He lifts his bandaged left hand up and touches the scar on his temple.

'I went on the bottle when I got back. Me wife, Bonny, our lass, left me. Me own fault that. I got a skin-full in me, one night and smacked her about a bit. That was the only time but she was right to go. I packed in me job at the post office, too.'

Watergate takes a pen out of his pocket. He rests the envelope he took down from the wall on a discarded table next to him and writes something on it.

'I got well and truly plastered for about five years. Then, when I finally sobered up, I got meself a caretaking job up here at Ravenswood. That's when I first met her. She'd seen lots more of them places – the camps – I reckon, than I had. Wrote most days but never spoke back then. Not a word. Just the letters.'

Watergate hands me the envelope.

'But maybe she'll talk to you now, son? It's been ten years.'

I look down and read:

Ari,
Alter Strasse,
Bezirke 24,
Wien.

Watergate's scribbled another address next to it. It's the one I was expecting to see:

Nizanna Oz,
4 G Windsor Mansions,
Faversham Estate,
Newcastle.

Under that, in capital letters, he's printed: RETURN TO SENDER. I look back up at him. I can see that his big jowly face is flushed; gone dead red.

'There was bairns in that camp, Billy. I used to dream about their eyes – little dark dots of nowt. Like something had burrowed deep down inside, and sucked every last bit of their innocence out.'

Chapter Twenty-Six

When I reach the tower block's lobby I see there's an Out of Order sign on one of the lifts. The red arrow light on the other shows it's already coming down.

There's a big ping as it reaches the ground floor and the silver metal doors of the lift, which are covered in red graffiti done in felt-tip, slide open. A lad and a lass, both about fourteen years old, are necking on in it. They come up for air and then step out of the lift.

The lad gives me a look.

'What are you staring at, ginger?'

He grebs a big hockle of spit at me feet, as he walks past. Him and his lass start sniggering. I get into the lift and hold me fingers with me nose. The stink of piss is terrible.

I press a button. The doors slide shut. I wait for the ping and stare at the red arrows above me head. Willing them to glow red and start pulsing.

I press the button again. Nothing happens.

The doors begins to slide open a bit. A big Dr Marten boot, polished black as a hearse, pushes its way between them.

Bino step into the lift. Blue Tear steps in behind him. He's brought his Alsatian with him.

Blue Tear smiles at me.

'Little Deeza and his lass said they'd seen a spindly ginger twat getting into the lift and you know what, Sir Isaac? Straightway, I thought of you. So I've given him half a bar to go fetch me uncle. He's in The Butcher's Arms down the road.'

He slaps a button with the palm of his hand.

The lift doors slide shut.

Another ping.

It starts to go up. The illuminated panel, next to the blinking red arrow, starts flashing up the number twenty.

BINO STANDS ON ME LEFT-HAND SIDE. HIS SHOULDER IS NEXT to mine. Blue Tear stands on me right-hand side. He's got his dog held tightly on a leash. Every time I even glance at the thing it starts growling and spitting.

Blue Tear takes a drag from his tab and lets the smoke drift out of his mouth. Then he flicks the butt off the edge of the tower block. It turns a little circle in the air before it tumbles out of sight. I stare down at the kids' playground near the door to the tower block. Me heart's pumping up and down like the pistons on James Watt's steam engine. From here, that swing and climbing frame look like models made out of matchsticks.

Me and Bino and Blue are standing straight behind a metal guard rail that runs all around the roof of Windsor Mansions.

'I'm here to see you, Blue, honest. About what you said in

the Legion. I was just wondering if your uncle still wants to see me?'

Blue Tear makes a thin sucking noise with his cheeks and, then, grebs some hockle at me feet. He leans over and starts patting the dog.

'See this fucking mutt of mine, he doesn't always do what I want. Set him on this darky, once. Only bit half his arse off. That's why we call him JJ, isn't it Bino? After that hippy slag, Janis Joplin, because when he only bit half that darky's arse off, I said to Bino, this dog, we got ourselves, is either some kind a daft peace-loving hippy, or a furry fucking faggot.'

Blue Tear stands up and hands the lead to Bino.

Bino looks all odd for a moment. Like something Blue said has really upset him but then smiles and starts to snigger. His little pink eyes glow a bit of a darker pink. In the bright sunlight, they look almost red.

'Can I, Blue? Can I?'

Blue Tear nods.

Bino kneels down with the lead in his left hand and twists on it. He runs his right hand down behind the JJ's back.

There's a sharp pulling movement.

The dog's eyes go wild. He jumps up; closes his slavering fangs around me arm. I lurch back, start to topple. Feel meself slipping out over the guard rail. Blue Tear grabs a hold of me hair and keeps me hovering over the side of the tower block. Bino grabs a hold of me left leg. The dog bites harder into me arm. I can see the lead twisting and tightening around Bino's fist. Blue Tear yanks on me hair and pulls me face up so it's close to his. I can feel his spit on me cheek.

His eyes are dark and wide and staring.

'I twist his fucking mutt-nuts, Sir Isaac! That gets his fighting dander up.'

I make me body go soft like a rag doll, flop me face into Blue Tear's chest. Make meself feel like nothing. Blue Tear grins when he feels me do that. A big wide sneer-smile. Bino jumps up. Swings his foot back. Kicks me in the arse.

'He's not here for you, Blue. He's not here for us. He's twisting your nuts, Blue.'

Blue Tear nods.

'Think you're something don't you, Sir Isaac. That you're so smart. Think I know nothing? That I learnt nowt at that fucking school. Newton's laws of gravity, I remember that. Not just you. Me too.'

I'm crying now.

Proper bubbling.

Blue Tear loosens his fingers. Lets go of me hair. I start to topple. Me arms are wind-milling through the air. He grabs a hold of me. Pulls me back in. I drop down onto the roof and prop meself up against the guard rail.

'Is that what you've been doing to me, Billy Quiz – twisting me fucking nuts?'

I gasp out an answer.

'I'm not in me uniform, Blue. I've got no post-bag, no letters. Why would I even be here without them if I wasn't coming to see you and Bino?'

Blue-Tear gives me a dead long hard stare. Bino pats JJ's back to calm him, and starts to snigger. Blue-Tear sucks his cheeks in and then grebs onto the floor. He thinks for a moment. Then he grabs a hold of me collar and starts hauling me to me feet again.

'You lying little arse-wipe. I'm going to put you fucking over.'

A hand grabs a hold of Blue's arm. Ossie Mingle's voice goes all deep and soothing.

'Careful, Blue, deep breaths, count to ten, why don't you?'

OSSIE MINGLE IS SITTING ON AN OLD WOODEN PACKING CRATE next to the ledge.

Blue and Bino are standing directly behind him. One on each side. Ossie takes a white handkerchief, with the initials OM stitched into the corner in red, and spits on it. He leans down and pats JJ, who's lying next to him, on the head with his left hand. Then he wipes away a small dark stain that's marking the toe of one them synagogue creepers, of his, with his right. He sits back up straight and stares down at me with his little blue piss-cube eyes.

'Feeling better, young William? A bit more relaxed, now, eh?'

I don't feel relaxed. I'm shitting meself. But I nod me head.

'Yes, Mr Mingle, much better, thanks.'

Ossie smiles.

'Hate has a patron saint, young William, did you know that? He's in the bible and everything. Numbers 25 is where you'll find him, St Phinehas is his name. Old St Phinehas, is a man, like me, who don't take to kindly to folks intermingling with other races. I expect you're more of St Valentine's man yourself?'

I shake me head. Me voice is all wavery but I manage to say something anyways.

'I don't believe in saints. None of us men of science...none of us do.'

Blue Tear and Bino start to snigger when I say that.

Ossie smiles.

'Me neither, son. Not really. But then, back in the day,

when I was in the League, the League of Empire Loyalists, in the fifties, I had an old mate, Wop Ernie, lovely Catholic gent, he was. Told me all about St Phinehas and, when Wop Ernie did that, I thought to meself, well, maybe, at last, I found a holy man I really can worship. A kindred spirit, so to speak. Like St Paul and the road to Damascus it was. Except with myself and St Phinehas it was the Old Kent Road. Me and Ernie used to have a pint in the Star & Garter there, after League meetings.'

The sun is beating down on the roof, making the black rubber that covers it a bit sticky to me touch. Beads of sweat are running down Ossie's head, from under his dyed-blonde hair line into his bushy eyebrows.

He dabs his brow with his handkerchief.

'Wop Ernie. That name ring any bells with you, son?'

I shake me head.

'No, I never heard of him.'

Ossie tucks his handkerchief away in his pocket.

'Ernesto Motta is another way of putting it. You heard of him, then?'

I remember the name as soon as he says it.

'The Motta Collection at the Hancock, is that who he is? That bloke who left all them Nazi stamps to the museum?'

'He didn't leave them, they was taken from him. But yeah, that's him. Me and Ernie were good pals before the war and after. I was a bit in awe of him, at first, I suppose. He came from Forli, near where Mussolini was born. In the twenties, they called Forli "El Duce's city." He was a black shirt right to his core, was Wop Ernie.'

JJ lifts his head and growls a bit. Ossie reaches down and pats him. Then sits back up again.

'I met him doing me nursing training at the London Hospital, over Whitechapel way, in '38. I collected stuff even then; memorabilia and such. He always was mad about them Nazi stamps of his.'

I'm still sitting on the sticky rubber floor. Ossie gets up off the packing case and takes a couple of steps towards me.

'But he didn't survive the war did my pal, Ernie, not in spirit anyways. They interned him in '39, in a stately home up here, over Durham way. Traitor, they said he was. Even after that, broken as he was, they came for him, again. Put him back inside in '55. He went back to home to Italy a couple of years later. Dead now is my pal, Ernie. Long gone, young William. Off to join St Phinehas in the sky.'

Ossie bends over a bit and pushes his face towards mine.'Them stamps of his are still with us, though. Just sitting there in that museum. And they mean something to me. A lot, actually. Sentimental value is part of it because he promised me one of them, in particular. The other part is the fifteen grand that particular stamp is worth. Except nobody knows which one it is save Wop Ernie, who ain't with us no more...'

Ossie taps his brow a couple of times with the tip of his finger.

'...and little old me.'

He stands up again and looks across at Blue and Bino.

'You don't buy no dog and bark yourself. That's why I got Blue and fucking Omo here to do stuff for me. You're a gift, young William, that's how I'm seeing it. I gave a little prayer up to good old St Phinehas and he delivered you unto me. So, I was thinking, either I can send these two fine young gentlemen to go a calling on your little Paki mate and her dear old mum over to them posh houses out Jesmond way – to persuade them to give me a set of keys for the museum...'

He takes a couple of steps towards me.

'Or you might find a way to get them keys for me, young William? How would that be?'

Another step.

Ossie's standing close to me now. He reaches out and grabs me by the hair. Pushes me face down into the tip of one of his crepe-soled shoes. I'm so close I can smell the leather. Then he leans in to me ear and whispers.

'Not a single word to the world from you, not to the coppers, or daddy at home, about our little chat, or next time we meet I'll leave Blue and Bino, here, to it. Meet me at the Hoppings tomorrow night at seven sharp. Can you do that for me, son? Get me them keys, bring them there, and stay silent about the getting of 'em?'

I blink me eyes a couple of times, so he knows I'm agreeing. Then say what I have to anyways, just to make sure.

'Yes. Yes, Mr Mingle.'

Ossie lets go of me hair and puts a finger to his lips. He flashes me a wink.

'Silence, young William. That's our motto.'

I'M LYING ON THE ROOF, WHERE OSSIE, BLUE TEAR AND BINO left me. I haven't moved for a couple of hours now. I'm holding me right arm. There's a torn bit of me Fred Perry jumper there, where the dog bit me.

I'm thinking about me dad. He's hardly spoken to me since I called Mrs Damoan a slag. He made an effort for a day, or two, but now he pretty much says nowt. Just the odd grunt is all I'm getting. I'm thinking about Watergate and how me and Ninder had him worked out all wrong. And about how daft

I've turned out to be for someone who thinks he's a man of science.

I'm thinking about me mam and how much I wish I could go home now and press our doorbell and hear Blue Suede Shoes. That she would open our door with her Lana-Turner smile and blonde hair with pink plastic curlers in it, wearing them rose-tinted Mars specs of hers, that let you see the world exactly how you want to see it, and give me a hug and cook up a plate of Birds Eye beef-burgers and chips and then get some Arctic Roll out the freezer. Because when I want to see the world exactly as I want to see it, that's what I always end up seeing.

I stare up at the black sky. At this time of year, on a cloudless night like this one, you can pick up stuff even without a telescope. There's a little dot to the left. That's Jupiter. On the right side is a small quarter of the moon. In the middle is Mars. And, right next to Mars, although obviously I can't see it, is Viking 1. "Only seven crucial days to go now," is what Patrick Moore said on The Sky at Night, yesterday.

I stand up and look out over the rooftops of the Faversham Estate. In the distance, down by the river, I can see the shadows of some of them Geordie Flamingos mam liked. They look dead scary now; more like a pack of robot-dinosaurs who only come out to hunt at night. I look over at the blue door that leads to the stairwell. I hope Ossie, Blue Tear and Bino have stopped prowling around for tonight.

I'm thinking, after today, I really understand now why I like the idea of Viking 1 so much.

It's an unmanned probe.

There are no people on it. No Blue-Tears. No Binos. No Ossie Mingles. And it's heading to a distant red planet where there are no people either. Truth is: a place like that – somewhere where other people aren't – is the only kind of place a kid like me could ever really feel dead safe.

And there's only one other person I know who understands all that stuff the same way I do.

THE BIG RADIO ON THE TABLE IS MADE OUT OF BAKELITE which was invented by a Belgian bloke called Leo Baekeland when he was looking for a replacement for lac. Lac is basically beetle turds. People used to use it to make a plastic-type-stuff called shellac and, sometimes, red dyes; that were the same sort of red as a dye called cochineal. Cochineal looks like dried blood; probably because it's made from crushed, dead insects.

Then this Leo bloke came along and replaced Lac with Bakelite.

Maybe the radio cabinet has been dyed with cochineal. It's a real dark red and has got one of them dials on it that, when you twiddle a brown knob, moves a little black pointer over the names of different cities from all over the world: Prague, Moscow, Budapest, Warsaw, and lots of other faraway places that I've never been to.

I used to love looking at this kind of radio in the Radio Rentals shop in the Grainger Market in town. They had a special section of them in there for all the grans and granddads to buy. I would stand outside that window with me face pressed against the glass and think that, if you twiddled one of them dials, it could take you to any of them places in an instant. 'Where do you want to go today, Sir?' the Radio Rentals man would say and whoosh, you'd be in Warsaw. Voom, and it'd be Venice. In me head, I used to add other places to it as well. Like stars and planets and constellations.

Mars, of course, was always me favourite. I'd shut me eyes and feel like I could get there just by adding bits of Martian Geography, with their funny Latin names, to the dial. All the places that Viking 1 is due to travel over in the next few days: Noctis Labyrinthus, Tharsis, Ausonia, Utopia Planitia, Olympus Mons and Chryse Planitia, the Golden Plain, where Viking's supposed to land, were on this imaginary dial in me head.

Nizanna puts a washing up bowl down next to the radio. It's got hot water and Dettol in it. She's starts dabbing me arm with cotton wool. The table in her living room is made of oak with an old fashioned white lace tablecloth on it. The radio is sitting in the middle of it next to two salt-and-pepper pots made from silver. A posh announcer says, 'This is Mo "Just a Mo" Morovitz with more Tunes of Yesteryear, on Late Night with Mo, coming up: Today's sacred platter is from Lady Day. But first, here's something else, a little taster from Mr Glen Miller." Music starts to play. It's what they call a big band sound with lots of trumpets and saxophones.

'You are being alright now, Postman? Better now?'

I nod me head.

'Yes, thanks.'

I look at me watch. It's nearly 1 o'clock now. I was worried about knocking on Nizanna's door this late but, when she opened it, she didn't seem a bit surprised to see me.

'Why were you up on my roof, Postman?'

I reach across and pick up the silver pepper-pot.

'Is it old? It looks old.'

Nizanna begins to fiddle with the white bead on the little chain she has tied around her neck.

She nods. I point to the picture on the mantelpiece.

'Was that your dad?'

Nizanna gets up and walks across the room. She picks up the picture.

'Yes, that was him.'

Her face changes. Goes still again.

I stare up at her, wondering where she's gone to inside her head.

'That is him,' she whispers. Her funny accent goes a lot thicker. It doesn't sound as though she's speaking to me, now. More like she's talking to someone else.

One of these people she's been writing her letters to, maybe. The music stops on the radio. Another track starts to play. It's more of a jazz track this one. Straightaway, I recognise it.

Nizanna hears it and smiles. When she does that she kind of comes back into herself.

'You like Lady Day, Postman. Billie Holliday is how people are normally calling her. You whistle this, remember? You and your father. From my window, I see you for the first time and you and he are whistling, Eeeny, Meany, Miny, Mo by Billie Holliday. Just a Mo Morovitz. He loves this track. He plays it every day. Calls it his Sacred Platter. You and your father you whistle it, and walk towards cruel men who scowl and strut and grin and bark, like the Alsatian dog they are holding on a leash.'

She puts the picture back down on the mantelpiece.

'When you did that, Postman, when I saw you do that, you remind me of me and my father.'

I put the silver pepper-pot down on the table and push it away from me.

'Me and me dad, we're not close like that, now, like you and yours. Not anymore. He's got himself a fancy woman. That's where he'll be going now I expect, after his shift finishes. Over to her place. He doesn't care about me anymore. He's even broken me mam's pepper-pot.'

Nizanna walks back to the table and sits down. She reaches across to the brown knob on the radio and begins to twiddle it. As she slowly moves the little black pointer across the dial, past Brussels, Paris, London and Lisbon, towards Vienna, static begins to crackle. I take a deep breath and pull something out of one of me pockets. Then I lay the letter Watergate gave me at Ravenswood Lodge on the table. Nizanna stares at it for a moment. She stops twiddling the knob and turns off the radio. She stretches out her fingers towards the envelope.

I can see that her hand is shaking a little.

She picks up the letter in her right hand and reads the address on the front:

Ari,
Alter Strasse,
Bezirke 24,
Wien.

Then she turns it over and reads the name and address that Watergate wrote on the back the envelope:

Nizanna Oz,
4 G Windsor Mansions,
Faversham Estate,
Newcastle.
Then in caps: RETURN TO SENDER.

Nizanna puts the envelope down on the table and pushes the envelope back towards me.

'My other postmen were better than you,' she whispers. 'They never brought any of my letters back.'

Utopia Planitia
Saturday, 17th July 1976.
3 days before Viking 1 lands on Mars

Chapter Twenty-Seven

Ninder is wearing a short red and black Bruce Lee kimono with the words Beware, Dragon Lady embroidered on the pocket. She yawns as she lets me in at her back-kitchen door. I'm surprised she's up. It's only nine o'clock and she usually sleeps really late at the weekend. Her hair, now dyed traffic-cone red, is sticking up in mad clumps. It looks like she must have been shagging the Van De Graaff generator Mr Tompkins used to demonstrate electrical current for us in school.

I'm glad to see her though. These days, me dad's pretty much giving me the complete silent treatment.

Ninder points at the pine kitchen table, which is covered in crap: used cups and glasses and a red plastic Whitbread Trophy Bitter ashtray that's filled with last night's tab butts. There's an envelope and a bit of paper on it too. I can see a printed logo on top of the paper, the letters NME, in red and black.

'They wrote back to me!' she says. 'The NME wrote back! They say they want someone to cover bands in the North East and they're looking to hire more women. What do you think of that?'

'Great, I'm dead pleased for you.'

I don't sound very pleased. Me voice is all flat.

I sit down on an orange knitted beanbag that's next to the table. Me arse sinks right into the middle of it, so me ankles and me Polyveldts stick up in the air. Ninder picks up an electric kettle from the Formica work top. Then she stands next to the sink and fills it with water.

'Still spending your time helping out that fat Nazi?' she says.

'You shouldn't have done it.'

'Done what?'

'Get them blokes from the Man and the Moon to give him a kicking.'

Ninder finishes filling the kettle. She puts it back on its metal stand and then flicks a button which glows red.

'Uncle Noor, Poirot, remember him? Me Uncle Noor who used to give me and you free Black Jacks and Hubba Bubba and stuff. He died in a fire, months ago, and you said that you'd help me find out who did it but instead you led me on a complete wild-goose chase to find a bloke who was a Nazi but who now turns out not to be, so you say. And a woman who you also thought was a Nazi, who turned out to be Jewish. Anyway, it wasn't me who sorted it.'

'I saw you with them. You need to at least apologise to him.'

'I said it wasn't me, alright?'

'You were with them outside the Man and the Moon.'

Ninder flicks the red button on the kettle back off. She walks back across to her back-kitchen door and opens it.

'Just feck-off, I don't want to see you again until you know for certain what happened to Noor. I need evidence, proper evidence. You were right about that bit. I can't go to the coppers when all I've got is a lump of dried-up dog shit, with a funny looking pattern in it, and a melted bit of black plastic that spells out the word us, and that's it. Not even a proper suspect.'

I sit there feeling like a right pillock on the bean bag with me ankles stuck in the air looking at her. I can't go yet. Not until I get what I came for. Ninder's face has gone all flushed to match her hair.

'Are you going to climb out of that fecking bean-bag or not?'

'Eureka.'

'What?'

'I'm here for Eureka.'

Ninder takes her hand off the door-knob.

'You said you don't like pets. That a concentration gerbil wouldn't help you. That's why I've been looking after him.'

'I changed me mind.'

Ninder gives me a funny look. She pushes the door shut and walks out of the kitchen towards the stairs. I count out thirty seconds in me head and then push meself up out of the bean-bag and walk, through an archway straight into her living room.

Mrs Lally has a small wooden desk with a typewriter on it and a few boxes of files. I glance back towards the stairs, which I can just see through the living room door, and then quickly sit down in Mrs Lally's chair. Me hands go straight to the second of two drawers that are set into the right-hand side of the desk. I know this is where Ninder's mam keeps her keys; I saw her put them in there one night. When I open the drawer all I can see is a couple of brown paper files and a packet of pink lacky-bands but as soon as I move the second file, I see the set of keys with the Roman Hat key-fob on it that she used to let us into the museum when we went to see the stamps.

I look back at the hallway. Still no sign of Ninder. I pick up the keys and put them in me pocket. There's a creak at the top of the stairs. I close the door. Then I run back into the kitchen and jump right into the middle of the bean-bag.

I hear feet padding down the stairs.

A tall bloke with very short, spiky blonde hair and a lass's stud earring stuck through his nose steps onto the balcony. Afghan Larry's wearing nowt except Ninder's Bruce Lee komodo, and he's holding Eureka's cage in his right hand.

'What happened to your hair?' I say.

He runs his left hand through his peroxide crop and gives me a big grin.

'I heard the Sex Pistols, man. Ninder's right, punk is all that's going to be happening.'

I point at the little chain he wears around his neck. His plectrum's gone but something else is hanging there in its place.

'What's that?'

Afghan Larry twists the end of the chain between his fingers and holds it up to the light.

'It's Johnny Rotten's safety pin, man, the one he was wearing when the Pistols played their very first gig at St Martin's Art College.'

LORD MUCKLESTONE LOOKS EVEN MORE LIKE PATRICK MOORE from The Sky at Night than he did the last time I saw him. In fact, now I'm standing here in front of him and he's dressed in his red fez and purple velvet suit, same as ever, it seems obvious they must be twins, or something. Especially with that monocle he's wearing, that goes up and down, every time he says What! What! What! Destiny Calling!

The Mucklestone machine is in its usual spot. Sitting in its glass case, inside a knackered old canvass tent at the Hoppings fun fair, next to a couple of fruit machines.

I can hear the different shouts of stall holders above the daft pop tunes like Fernando by Abba and one me dad likes, that's top of the charts right now, called The Streak by Ray Stevens – where a bloke takes all his clothes off, in a super-market, and runs about in front of a woman called Ethel, who's standing near the kumquats. The music is playing out loud from the big rides like the dodgems or the Waltzer. There's bad smells everywhere – greasy chips, candyfloss and toffee apples.

Ossie told me to meet him at seven o'clock outside one of the gypsy caravans called Madame Ormalu's. It's about ten to seven now. I can see this Madame Ormalu's, about thirty-feet away, right on the end of a row of three others. It's got a hand-painted red sign that says: Tell me your dreams, and then I will reveal to you the Universes deepest secrets! Whoever's painted this sign has missed the apostrophe out of it. The way they've done it makes it seem like there's lots of other universes out there, existing side by side, one after the other. There's an American scientist called Hugh Everett, who did a bit of thinking about a thing called multi-verses. This Hugh bloke decided there really are loads of universes out there. Each one of them only a tiny bit different from this one. So, maybe, this sign writer could be onto something.

I push me hand into the top pocket of me Levis jacket and

hunt around for a 10p. I can feel Ninder's mam's keys in there as well as the folded-up Ari letter. Nizanna wouldn't take it back the other night or tell me nowt else about it. I dig out a coin and bung it into the slot of the Mucklestone machine. It rolls down and clangs into the money box inside. I hear something mechanical make a click inside.

I look about the floor of the tent.

It's covered with the pink cards that come out of the Mucklestone machine. All sorts of different futures that people have paid their 10ps for, read, and then thrown away, probably because they don't fancy them, that much.

I kneel down and pick one up it says: Future is: comical, laughter is life's greatest tonic. I pick up another it says: Future is: troubled, but dark clouds always part, then sunlight will guide your way.

I look up and see Ossie Mingle step out of the Madame Ormalu tent. He starts walking across the grass towards me. There's a whirring, buzzing sound and then Mucklestone prints out another ticket. I stand up and take it out of the machine. It reads: Future is: now dark but a golden one will surely find you.

'ALRIGHT, YOUNG WILLIAM?'

Ossie steps inside Lord Mucklestone's tent and stands in the middle of all them pink tickets. I feel meself tense right up but he seems a lot calmer today than when we last met, on the roof of Windsor Mansions.

A lot less twitchy, relaxed even.

'I'm fine, Mr Mingle.'

I don't feel very fine. I just want to give him the key and go but I need to make sure of something first.

'No Blue and Omo, with me today, son. You'll be glad of that, I expect. I stood them down. Reckon they need a rest from each other. That albino, he gives Blue some funny looks, from time to time, you ever noticed that?'

I say nowt. Ossie holds out his right hand.

'Come on then, son, had no grub this morning. So I'm needing to get me some nosh, pretty soon. You got what I need?'

I take a small step backwards.

'You won't need to see Ninder or her mam will you, Mr Mingle, if I give you the key for the museum, like I said I would?'

Ossie smiles and looks around at all them pink slips on the floor. He kneels down and picks one up. Then stands up again. He holds the slip out in front of him and reads it out.

'"Future is: Rosy – as red as the roses in Eden's garden."'

Ossie crumples up the pink ticket and drops it back onto the floor.

'Future is rosy, eh? Not for everyone though, am I right? Not for us all. My old mum ran off with a fucking Yid, young William, when I was ten years old. Did a right skip and bunk she did with a pawn-broking Yid, that owned a fucking three-ball, down the Whitechapel Road. She gave up our nice seafood stall on the front at Hastings, to run away with him.'

Ossie takes another step towards me.

He pushes the middle finger of his right hand against his temple and stabs at it a couple of times.

'I can see that stall sign now, son, when I close my eyes. Hear the seagulls crying out, smell the Sarsons, see them glass pickling jars, filled with cockles and whelks, and Mum, in amongst it all, winking at me.'

I take another step back. Now I'm standing against the Mucklestone machine.

'You ever looked in a pawnbroker's window, young William?

I nod me head.

'Yes, there's one along where me uncle lives.'

Ossie smiles. He seems dead pleased at me saying that.

'Full of stories they are, them windows, little bits of yesterday people had to leave behind, when things got so tight they couldn't cope with tomorrow. After she left, and my old man told me who with, I used to go to one, over St Leonards-on-Sea, and press my face to the window. Thought I might spot her there amongst all the stuff people had left behind. Nonsense, of course, young William, since him that took her was a Whitechapel Yid, but I was only ten years old. Too young, back then, to understand just how sour a man's sweetest dreams can get.'

He looks down again. Moves his head, left and right; points to the leftover Mucklestone tickets on the ground.

'Back in them days, I thought I'd get myself a ten-bob note, and a pawnbroker's chitty and buy Mum back, somehow, bring her home to my old man and me. Dust her down and set her back in her rightful place at our kitchen table.'

Ossie takes another step towards me. Me and him are standing up close together now. His blue pupils look a bit lighter. Softer, even. His voice goes dead soft, too.

'Was I fool to think like that, young William? A soft-hearted young fool?'

I shake me head again. Me words come out real loud. A good bit louder, I think, than both me and Ossie are expecting.

'No, you weren't! It's not daft to think like that!' Me voice drops back down again. 'I mean I don't think so, Mr Mingle.'

Ossie turns his head from side to side again; looking down at the tickets on the floor. He goes all quiet for a few moments. Then he looks back up at me, and takes a couple of real big sniffs of air.

'Smell that, son, lovely grub, that. Hot-dog and fried onions. I used to love them when I was a nipper. A mate of Blue's got a stall up near where the big dodgems are. Let's me and you go and have ourselves some nosh.'

THAT RAY STEVENS SONG, ME DAD LIKES, IS BLASTING OUT from the tannoy on the dodgems. There's a little queue of people in front of the white hot-dog van.

Ossie's standing by the side of it, a couple of feet away from where I am. He's munching on a hot-dog and talking to a middle-aged man with long black hair, a gold tooth and two small hoop-earrings. This bloke's wearing a purple pork-pie hat and yellow riders.

I recognise him straightway. It's Jimmy Knight, the one they call Jimmy Segs, the one who used to come in the club sometimes. The bloke me dad told me was a real bad 'un, and Ninder said came around her Uncle Noor's shop, that time, and asked her to say he'd come about "The usual."

Ossie and Jimmy Segs take a couple of steps away from me and step behind the side of the van.

I look down. There's two new sets of footprints in the mud. One set, where Ossie was standing, is the flat pressed shape of his crepe-soles. The other set, where this Jimmy Segs was, is different. There's a sharp imprint from the soles of his yellow riders.

Something else, too, though. Funny Blakeys, odd-shaped, like the plastic knight's shields, I used to see in Fenwick's toy shop, when I was a bairn. Exactly the same shape, in fact, as the ones I found in the dried-up dog shit outside Uncle Noor's Marvellous Emporium.

Ossie walks back from around the back of the van. He bites down on the last of his hot-dog and then drops the greaseproof paper on the muddy ground. Then he says what I thought he might, like. The thing that's been scaring me the most.

'I'll make no promises about your Paki pal and her mother. But I'll have them keys from you now, son, just the same. On my life, I will. You and me we're going to pay a little visit to that museum in a night or two.'

I put me hand up to cover the top pocket of me Levi's jacket, where the keys are.

'But you said you wouldn't send Blue and Bino to Ninder's, if I brought you the key, and I have done. You promised?'

Ossie reaches across and grabs a hold of me hand. I try to keep me fingers tight hold of me fastened pocket. But he begins to loosen them. Dead slow, like. Them nasty blue eyes of his fixed on mine. I can see he's really enjoying himself.

'Billy Quiz. That's what they calls you, young William isn't it? A question then, for you, Mr Quiz.'

I keep staring down at the pocket of me Levi's jacket. Ossie carefully lifts the last of me fingers off it. He begins to unclip the button.

'Zyclon B, you heard of that?'

I nod me head.

'Yes, the Germans used it, in the war, at them camps, like Treblinka and Auschwitz, used it to gas people. I seen it on the World at War, on the telly.'

Me pocket pops open. Ossie smiles.

'Lice was what Zyclon B killed first, a delousing agent. My old pal, Ernesto Motta, worked as a researcher for the I.G. Farben chemical company. Then as a salesman for them, before the war and during. Went all over Europe selling Zyclon B. Not to Auschwitz, not to Sorbivor, not to Treblinka. But he sold it to the people who sold it to the people, who sold it to them places. Insects, lice, general extermination of all types of vermin. That's how Wop Ernie could afford them stamps of his.'

Ossie's fingers delve deep inside me pocket. He takes out the keys. Holds the Roman Hat key-fob between the fingers of his right hand and shakes it from side to side.

I stare at it. So does he.

His hand stops moving. The keys stop swinging. His face goes a funny colour. A bit flushed and pinky. The middle finger of his left-hand points at me open pocket.

'What's that?'

I look down at me jacket. The top of the Ari letter is peeping out. I can just make out a few bits of Nizanna's handwriting on the edge of it. I try and cover it with me hand. But Ossie flicks me arm aside and grabs the letter.

'Where do you get this?'

His voice cracks a bit. He sounds dead scared. Almost terrified.

'The post office. I found it in the Returns Box at the post office.'

Ossie rips the letter out of the envelope and reads it. He begins to twist at the paper.

'My sweet dream, just turned sour again.'

He shreds the letter into little pieces. Watches them flutter down onto muddy ground.

'Lice is right is, young William,' says Ossie.

He looks back up at me. A horrible glint floats into his eyes.

'Kill all the fucking lice, I say. Kill 'em all.'

THE LIFT GOES PING AS I STEP AWAY FROM THE SMELL OF STALE piss onto the fourth floor.

I stand in front of the door with the flower basket and press the white door bell. I wait for a minute. I press the bell again. Nowt happens. I roll me hands into fists and start banging against the yellow paint.

Footsteps, I hear footsteps in the corridor.

There's a tiny rattling sound that seems to echo right around the whole corridor as the chain comes of the sneck.

Nizanna's green eye finally appears in the space between the door and the frame. She's only holding the door about an inch wide.

'There's a man called Ossie Mingle. I think he knows you. He might come here.'

'Not now, Postman. Now is not a good time, I think.'

'It has to be now.'

I push me foot into the crack between the door and the frame.

'I'm not just here about him. You wouldn't say nowt last time. I need to know why you write them?'

Nizanna looks down at me big daft Polyveldt stuck between the door and the frame. Then back up at me. Her face is all still. I don't know what she's going to do next. She's got her Weather Head on, today.

Nizanna opens the door a little bit wider.

'No, I said, no. I cannot be here now, amongst all this.'

I put me hands down and step back out into the corridor when she does that. She points at the "Witch" graffiti on the corridor wall.

'Spells, Postman, incantations, curses, a calling down of demons. Is that what you think my letters are? Maybe these people do, too, but they're wrong, Postman. They're wrong…'

'I need to know.'

Nizanna steps back into her passage. The door begins to close.

'Not today, Postman. Some other day, maybe. But, perhaps, never.'

There's an echoing thud as the yellow door slams shut.

I take two big gasps of air.

I kneel down. Pull up the metal flap of Nizanna's letterbox with me right hand.

Then I start shouting through it.

'Me Mam's dead. An accident; two years ago there was an accident. The Newcastle coppers said Mr Pontefract, the insurance salesman did it. He'd eaten too many pies or something and had a heart attack at the wheel of his Hillman Imp. I'm a man of science, so I had a theory: that it was the cheese plates, the cheese plates at the Comrades Club that had killed me mam, as well as him. I got meself a stopwatch and did some tests. It wasn't the big plate, or the small plate that done it. It must of been the middle plate! I deduced that because she had a very lady-like bite….

Me voice is going dead hoarse now. But I carry on shouting.

'... it was the middle plate, the middle plate that killed her! That's what I told me dad afterwards, anyways, and it seemed to make him feel better when I said it. Because then he knew it was nobody's fault because any little thing can kill you. That's what he wanted to believe, I suppose, because it made him feel better when he believed it. Little things like that you can put down to Fate. Me dad, the women at the club, most people, they all love Fate. Believing in Fate makes them feel safe; like, as if someone is looking out for us all. But no one is really! It was somebody's fault! It wasn't really anything to do with Mr Pontefract, or the middle-sized cheese plate, that she went. It was me...I did it. I'm the reason me mam's not here anymore. I'm the one that killed her!'

I hear a clicking sound.

Nizanna's door swings back open.

Chapter Twenty-Eight

Next to where I'm sitting, on the other side of the table, is a blue bottle full of Quink ink and a green tortoise-shell fountain pen with a silver nib on it. There's a blank sheet of letter paper sitting next to them.

Nizanna brings a cup of tea through from the kitchen puts it down next to me and then sits back down herself, next to the pen and the envelopes.

I take a swig of the tea. It's strong and sweet. Then I lean forward; start talking again.

'It's got Moons. Demos and Phobos is what they call them. Every time I close me eyes all I can think about is them moons of Mars. Fear and Terror is what Phobos and Demos means in Greek. Then all I can see is Blue Tear and Bino and Ossie Mingle. I want to talk to her. I want to talk to me mam but I can't anymore because of what I did. Me dad won't talk to me anymore because I don't like him seeing his fancy woman, Mrs Damoan but I can't bring meself to tell him anyways. I've been thinking about it for two years. Wanting to tell him, all that time wanting to, but I just can't say nowt.'

Nizanna reaches across the table and twists the brown knob of her red Bakelite radio.

There's a crackle of static.

Some jazz music, that I don't recognise, begins to play.

'No Just a Mo today, Postman. Too early for his show, but he's off anyway. Off sick, the announcer says so there will be no turning on a deck of his sacred platter.'

I pick up me cup. Take another swig. Put it down again on its white, slightly-chipped saucer.

'Why do you write them?

Nizanna looks away from me. Then back again.

'There was dancing in our house, when I was younger, Postman, much dancing. Even though we lived on Teufal Strasse, Devil Street.'

'Devil Street?'

'Kuppelwiesergasse was its real name. In 1938, when I was thirteen years old, Postman, there was a poisoner, who lived near us in Kuppelwiesergasse, next to Hugle Park, Martha Marck, she was being called. After this lady was convicted, small boys used to tip-toe down our street and shout "Das ist Teufal Strasse," and then run away. It was the year of Anschlaus, when the Nazis took over Wien. Afterwards, my father, used to laugh, when the boys would come and shout after them "The Devil doesn't just walk down this street, boys, now he owns the whole city." But before that, before the Nazis were coming to Teufal Strasse, there was always dancing.'

'I need to know, why? Why do you write them?'

Nizanna reaches out and turns the music up a notch. She stands up and stretches out her arms as if she was doing one of them posh dances like a waltz, or something. She does a couple of turns around her old blue rug. Then she sits back down again and rests her head on the back of the oak dining chair and looks away from me up at the ceiling. She's gone to that place now. Lost inside her mind. A minute or two, maybe more, goes by. Then she speaks.

'Kamm und uns. Uns und kamm. Them and us, Postman, us and them. A simple choosing that happens every day, every-where, and in every place, does it not? Eeeny. Kamm. Meany, uns. Miny, kamm. Mo. Eeeny and Meany. Miny and Mo. Kamm und uns. Uns und kamm. You too make these choices do you not? You sit on the bus next to this person. not that one, you enter a room and move this way, towards, this lady with the soft, dark hair but not that way, towards this other whose suit is a little too tight, hair too blonde, scent a little grubby, perhaps, a little downmarket, too common, perhaps? Like your father's friend that we discuss, Mrs Damoan. The smallest things insist that we decide – the edge of someone's laughter – makes us move away. Towards this person we are drawn only because of the greenness of their eyes, to another because their face possesses some kind of banal symmetry. Away from this other, why? Can we even discern our reasons? Their nose is a little too long, perhaps. Their teeth too yellow. That dress? Well, my dear, it is simply zu auberordentlich, too extraordinary.'

There's something kind of hypnotic about her voice with its funny accent that's making me feel, even though I know it's daft, that the ceiling and all the other floors of Windsor Mansions above me head has disappeared, and all me and her can see are the same twinkling stars and planets that I stare at every night through me telescope. That's exactly how it feels. Like she's talking to them, not me.

'We Uns, Us, we know, are better than Kamm, better than Them, and so, in time, we, too, begin to despise them just a little. In turn, others make these same choices around us, do they not? Around you and around me. Our skin may be a little too pale for them, our face too gaunt, too Hebrew, too Arabic, too African. Our hair too blonde, not blonde enough, too dark, too red. Kamm und uns. Uns und kamm. Them and us, us and them.'

Nizanna turns her head towards me.

'On every day, in every minute and in every moment, Postman, we – all of us – decide these things, do we not?'

I nod me head.

'Like me and Mrs Damoan. That's how I've been with her.'

Nizanna turns around in her chair and stares across at me.

Her face goes a bit softer. She smiles.

'It was not strange – the place I came to in the war, Postman. Not to me, at least. It was not alien. It was not inhuman. It was not, as people said afterwards, a freak occurrence. No aberration. No perversion. It was not abnormal. Those are just the words we use to push it away from ourselves, to make it seem that these things, these acts, can only happen somewhere, some place, else.'

Nizanna looks into the distance. Then back at me.

'Most of all, Postman, and I am realising this as soon as I truly understood its purpose...it was logical. There had been plans, there were blue-prints. Meetings, where the most efficient methods of disposal had been analysed and discussed. Eeeny and Meany. Miny and Mo. Kamm und uns. Them and Us. Uns und kamm. Us and Them. Make the choice. Allow some time. Let the world divide as it will, and you will always end up in a place like that eventually.'

I pick up me cup. Take another swig of tea. It rattles a bit when I put it back down in the saucer. 'Always?' I ask. 'Do you think so?'

Nizanna nods.

'In all of history, there could be no more logical a place than the one I found myself in – at the end of a railway line in the April of 1942. That's how I feel anyway, because the carriages were full of Uns, Us, and, waiting there, wearing black polished boots, and holding dogs that strained at the leash in the cold night air, there were Kamm, there were Them.'

NIZANNA COMES BACK IN FROM HER KITCHEN WITH A BLUE-and-gold plate with a piece of Kaischerschram on it. She puts it on the table and sits down.

She takes a silver knife and cuts it into two.

'My last piece, Postman. Our last piece.'

She leans forward and twists the brown knob on the radio. The pointer on the black dial races past Berlin and Belgrade and rests on Vienna.

The music stops. Crackling static fills the air. I lean forward and stretch me hand out towards the upturned piece of white letter paper in front of her.

'I still don't understand, why?'

Nizanna rests her hand flat on top of the paper, so I can't turn it over. I sit back up. She points at the picture of the modern house that stands next to the one of her and her dad, on the mantelpiece.

'There was dancing in that house, Postman. Dancing under a chandelier. A spectacular chandelier in the ballroom. Over two thousand pieces of white glass specially commissioned from the Barovier & Toso glass factory in Murano, Venice, set against a cloth of darkest blue velvet. My father was an architect, a famous one in Austria. He had the chandelier built for me; a present for my seventh birthday. Two thousand white pieces of glass to represent the stars visible from Vienna on the night I was born. So my father and I would always be able to stand beneath it and look up into the heavens like we used to do in his friend Uncle Rudy's House, when we took my little brother and his red hoop, who loved it so, to visit there before the war.'

Nizanna smiles.

'Uncle Rudy's ice-cream house.'

'An ice-cream house? Your uncle was an ice-cream man?'

Nizanna shakes her head.

'My father's friend, we thought of him as uncle because he was so kind to us, was a merchant, a wealthy one. Rudolf Konig, he was called. But he loved astronomy, loved the stars as you do. He built a famous house, near ours, in Kuppel-wiesergasse. A white cupola on the top of it, something magnificent, in which our Uncle Rudy kept his own – his very own – large telescope. Its white cupola made Uncle Rudy's house look a little like a very big, how you say, a cone? So, my little brother, Alter, when he was only three years old, took to calling it "Das Eistute Haus," the Ice-Cream House.'

I lean forward in me chair.

'Your brother's name was Alter?'

Nizanna nods. Then looks across to the mantelpiece at the photo of her dad.

'"To Wenig Sterenlicht with all my love." My father had written a card to go with the chandelier, when he showed it to us. Wenig Sterenlicht, Little Starlight, was a pet name he sometimes used for me.'

'Wenig Sterenlicht – W.S?'

'Yes.'

'Alter – Alter Strasse!'

Nizanna points to the family photograph on the mantelpiece.

'My brother was a sick child. Alter is a name that my people often give to sick children, to bring them luck and help them live and prosper in the world. And Alter did live. A "miracle child," so my mother often said. His red hoop I am holding in the picture. My brother, Alter, loved to play with that red metal hoop.'

I lean further forward and grab a hold of the paper. This time she lets me do it. I pick it up in both hands and stare at it. I look up at her.

'There's nothing on it.'

'I have talked a lot, in these last few weeks or so, used so many words, Postman. When I talk, I can't hold onto them.'

'Hold on to who?'

'I had to believe, Postman. In that place at the end of the railway line only those who believed, survived. And I did survive. Then, in time, perhaps when I became unwell, perhaps before then, I began to believe for everybody.'

She reaches out and picks up an envelope from the desk. It's cream coloured. Different to the pile of white envelopes, near the green pen.

'Well, almost, everybody.'

I can see it's got loads of creases in it, where it's been folded and opened again loads and loads of times.

It's fatter too. There's a letter inside it.

'So many nights, before the war, my father would sit with Alter on his knee in Uncle Rudy's Eistute Haus. They would each take turns looking up at the stars, through the big telescope.'

Nizanna pushes the cream envelope across the tablecloth

towards me. I stare down at it. Even though it's obviously dead old it hasn't got a stamp on it, like the ones at Ravenswood.

I look up into her eyes, filled with them far-away twinkles.

'Maybe you can do that for me now?' she says. 'For your mother also? Can you believe too?'

I stare at Nizanna. She stares back.

'My little brother was a wonderful creature, Postman, full of life and mischief. But the greatest part of his charm came from his innocence.'

Nizanna slides the envelope a little closer to me.

'This is the first letter, I ever wrote. I could not bring myself to send it. Not then. Not now. I believed for me, Postman. I believed for everyone else. I do still. But, somehow, I cannot believe for him. Perhaps you can do that for me?'

I read the address written on the letter:

Alter Oz,
Alter Strasse,
Bezirke Veindenburger
Wein.

I look back up again at Nizanna, straight into them eyes with their faraway twinkles. I stretch out me hand and pick up the letter.

Chapter Twenty-Nine

I read this Alter letter Nizanna gave me loads of times when I got back to me room last night. It's a bit different to all the others. Most of them, I reckon, she must have written with her Weather Head on. If this one's the first that she wrote, after her husband, this Captain McNeil, died, like Watergate said, maybe she wasn't quite so ill when she did it. Maybe she wrote this one just before she started to go a bit doolally tap in her head.

I pick it up and start to read again.

Dear Alter,

Ich Sehe Sie,

I lost you once.

Your hand, so small and soft, pulled away from mine.

I was sitting on the wooden bench under the old sycamore tree in Hugle Park, reading. I turned the pages slowly; listening out for the reassuring spinning sound your metal hoop made on the ground.

My eyes closed, only for a second, I opened them again.

You were gone.

In that moment, for the first time in my life, I experienced terror. I was only eleven years old; how would I be able to explain to mother and father that their miracle child could not be found?

But then...

I did not run, I walked, such was my certainty; under the flowering linden trees, down Kuppelwiesergasse.

Turned down the path, knocked on the red door. Went up the dark oak stairs that led to the white cupola.

Your face, full of mischief, turned toward me as I arrived.

"Ich sehe sie," I whispered.

"Das Eistute Haus, Das Eistute Haus," you cried.

A person can never be truly lost as long as someone else keeps looking for them, Alter. You are not, then, gone from me, forever.

I will not believe it.

It is simply that I have not, yet, found you.

Ich Sehe Sie, Alter

Your W.S

There was something else in the envelope too. A drawing – pretty much like all the other ones Nizanna's done. It's on normal paper but it looks like the ones architects do when they're making plans.

This one is a little bit different, though. It's got a tower on one side of it with a big round roof. Little Alter was right. The cupola bit does look a bit like a giant scoop of ice cream sitting on top of a cone.

There's a noise in the alley, outside me window.

Down towards one of the lock-up garages I can see a bloke pushing up the metal garage door. I can't make out who it is at first but then he steps back into the moonlight. Dad glances around; first left and then right. Then he goes inside the garage and pulls the metal door down behind him.

It takes me a couple of minutes to get me jeans and jumper on. Then I pull me Polyveldts on too, without bothering to tie the laces. I walk down stairs; go into the kitchen.

The back-door into the alley is already open.

DAD'S LOCK-UP IS THE FIFTH GARAGE DOWN FROM WHERE OUR back-door is. When I get there I can hear him rummaging around inside. Although the door is closed, it's not locked shut. There's about two inches of space between the metal base and the concrete of the garage floor. I can see a bit of light moving about inside.

He's got a torch in there.

I bend down and take hold of the bottom of the doorframe with both hands. There's a rasping sound of rusty metal. The chain swivels round in the mechanism as I push the door up.

Dad's standing next to six big sacks that are all pushed to the very back of the garage. He spins around and sees me. At first, he tries to stand in front of the sacks so I can't see them. Then he realises that's not going to work, and there's a click as he switches off his torch. Everything goes dark apart from the moonlight in the alley outside. I can't see me dad's face. He takes a step forward and sits down in an old raffia chair with a broken leg.

He switches the torch back on and moves the beam upwards and starts running it over the sacks piled up in the back. As the light passes over them, I see they've all got the letters P and O printed on them in white. They're from the post office! The big brown sort the mail comes in, when it arrives at the depot. Out of the top of each one of them, I can see loads of stuff sticking out – parcels, post-cards, brown bills and letters.

Dad sticks the beam of the torch just under his own chin so I can see his face. His eyes are all glassy, with big dark shadows under them and he looks scruffy because he hasn't had his shave yet.

'People say I'm a laugh – Oh, Bobby Agnew, he's always good for a joke, or a tune. I had to try for you, son. Try to be meself. After she went, I'd just leave for the post office whistling in the morning, same as always. Then come back whistling in the afternoons.'

He turns around again and shines the torch back on the sacks.

'The first two weeks I managed it. But, then, I had a blip. Threw a wobbly. Nervous what-do-ya-ma-call-it. Losing your bottle. That's what it was really. I lost mine.'

I walk across to one of the sacks and pick-out a postcard that has a picture of a blue sky and sandy beach and donkey wearing a sombrero on it. It's got "Greetings from Benidorm" printed on it in pink.

'You've interfered with the Queen's mail, Dad. Not delivered it!'

'Big deal, I didn't deliver the mail for a couple of weeks, so somebody somewhere is missing a post-card of a stupid bleeding donkey, wearing a sombrero. I'd just go to the depot pick up me sack and bring them here and sit on this daft chair, that we got in Farnons for ten bob, twisting knots into the knackered raffia. Thinking of all the good times we had, me, you and her. It was a week, that's all. Ten days, tops. I've been re-delivering them ever since. Just a few each day in me bag, so no one will notice.'

Dad leans down and puts his hand into a old tin biscuit box that's sitting on the floor. He takes out a pair of me mam's red Mars specs and puts them on.

'Remember these, son?'

I nod me head.

'Yes.'

'I can still see your mam, watching that film, at the Odeon in Leicester Square on our honeymoon. In the middle of it there was a bit where the lass who was the star, Phyllis Kirk, well, her face was, like, massive on the screen.'

Dad reaches up and straightens the glasses he's wearing.

'Huge, it was, coming through the darkness towards me. Right then, I looked across at your mam. She was just staring up at Phyllis. Then I looked back at the screen and I thought to meself: not a patch, Bobby, son. Hollywood star or not, 100 ft. high, or higher still, this blonde bombshell, Phyllis, she's not a patch on your new Mrs.'

Me dad reaches up and takes off the specs and drops them back in the tin box. Then he gets up from the chair and walks towards me.

He puts his hand on me shoulder.

'They don't work, son. Them Mars specs of your mam's. She used to say they were rose-tinted. That they'd let you see the world however you want to see it. But I've been wearing them for months now, coming in here and sitting in her old raffia chair with them on. But the thing I want to see more than anything else in the world, her face, next to mine, looking just like it did that night in Leicester Square, I just can't make meself see it.'

Me dad pats me on the shoulder for a second time.

'I'm sorry I slapped you, son.'

I step away from him and sit down in the chair. There's

loads of knots in the side of it where Dad's been twisting the raffia. I find a fresh long bit sticking out from the corner of the left-hand side, and start twisting it between me fingers. Same as he's been doing.

'You could go to prison, Dad. A bloke in the Carlisle Depot did it once and he did. There'll be cheques and postal orders in them sacks.'

'I know, son. He got eighteen months. Everything's fucked-up, our Billy. And it's all my fault.'

I can't look up at me dad when I hear him say that. I stare down at the Mars specs in the box and twist a bit of the raffia around and around on the side of the chair.

At first, I can't make meself say what I need to say, then I do.

'It wasn't cheese and crackers, Dad. It wasn't cheese and crackers that killed me mam. We had an argument, me and her. She wanted me to go to church. I told her that Jesus, angels, the gospels; all that stuff...it doesn't make any sense. She started doing the dishes; banging the pots against the taps. Then she said I was "being daft!" I couldn't stand it when she said that. I went mad with her, all shouting and bawling, like a little bairn, saying she was the daft one. Her, not me! Believing in all that mumbo-jumbo. Same as the other women who went to the club, who were always talking about Saturn being on the cusp.'

I can't look up, can't make meself do it, but I feel me dad step a bit further away from me.

'That you and her were the daft ones. That you read daft books. and liked daft songs, and daft stuff like dancing at the club and doing silly impressions, and had a daft door-bell that played Blue Suede Shoes. That you couldn't be me real mam and dad. She didn't say nowt; just picked up her coat and went off to church, like she always did. That's why she stayed longer in the club than usual…because she didn't want to come back and see me, after what I'd said to her!'

I still can't make meself look up at him. Not now, after saying what I've said.

There's a click as he turns off the torch. Then he's gone.

I pick up the Mars specs and put them on. Then I just sit there on the knackered chair twisting and twisting away at another bit of raffia.

WHEN I GOT UP THIS MORNING AND WENT IN THE KITCHEN ME dad looked up, picked up his tea, and his Daily Mirror, and went out.

I didn't say nowt to anyone at work; just got on with sorting stuff but I could feel me Mucklestone Moments pin-cushion head getting sharper and sharper all day, and the way I sorted the letters getting slower and slower; so, by the end of the afternoon, it must have looked to the other sorters that I was sorting on the surface of the Moon, or something.

Normally, on the Mucklestone Moments days, I go to the library and try and read meself better but I can't do that anymore. Not since Ninder and her big gob got me banned. I wanted to go back to Windsor Mansions and see Nizanna again, talk things through with her. But I can't face Blue and Bino and that dog again.

After work, I even went around to Watergate's house to see if I could talk to him but his sister said he was at the hospital having his bad wrist checked out.

I've rung Ninder's house loads in the last few days, to tell her about Jimmy Segs and his yellow riders with the funny

Blakeys pattern on them, but she's never answered. Her mam's away in Belfast visiting relatives at the moment, and Ninder's always out. Probably over at Afghan Larry's.

Worst thing is I've got to meet Ossie Mingle tomorrow night outside the Hancock Museum.

I feel a lot better now though. Now I've decided. Decided that when I get home tonight I'm going to do what I should have done ages ago, and tell me dad all about it.

IT'S GONE SEVEN WHEN I GET BACK FROM THE POST OFFICE. There's a note propped up against the Fred Flintstone salt-shaker in the kitchen and twenty quid stuck underneath it.

I pick it up and begin to read.

I've got a chitty from Dr Mohammed about me nerves not being right so I don't have to go into to work until next week. Gone to stay with Brenda for a few days to get me head straight. It upset me what you said, son, about your mam and that argument and the cracker plates. Look after yourself for now. I'll be back on Saturday, then we can talk things out.

Dad

PS: (Brenda's not a slag, she's a Catholic. She's only ever done it with me and her ex-husband, Norman, before he ran off with a lass he met at Pontins who worked for the Green Shield stamps.)

Chapter Thirty

The great white shark hangs there in the darkness. Like it's swimming through deepest space; sucking up any plankton, pilchards, fairy cakes, people, or orbiting probes that happen to be passing. Blue gives me one of his best sneer-smiles then slips the key back into the pocket of his Levi's. He punches in the code, that's handwritten on the back of the fob, into the old alarm and then pushes the massive wooden door of the Hancock Museum shut behind us.

He and Bino take out a couple of small torches and head under the shark through a door that leads to an area called the Evolutionary Hall, which has loads of dinosaurs and stuffed animals in it.

Ossie whispers after them.

'Oi, you, Psycho. Remember what I said.'

Blue turns back around. I see something peeping out of the top of his jacket pocket. It's the marmalade jar; the one he had with him at the Rocky Horse Park.

'Take nothing of real value, son, but mess it up a bit, so it looks like vandals,' says Ossie.

Blue points up to a sign on the wall that says: This way to the Hancock Beehive, and grins.

'Don't worry, Ossie; me and Bino are going to be busy. I got some of that phosphorus with me.'

He taps the jar in his pocket.

The image of the melted plastic lid I found at Uncle Noor's comes into me head. Then it hits me. US! Of course, that's it. Them two letters don't mean the word us. Now, I'm remembering what Ossie said about Blue being a mate of Jimmy Segs. I must be daft for not seeing it. That lump of plastic is from school. It's a melted bit of one of the containers we used to use for chemicals, until they all got nicked. The u and the s are the last two letters of a word – phosphorus. Ninder was right. Blue must have given it to his pal, Jimmy. There's nowt I can do about it now, though. I watch him and Bino go through a door into the main hall.

Ossie slaps me on the back.

'Come on, son, you're with me.'

He steps further into the middle of the museum foyer, next to one of the wooden reception desks, and takes a torch out of a little canvas bag he's brought with him.

'You thought we'd take them keys and come on our own, eh?

He shakes his head; shines the beam of the torch onto a sign, next to the stairs, with old-fashioned white letters on it, that has got Coins, Stamps and Incidentals written on it, next to a white arrow that's pointing up. Ossie's thin lips slit into a tight little smile.

'Welcome to collectors' paradise, young William.'

He reaches out and pats me on the left shoulder. Flashes me a dead nasty wink.

'Glad you could join me, son, I was, in fact, going to come

without you. Until I seen that letter. When we're done here, you and me are going to have a nice little chat about what you know about it. Never mind though, eh, young William? Two's company, as they say.'

Ossie turns right and starts walking up the big concrete steps on the opposite side of the foyer to the ones the shark is hanging over. I follow him. After a minute, or so, me and Ossie come to the landing that looks over the auditorium that houses the Destination Mars Exhibition. I can't help thinking about how close Viking 1's lander is to touching down on the real Martian surface.

Ossie stops in front of one of the display cases. He pulls back its green felt cover and then runs the beam of his torch down the front of the wood cabinet. It picks out rows and rows of stamps: swastikas, storm troopers, Stuka dive-bombers, Panzer tanks and, repeated over and over again – Hitler's white face, staring eyes and little black moth of a moustache.

Ossie hands me the torch. He takes out a glass-cutter from his bag and presses it against the edge of the cabinet; where the glass meets the wood. He starts to score around a small glass panel that's about six inches square in the bottom left-hand corner of the display case

'The cheesecloth-wearing sandal-prancers who run this place have been sitting on a gold mine and they don't even know it. A collector came into my shop a couple of months back and asks about a certain stamp. Tells me there were only a few of them ever printed. He'd pay me fifteen-grand if he could get his hands on one. So, I'm here for the dosh, sure, but not just that. The reason I really came is because Wop Ernie Motta always said I could have it, and because I'm in love with its story.'

There's a thin grating sound as the glass starts to break.

OSSIE LEANS DOWN AND RESTS THE GLASS AGAINST THE WALL, next to his canvas bag. He flips open the top of the bag and takes out a small panel of glass, exactly the same size as the one he's just removed, and a small white tube of putty and rests them against the wall next to the glass he's just taken out. He stands up and leans dead close to me. His yellow face looks all wrinkly, like parchment; as though he should have its own display case next to Bakt-Hor-Nekht.

'Little museum like this one, even the people who run it don't expect to have anything of any real value. They don't know what they've got. We're going to put everything back nice and tidy. Just as it was. When they check the log on that alarm and see someone's been here that shouldn't, all they'll find is the little bits and bobs of aggravation that Blue and Bino are up to, and blame it all on vandals.'

Ossie takes a small square of yellow paper out of his pocket and rests it on the wooden edge of the case, and places a pair of tweezers next to it. I stare down at the stamp. It's got Hitler's head on it and Deutsche Reich printed on the bottom – same as most of them in the case.

He leans into the case and picks up one of the stamps. Holds it in front of his grinning face, side by side, with the one he pulled out of his pocket. I have to lean forward in the half-darkness to get a proper look but when I do I can see they're the same. Both yellow with Hitler's head on it. Even the little bit of frank-mark that's on them is a match. And that's when I realise about the colour. That, of all the stamps in the case with Hitler on them, the only one that's yellow is the one Ossie just picked up. He grins.

'Snap, eh? I know a bloke in the Whitechapel Road who

can paint better than Da Vinci; provided I give him reference. Stamps of the Hancock Museum came in handy – 10p from the gift shop, last time I was up here.'

Ossie puts the stamp from the case down next to the one he brought with him. He holds it down with the middle-finger of his left hand and takes his thumb nail and starts to rub gently at its bottom right corner. The picture of Hitler begins to lift and bobble a tiny bit. Ossie picks up the tweezers and grips the lifted-bit of the stamp with them. As he lifts the tweezers up, the image begins to peel away from the rest of the stamp.

There's another picture beneath it. The picture of Hitler on top must be a fake. Something Ernesto Motta had stuck on top of the real stamp underneath it.

'I went to see Ernie before he died. They had him in cancer ward. He'd always said I could have this stamp when he'd gone. I knew the value of it. Worth five-grand, even then. He was babbling, half-crazy. I kept on at him. Finally, he reached out and nipped me cheek with his bony dead man's fingers, and started laughing. Giggling like the Reaper himself was in the room, and had decided to grant Ernie one last big belly laugh – a thank-you note for all that Zyclon B he'd flogged. "He's got a fever, same as you have, the one that's got it, Ossie, of all them little Adolfs of mine, only one of them's got a fever." That's what he said.'

Ossie puts the tweezers into his pocket.

'Stumped me all these years – never could work out what he was on about. Then, a few month back, I read that book again, Stamps of the Hancock, and it mentions there was only one yellow stamp in the whole of the Motta collection. Only one of them Adolfs, had got a fever – a jaundice like mine.'

I stare down at the new picture. It's yellow too but other-wise it's completely different from all the other stamps in the cases. Hitler's sitting down around a table in it, for a start. Next to him is bloke in an ordinary suit that I recognise from the time me and Ninder were here, talking to her mam. Ossie taps his finger down on the bloke.

'Know who that is?'

I nod me head.

'Albert Speer.'

'And who was Albert Speer, Billy Quiz?'

'Hitler's architect.'

Ossie smiles.

'They had a dream together – Adolf and Albert. A sweet dream. A new Berlin – Weltahauptstadt Germania, World Capital Germania. A capital city on a scale no one had ever seen before. If the Reich had conquered the world, they would have built it.'

Ossie leans over and puts the other stamp – the one he brought with him – gently back into the exact place in the case that the original was. Then he slips the real stamp into his pocket.

'When I had the jaundice they give me morphia for it. Such dreams I had on them ampoules. I dreamt Germania risen and me strolling down the Avenue of Splendours towards the Volkshalle, the people's hall – a huge white dome sixteen times bigger than St Peter's in Rome.'

'But...'

'Yes?'

'It doesn't exist. They didn't win.'

Ossie grabs a hold of me by me throat with his right hand and forces me into a space between two cabinets, so me legs are pushed up against the balustrade that surrounds the museum's courtyard, where the Destination Mars exhibit is.

He jabs two fingers of his left hand into his own temple.

'It exists in here for me.'

His eyes have gone all glazed and a bit crazy.

'I believe you, Mr Mingle, I believe you!'

I shout the words but he doesn't seem to hear me. I feel his fingers relax around me throat. He's looking straight past me now; over me shoulder.

'How the...'

He points downwards into the courtyard. When he speaks his voice breaks up a bit.

'She is a fucking witch. I always knew it.'

I turn round and follow his gaze.

There's a woman dressed in black standing on the Martian surface, next to the spacecraft. She's staring straight up at me and Ossie and, in the red glow of the lights that surround the model, looks as if she's just stepped right out of the Viking lander.

'You show me that letter, young William, and now here she is.'

Ossie's whisper is so low I have to lean me head towards him because I can hardly hear it.

'MacNeil...Oz...Nizanna Oz – the Letter Lady.'

OSSIE RUNS DOWN THE STAIRS. I RUN AFTER HIM INTO THE main hall. Nizanna is standing right next to the Viking lander on the Martian surface. She's holding something tight in her arms though; cradling it, like it was a little bairn. It's one of the fire axes that's usually stuck to the wall, near the doors of the museum.

Ossie stares at Nizanna, and then glances across at me.

'Do you know what the scariest dreams are, son? The ones

that start off good and then turn into something else. A sweet dream that turns sour.'

I get a real chill in me bones by the way he says that.

He turns back towards Nizanna and holds out his right hand.

'Don't be afraid, Miss Oz. It's me, Nurse Leech, from Ravenswood Lodge. Maybe you should just give the axe to me?'

He sounds all in-charge when he speaks. Like this kind thing has happened to him a lot. And I've never seen Nizanna's face look so still before. Then something changes. She looks at me and smiles. Her green eyes fill with all them far away twinkles.

Ossie takes a step onto the Martian surface.

Then another.

'The axe, Miss Oz, give me the axe.'

Nizanna's staring down at the footprint Ossie's left in the red dust, like it was Neil Armstrong's on the moon, or something.

She looks back up at him. Then at me.

'After the war, Postman, I came home to Kuppelwiesergasse, house number 6, near Hugle Park. It was not existing anymore. In the distance, I could see a broken cupola. All that remained of my Uncle Rudy's observatory – the ice-cream house my brother had loved so much. Where had they gone? My father? Alter? The neighbours and friends who had danced in our ballroom? Our beautiful chandelier with its pieces of glass, each one representing a star above the city, on the night I was born, had disappeared. Only a few tiny fragments remained.'

Nizanna closes the fingers of her hand around her necklace.

'Then, amongst the dust and debris on the floor, one of them twinkled.'

Her fist clenches around the little white bead.

'I'd had to believe to survive, Postman. Right then and there, I decided to believe for everybody. This I am reasoning to myself – they all had to be somewhere.'

'Somewhere?'

Ossie takes another step forward as he asks the question. Nizanna raises the axe above her head.

'Somewhere else.'

Ossie takes a step back.

Nizanna lowers the axe a little. Then she turns away from us and faces the Viking I lander. Raising it again, she kind of whispers to herself.

'It's an unmanned probe, Postman, that is what you say to me at my house. That is why you like it.'

I nod me head.

'Yes.'

She raises the axe little higher.

'Others will come though, other spacecraft, to Mars and beyond, and they will have people on them.'

Then she brings it down on the lander's big, white satellite dish.

'No!' Me voice echoes around the room.

I run towards her. Grab her arms. Hold them and the axe above her head. Me face is dead close to hers. She closes her eyes. I feel her arms go soft. Her fingers loosen. I can feel that she knows. Knows how to let other people feel they've won; same way I do. I take the axe from her and turn back towards Ossie. He leans in close. Takes it from me. I can smell his dead cheap aftershave as he whispers in Nizanna's ear.

'I can heal you from the sickness in your head, pet, heal you just like I did last time.'

There's a click as he turns off the torch. Then all I see is the shape of Ossie's hand, and the dead heavy torch swinging through the darkness towards me.

Olympus Mons.
Monday, July 19th, 1976.
Only hours until Viking 1's lander lands on Mars

Chapter Thirty-One

When me old pal, Sir Isaac, investigated light he used to do experiments like pushing a big needle into the back of his eyes to see how it would change the way he saw patterns, and staring at the sun until he went blind After he did that sort of stuff, his bonce must have felt like mine does now – like a gang of Irish builders have mistaken it for a bit of tarmac.

I open me eyes and wince.

I blink a couple of more times, all I can see is a kind of white texture in the darkness.

It's not light though. I can tell that, now. I sit up, blink some more and look around me. Now I can see it.

I'm lying under the red lights, next to one of three big rocks on the Martian surface. In the distance, through the open door that leads to the stairs, I can see the white shark.

I put me hand up to me right temple. There's a massive bump on it, as big as some of the snake eggs they keep in the cases here. Then I notice it. Nizanna's white bead lying in the red dust. No sign of her, though. I pick it up, put it in me pocket and then walk past the buffalo in the case, into the reception area.

I'm almost standing directly under the shark before I see Bino lying on the stairs. His pink eyes are wide and staring. Like they're about to pop right out. There's blood streaming from his nose. One of his eyes is already beginning to turn black and blue. His voice is just a whisper.

'Blue tried do me. I know stuff about them – him and Ossie.'

He dabs at his nose with his shirt sleeve to stop the blood. I take a step towards him.

'Have they got her with them? Nizanna, the Letter Lady?'

Bino looks up at me.

'They've taken her, yeah, but I don't know where. Ossie don't' sleep no more, so Blue says. Paces his room every night. Too scared to close his eyes, in case he goes to the land of nod. Bastard calls me Omo and fucking Ghost-boy, shite like that. But, I could tell just by the way he was looking at the crazy fucking witch-woman from Windsor Mansions, that she's got inside his head, got him proper haunted.'

He starts to shiver a bit.

'They might come back for us,' he says. 'Me and you need to be someplace else.'

Bino tries to get up. His right foot gives way beneath him. It looks knackered. He starts limping towards to the door. I race past him.

'I'm going to get the coppers' I shout. 'We need help.'

I TEAR UP THE BIG STONE STEPS AND PUSH OPEN THE MASSIVE door of Market Street police station.

The reception area is packed with coppers and football fans. I run past a queue of pissed-up Rangers supporters wearing blue and white scarves, all with a couple of PCs standing on either side of them, waiting to book them in for the night.

I push me way past the rest of the queue and stand at the front desk.

'Something's happened!'

A big fat sergeant with a red nose looks up from the book he's writing in and stares at me.

'Right first time, Einstein. Rangers lost 2-0 in the friendly tonight and, right now, their fans are smashing up half the city. Now get to the back of queue and wait your turn, son.'

'Someone's dead! Nearly dead anyway.'

The sergeant stops writing and looks up again.

'Nearly dead, where?'

'The museum.'

The sergeant sighs.

'Aye, son, you're right. I was there two weeks ago with the bairns. Her name is Bakt-Hor-Nekht.'

'A woman's gone missing, too.'

I reach across and grab hold of the sergeant's hand.

'It says US. But US was them. The melted lid says US. The ones in the chemistry labs at school all have black plastic tops, like that. It was obvious all the time! But I couldn't tell because it was too melted. They were US! Blue Tear and Bino. They gave the phosphorus to Jimmy Segs. Sold him it, or they were with him, or something, and now the Letter Lady's gone missing from the Martian surface.'

The sergeant stares down at me hand. Then back up at me. 'Last chance, sunny, back of the queue or I'll be locking you up in the cells with the rest of them.'

THROUGH THE DOOR OF THE RED PHONE BOX, OPPOSITE THE police station I can see another jam-sandwich full of hammered Ranger's fans pull up. I keep thumbing through the W section of the phone book. It takes a minute to get through all the Woods and the Wooltons. Then, there it is. I dial the number. It rings. Once. Twice. Three times. Someone at the other end picks up. The pips start.

I ram in a 10p and a couple of 2ps.

'Tommy, it's me, Billy. She's missing, gone, the Letter Lady. She's been taken.'

'It's not him, donkey bollocks! It's me.'

Ninder's voice sounds thick and a bit blurry, she's had a few.

'What you doing at Watergate's house?'

'I came to apologise about breaking in and getting him beat up and that, although it wasn't me that organised that, it was that fecking arse Afghan Larry, so he could get into me knickers, but you'd already made your mind up that it was my fault. I was at the pub, I had a couple of pints of snake-bite, I thought about what you said and then I got in a mini-cab and came here.'

'I need to speak to him now! Someone's dead. She might be.'

'Dead?'

'Just fucking get him, Ninder, man...'

I hear Ninder put the phone down on the table. The pips start again and I slam in more 2ps.

'Alright, Billy. What's this young Ninder's saying?'

'They've got her, Nizanna. They've taken her away somewhere. I've tried to tell the coppers but they won't listen.'

'Calm down, son. Calm down. Take a couple of breaths, speak slowly.'

'A skinhead called Blue Tear. He's the one that helped Jimmy Segs set fire to Ninder's Uncle Noor's. I know it was him because this Jimmy Segs used phosphorus to torch the shop. I found the lid of the bottle on the floor there. Blue and Bino they done the school chemistry lab ages ago, nicked loads of stuff. I mean I don't know for sure they were there, but it must have been them that gave him the phosphorus. Now Bino's been battered and Blue and his Uncle Ossie, they've kidnapped Nizanna from the museum.'

'What's the uncle's name?'

'Mingle, Ossie, Mingle but then to her, to Nizanna, he said Leech.'

'Ossie Leech?'

'Nurse Leech, he said.'

The pips start going again. It's Watergate's turn to shout now.

'I know Leech. Did that slimy bastard say anything else? Think carefully, son.'

I hunt around in me pocket and find me last 2p. I ram it into the slot.

'He could heal her. Yes, he could heal her. That's what he said.'

Chapter Thirty-Two

The headlights pick out the stone wall. The post-van speeds past it, in the pitch darkness. I'm sitting in the passenger seat. Ninder is in the back, behind the van's metal grill, lying next to a couple of empty post office sacks. She's said nowt since we left Newcastle. Her eyes are all puffed up and her mascara's running where she's been bubbling. I know she's thinking about her Uncle Noor and the phosphorus and Jimmy Segs.

Watergate puts his foot down hard on the accelerator.

'He was always a scum-bag, Mingle. Back then, he called himself Leech. We didn't know it, but later, it turned out, he'd caused some trouble for the Med Corp when he was out in Malaya. A rumour about a massacre, or something, it got hushed up. We never found out exactly what. They were going to strike him of the medical register, wouldn't let him work as a nurse no more, so he changed his name to Leech and fixed himself up with false papers. He only started working the Lodge in '56. Her letters, Nizanna's letters, were everywhere by then. All over people's walls and desks. Every place she couldn't see them, anyways. We always kept them out of her sight, so she'd keep on believing we sent them.

I could tell straightaway Mingle didn't like them letters. Made comments, he did. Smart-arse cracks about her being Queen of the Fruitcakes. Nothing racial. He was careful, at first, to hide all that. Then some of the letters started disappearing. I'd find 'em burnt near the bins or in little piles out in the woods. He started saying things to set the other patients against her, too. That she was the witch they'd burned at Ravenswood, the one who sent the ravens away, come back to haunt them. Malice, I thought. Pure malice from the bastard. Sometimes though, the way he went on and on and on about it, well, I could see there was part of him beginning to sort of believe that maybe she really did have supernatural powers.'

I spot a phone box just as the van speeds past it.

'Maybe we should try the police again, Tommy, give them a ring?'

Ninder leans forward. She dabs at her eyes with one of her "What are little girls made of?" hankies.

'Yeah, maybe?'

Watergate shakes his head.

'From what you've said, Billy she's too fragile. I've seen her like that before. At Ravenswood, sometimes she would be all calm and serene. Other times you could feel most of her had drifted right away from you, and the bit that remained was stretched so tight it might snap and she'd be gone forever. If the coppers get her first, they'll get her sectioned again. I don't think she could take that this time, do you?'

He stamps his foot down on the accelerator.

'That's how that shit-bag Leech, likes to see her. Back in them days, he waited until there was no one around. Then he brought a whole box of her letters into the ward and scattered them all over her bed. Made sure she couldn't not see them. So she knew they hadn't been posted. She scratched his face, started screaming, started speaking – speaking after all that time – saying crazy stuff. The lousy sod liked that – the pain in her voice. I reckon, it was her not speaking that he'd always hated the most.'

'Did she stop then, after he did that, stop writing the letters?' says Ninder.

Watergate moves the gear-stick from fourth to third. The van goes around a sharp bend near a wooden farm gate.

He shakes his head.

'Not at first. He kept working on her though. Slipping old letters under her pillow, in her washroom, other places too, I expect. When she reacted, he'd tell the docs she was getting worse and, maybe, they needed to give her electroshock.'

'Electroshock, what's that?' says Ninder.

Watergate turns his head towards me.

'One for you, Billy?'

'Electro Convulsive Therapy is what they call it these days. If you're dead sad all the time, they strap you down to a bench and give you shocks on purpose.'

Watergate nods.

'Yeah, that's it. In the end, after he'd asked them enough times, they gave in and said yes. Mingle administered the treatment himself. She never wrote any more letters after that. A few months later, she started to speak a lot more. A year after that, they let her out.'

'So the shocks made her better?' Ninder says.

Watergate shrugs. Puts his foot down.

'In one way yes, not in another.'

'How do you mean?', I shout dead loud over the noise of the engine. He looks across at me.

'He left her just like them little bairns I saw in that camp at the end of the war. There was nothing left inside her after he done what he did.'

The van shoots over the brow of another hill and I get me first glimpse of the abandoned hospital's knackered old stone tower.

WATERGATE PARKS AT THE BACK OF THE HOSPITAL, NEXT TO A couple of upturned industrial bins and a busted fencepost. Me and Watergate get out. Then I pull the seat forward and unclip the metal grill, so Ninder can scramble out of the back. Her pink Doc Martens crunch down onto the gravel.

Watergate takes his torch out of his pocket and leads me and Ninder down a little overgrown path, past a couple of smashed vegetable frames and some old red flowerpots towards the front of the building. Then he goes to the arch-shaped window that's next to the big wooden door.

He reaches through the busted window and unloosens the catch. I push at the frame and it opens. I jump up onto the window sill and then step down onto the cardboard boxes with the words SANIJAB SYRINGES written on them.

As I jump down on the ground, Ninder scrambles up onto the sill behind me. I put me hand out. She takes it and climbs through. Watergate's wheezing a bit. A drop of sweat trickles down from underneath his comb-over and runs down his bald white head. He forces his fat gut through the tight window frame and then drops down next to us.

I stare out of the window. A yellow moon is shining down between the trees in the wood and lighting up the empty court-yard at the front of the hospital.

'They're not here yet.' I say. 'Maybe they've taken her somewhere else, Tommy?'

Watergate takes a torch out the pocket of his jacket and shines it in front of him. There's an old metal bed-frame that's been turned on its side in the middle of the corridor, about twenty feet in front of us. Beyond that, an open glass door with a smashed pane.

'Don't worry, son. They will be.'

THE LETTERS AND DRAWINGS THAT ARE STUCK TO THE WALL OF the Community Room lift and flutter a bit, making them look dead like a colony of bats again.

When she sees them Ninder comes to a stop in the middle of the room. Watergate runs his torch around the walls picking out letter after letter, drawing after drawing – houses, shops, theatres, restaurants; this time I notice there's even a real canny pencil diagram of a swimming pool.

Ninder spins around and around as she follows the path of his torch. It looks a bit like she's dancing in her pink DMs. Then she stops twisting and turning, stands completely still and stares at Watergate.

'In here they don't feel like letters anymore. It's like we're walking through a graveyard.'

Watergate nods. He walks a little closer to the wall near the broken patio doors and holds the torch up over his shoulder, so he can see to read a few of them.

'You're right, pet. Dear Artur...Dear Sigmund...Dear Rina...After a while, when you're read as many of them as I have, they feel like ghosts; the remains of living breathing people that in some weird sort of way you feel you knew once.

Someone, maybe, you sat next to in a café one time, or passed in the street on the way to work.'

I walk across the room and stop at the back, near a knackered patio window that lets the breeze into the room. I stare down at one of the envelopes that's resting on top of a broken bookcase. I pick it up and look more closely at its orange stamp. Hitler's face stares blankly back at me. There are two letters franked over him: a V and an S.

'This stamp is like the first one I found, Tommy. It's got the same franking mark on it!'

Watergate nods.

'Auschwitz. There was a post office there for the officers and guards. They let prisoners send cards and letters home, not the Jews, but some of the others. Censored, though, of course. The stamps are easy enough to buy on the open market because thousands and thousands of letters got sent from there during the war. I bought a job lot of them off a bloke I used to know at the GPO, a big stamp collector, and gave them to her, when I worked here. Once I knew her story, well, somehow, it just seemed to make sense.'

I put the envelope back down on the bookcase. Ninder turns towards me. She looks puzzled.

'Why would Blue Tear beat up Bino, Billy? Why would he give his mate a kicking like that?'

'I don't know.'

I lean down and pick up one of the letters that's fallen on the floor. Rest it on top of a little coffee-table that's standing to the left of the patio doors, and point at it.

'They're not ghosts,' I say.

She shrugs.

'They feel like they are, to me.'

I grab a hold of the patio doors with both of me hands and

try and force them properly open but they're stuck. I turn back around and face Watergate.

'She doesn't think of them like that. She doesn't think of them as being dead. To her, it's like they're alive. All this time, in her head, she's been writing to the living.'

There's an old purple velvet curtain covering the patio doors. I stretch me hands out and grab a hold of the right-hand side of it.

Watergate walks towards me. Puts his left hand on me arm.

'What you doing, Billy Quiz?'

'She stopped writing because of the electroshocks, Tommy, I see what you mean about that. But then she started again. Why do you think she did that?'

Watergate turns the torch back on the walls again – it picks out more letters.

'I don't know,' he says. 'Drugs maybe. She'd be getting prescriptions after her release. Most people would, who'd been sectioned like that. Valium or some other anti-depressant. Maybe she ran out?'

I nod me head.

'Yes, that's probably part of it. But when did she start again, Tommy? When did you see the first new letter?'

Watergate turns towards me.

'The one you found in the Returns Box, that was the first new one I'd seen in years.'

I grip the velvet curtain hard with both of me hands and yank it back. A massive cloud of dust shoots up into the air. Me and Watergate and Ninder all start coughing. Moonlight lights up the room.

'What the feck you doing you idiot?' says Ninder, still gasping for breath. I look up at the night sky scattered with its thousands of little pin-pricks of light. I reach down into the pocket of me jeans and take something out. I hold it up. Nizanna's white bead glints a little bit as it catches in the moonlight.

'This glass bead, she always hangs around her neck, it's from a chandelier her dad built in her house that represented all the stars that could be seen from Vienna, on the night she was born. I think I know where it is.'

'Where what is?' says Ninder.

'District 24, Alter Strasse, in her mind she's built it somewhere up there.'

Ninder walks towards me and holds out her palm. I drop the bead into it.

'"Others will come…other spacecraft…to Mars and beyond, and they will have people on them." That's what she said to me at the museum. In her mind, she's built Alter Strasse up there because other people can't go there, and, where other people can't go, that's the only place Nizanna believes they could ever be truly safe.'

Watergate takes a couple of steps closer to me and Ninder. He stares down at the bead in me outstretched hand.

Shakes his head.

'No, it's not up there, among the stars,' he says. Then he fishes around in the pocket of his brown cord pants for a moment. Ninder looks up at him.

'He doesn't mean really, he just means...'

Her voice trails away as Watergate takes out a key and holds it up in front of us. Me, him and Ninder all stare at it.

'It's not up there,' he says, 'It can't be. I've already built it someplace else.'

THERE'S A DOOR AT THE BACK OF THE COMMUNITY ROOM that's been wedged open with a couple of rusting metal oxygen bottles. Almost as soon as we get through it, the yellow-and-blue painted corridor narrows and we come to what seems like a dead end. There's another purple velvet curtain hanging down from brass rings. Watergate reaches out and pulls it back.

Lying behind the curtain is a dead old black wooden door, like one of them you'd see in a church or a cathedral. It's got a rusty metal padlock on it. Watergate leans down and puts his key into the lock. He jiggles about with it for a moment or two. There's a bit of grating sound, followed by a couple of clicks and then the door begins to open.

'This is the tower, the old tower where, back in the day, they burnt that woman, the one who scared the ravens away. There's offices through here, where the doctors used to sit, also a couple of treatment rooms where they sometimes did the shock treatment. Always was a maze this place.'

Watergate steps back from the door. He gestures with his hand for me and Ninder to go in.

IT'S DEAD DARK IN THE ROOM ON THE OTHER SIDE OF THE door, although there is some light coming through cracks in the floorboards from the room right above us. This place seems dead big though. Much bigger than I thought it would be from looking at the tower from the outside. Staring up into the rafters I figure it's got to be as much as a hundred-foot long and fifteen-foot high. Looking around, peering into the shadows, I can just make out the wooden legs of some trestle-tables.

Watergate flicks a small green metal switch that's stuck to

the wall just next to me head. A row of six safety lights, three tied to each wall and connected by big red rubber-encased wires, flicker into life. They blink, on and off, a couple of times and then flood the room with the eerie glow of very dull red light.

Ninder takes a step towards the trestle-tables, which cover most of the floor space in the room. I step forward and move towards the right-hand side of them. I kneel down.

Me chin's resting on the table.

Everywhere I look, I can see the same things: spires, pointed roofs, the tops of trees, street upon tiny street of the kind of houses that people built in Vienna before the war. Street upon tiny street of the kind of restaurants, schools, synagogues and swimming pools that Nizanna has drawn in them little pencil diagrams in her letters. The same ones me and Watergate could see in the Vienna book in the library.

Ninder leans down on the other side of the table and looks across the rooftops, tiles and chimney pots. I can see her brown eyes and red hair peeping out over the roofs of two little houses.

There are hundreds of them.

At first, they all look the same, like, but, when I look closer, I realise they're all, in fact, a canny bit different. One, right in front of me, has a red painted door, another blue; some have rounder windows, others square. A little house that begins a street that's about a foot away from me has two large square windows which are made of a kind of stained glass with pictures of tiny Chinese Pagodas drawn on them.

Ninder reaches out across the table. Her painted nails close around a big house with a green tile roof.

'This one's exactly like one of those drawings in the other room, Billy.'

Watergate takes a couple of steps forward. Then he gets down on all fours and crawls under the nearest table. He stands up in a space he's left, about four-foot square, in the middle of the room. He's now completely surrounded by six tables and the rows and rows of little models he's built on top of them.

There's a book in the library called Gulliver's Travels where this bloke Gulliver visits all kinds of funny places before he discovers that people aren't nice and he much prefers horses. He goes to a land called Lilliput where all the people are dead small so, to them, he seems like a massive giant. Watergate looks a bit like that now; standing there in the middle of all them little houses he's built. He leans down and picks up a building with a couple of round towers on it that looks like it's supposed to be a synagogue.

'Once Nizanna stopped writing I left here – asked for me P45 straightway – went back on the booze. All I could think about was stuff I'd seen in the war. Mostly them little kids. Reading the letters, talking about them, what they meant, who the people might be, what the stories could possibly be behind all those lives she'd described – it had been like a kind of therapy for me. It was the same for a lot of the people here, I think; nurses, doctors and other patients. It was hard when she stopped. Not just for me, for everyone. I can't really explain it, but it was dead hard to take. A few years later, I heard about this place closing down. I still had a set of keys. I drank a bottle of whiskey one Sunday and drove out here. One of the shrinks, Shateri, Iranian, I think he was – little bloke with a frizzy barnet and a tash. Smart as a whip. He always treated her well...'

He stabs the middle-finger of his left hand into his head a couple of times, to make his point.

'I broke into his office, and found his notes and a huge

stash of her letters. There were even more in a storeroom in the tower. I stuck a lot of them up on the walls, too.'

Watergate puts the synagogue back down on the corner of a little junction.

'I just made one house at first. It felt really good. So, I made another. In the end, I was driving out here nearly every night. Years went by. I couldn't stop. It took me over. Sometimes, I think, I believe in the people of Alter Strasse and them letters more than the real flesh and blood I see walking around Newcastle.'

I take a step towards him. 'But who were they, Tommy? The people in the letters. Her brother was one of them. The first one. I know that. But, the rest of them?'

Watergate stares down at the city he's built.

Then back up at me and Ninder.

'The Iranian doc, he'd talked to her loads but she'd never say nowt. So, he got in touch with a woman who had been in the camp with her. This lass said, one day, her and Nizanna had to take a message to a guard. When they got there, the guard called them over; like he wanted to share a secret. He pointed to a spy hole in a metal door.'

Ninder looks at me. Then back at Watergate.

'What could they see, Tommy?' I say.

Watergate taps his fingers on the table.

'They were all crammed in. A hundred of them. So packed together they couldn't even fall down. Standing up straight, they were, Mams and dads. Bairns too. Dead. Gassed. Gone…'

Watergate's fingers stop tapping on the table. He doesn't look at me and Ninder. He just stares down at the little rooftops and chimneys of this mad town Nizanna's built inside her head.

His voice goes dead low. I have to take another step towards him; just to make sure I can hear what he's saying.

'Afterwards, Nizanna couldn't stop talking about how they'd been standing up, this lass said. How they looked like they were in queue, how they looked like they were going somewhere. Then she went silent, not just for hours, or days, but weeks.'

Watergate looks up. His fingers drum on the table two more times. Then stop. I look around the room.

'But there are thousands of letters, Tommy, loads more than a hundred. Who are all the rest written too, then?'

Watergate walks across to a green metal filing cabinet that's standing in the corner of the room. He opens it and takes out a manila file that's bursting with bits of white and pink paper.

He walks back towards me and Ninder and drops the file on the edge of the table.

'The Iranian doc had a theory,' Watergate taps the file with his hand, 'it's all in here. She started with her brother, like you say. Then the ones she saw through the peephole. Then...Dear Everyone, that's what the doc says. Every face she saw in that camp that didn't make it through the war, Nizanna's tried to sit down and write to each one of them. Couldn't know all the names, obviously – impossible. So she christened them again; like they were new born.'

Ninder stands up and looks towards the far end of the room beyond the sixth table. There's another green curtain hanging down from the ceiling, next to a big sign that's pointing towards a Fire Escape

She walks towards it and pulls it back.

Behind it there's another whole room filled with the same

kind of tables and the same kind of models and beyond that we can see another room with even more of them.

The safety lights flicker and go out, then flash back on again, this time glowing a little sharper and redder. Watergate smiles across at me over the tiny rooftops.

'Main generator in the basement's been switched on, son. She's here.'

He stares down at a little Alter Strasse synagogue, near some traffic lights at a junction.

'They are.'

Watergate takes a blue handkerchief from his pocket and hands it to me. He walks across to a metal cabinet and opens it. There's rows of clear glass bottles in it. They must chemicals the doctors here used. He chooses a bottle with a clear liquid in it and Trichloromethane written on the label.

'Me fighting days are over, Billy Quiz, but I've got a bit of a plan. Know what this is?'

I nod me head.

'Chloroform,' I say. 'Trichloromethane is another word for chloroform. They used to use it in the old days to send people to sleep.'

Chapter Thirty-Three

A low whistle echoes around the black stone walls of the tower.

Me ears prick up even further when I hear a foot crunching down on some broken glass and a dog barking. I'm crouched down behind one of the trestle-tables. Ninder is standing up next to me but, when she hears the dog, she crouches down too. There's a creek as the black door at the end of the corridor is pushed a bit further back.

I look across at Ninder. I can see she's shitting bricks same as I am. I open me gob to say something. She puts a finger up to her mouth to shush me.

Voices in the corridor; one of them sounds like Ossie's.

'Bring her in here,' he says.

More footsteps. This time they're soft padding ones.

JJ appears in the doorway.

'Shit and bollocks, Billy. We're cheese on toast,' says Ninder under her breath.

The dog's grey fur is tinged pink because of the safety lights. It takes two steps forward then leaps up onto the trestle-table that's closest to the door. He starts walking slowly between the houses on the model's main street. Takes a moment to sniff a little a tree, then pushes his pink tongue out and licks a tiny chimney pot. Then he sniffs the air a couple of times and looks up.

As soon as he spots me, he starts barking.

OSSIE'S GOT A KNIFE IN HIS HANDS. THAT FAIRBURN-STYLES fighting knife. Blue Tear's next to him, in the doorway. Nizanna is standing about two feet away from me. She's never stopped staring at Watergate's model since she came into the room.

Ossie walks around her and stops at the edge of the Alter Strasse model. He reaches across and picks up one of the houses and then plunges the tip of his knife into it, so it goes straight in through the little blue front door; skewers it.

'Worrel built this, you say? I get that. He always was a sentimental arsehole. What I don't get is where he is now? And how you and this Paki tart got out to Ravenswood in the first place. young William?'

Ossie moves slowly across the room holding the knife, with the little house stuck to the point of it, about six inches in front of his face. He stops next to me and Ninder. Waves the knife, first right in front of me face, then in front of hers.

'I'm a collector. You remember that?'

He takes the house off the tip of the knife and drops it on the floor. Then he grinds it flat with the heel of his crepe-soled shoe.

'This knife here has a story. A story about little yellow ears and toes that someone came along and snip, snip, snipped away.'

Ossie smiles. His voice goes dead soft and low.

'My story. All mine. Collecting stories is one thing, creating them, being their author, so to speak, feels even sweeter.'

Nizanna walks forward.

Blue Tear stares after her.

'Where you going, witch?'

She looks at him but her expression doesn't change a bit. I watch her face and them twinkling green eyes. The way she is – all calm and in control of herself – it doesn't even seem like she's in the room with us. More like she's walking, all serene and peaceful, in a field of flowers somewhere, or by a dead pretty lake.

She takes a few steps towards the model. Then she stretches out her hand and points to a house with red roof and a green door. 'Dear Gretchen.'

She walks across to the other side of the table and points at another one.

'Dear Aaron.'

Her fingertip moves to another one with blue curtains and a tiny carved window box attached to it.

'Dear Elijah, ich sehe sie.'

She turns towards Ossie, me and Ninder.

'I knew, Postman, when I looked from my window and saw you and your father whistling. Walking towards those brutal men with their barking dog just as my father and I once had to do. Then I realise I must write again. Write again because a miracle is beginning to happen.'

Nizanna stretches out a hand and touches the roof of the model synagogue.

'I always believed. I always knew. First that miracle, and now this one.'

Blue Tear's right hand twists on JJ's leash.

'Knew what, you mad bitch?' he says.

The dog jumps up; snarling and barking. Nizanna turns round and walks directly towards them. Ninder takes a step forward.

'Leave her alone.'

Ossie flicks out the back of his left hand and smacks Ninder right in her gob. Then he moves the tip of the knife, first towards me, and then back in her direction. Ninder lifts her hand to her lips and starts to bubble a bit.

Nizanna leans down in front of Blue Tear and rests her hand on JJ; just like she did the first time I met her. First, he stops barking. Then, he stops snarling. Blue Tear looks down at the dog and then back at Nizanna.

'Knew what?' he says again; his voice has gone all thin and weak, like he's scared of the answer.

She looks up at him. Kind of stares right through him; as if he doesn't really exist.

'That one day, in some strange way, my letters, all my letters, would be answered.'

Nizanna stands up, reaches out towards Blue and touches his drawn-on tear.

'What was it?' she says.

For a moment, I think he's going to slap her but then he lifts up his right hand and touches his tattoo too.

'What was what?'

'The thing you regret so much?'

Something happens to him when she says that. The blood drains away from his face. His cheeks thin out and whiten. I've never seen him like this before. She's got him dead frightened.

Like a little bairn who's got lost in a dark room, and doesn't know how to get out.

'We was messing about,' he whispers, 'me and Bino, messing up stuff in the museum like Ossie said we had to.'

Blue reaches into the pocket of his jacket. He takes out his glass jar. It's stuffed, right up to the brim, with a big black blob of dead insects.

'We were having a right laugh...Then we came to the hive. Me and him, standing there, staring at all them little crawling things through the glass. I could see his pink eyes reflected in it, and then a weird soppy look came into them. I was alright just knowing. I already did, really. The way he stared over at me sometimes. Like I was the King of fucking Persia.'

Blue Tear walks across to the model. Ossie takes a couple of steps towards him.

'What's done's done, son. Leave it be.'

Blue puts the jar of dead bees down next to a little post-box in the middle of the nearest street to him.

He turns towards Nizanna. Then back towards his uncle.

'Then he said it.'

Ossie's voice goes all harsh and growly.

'Said fucking what?'

Ninder stretches out her right hand and takes a hold of mine. When I give it a squeeze I can feel it trembling.

'I love you, Blue,' says Ninder. 'That's it, isn't it?'

Ossie looks across at Ninder and then back towards Blue.

'So, Omo was a fucking homo. Big deal! I never understood how you couldn't see it, son...'

Blue takes a couple of steps back towards Nizanna. The dog pads towards her and then sits panting near her feet. Blue stands in front of her staring into her eyes.

'He was me only proper mate but I smacked him. He was a

hard bastard, always was, but he just let me do it. Like, some-how, he wanted me too. Like it was a big fucking relief…'

Nizanna looks across to Ossie. Then back up at Blue.

'Sometimes just the sound of this strange word love is the thing we fear the most.'

Ossie takes three quick steps across the floor and grabs hold of Blue Tear's shoulder. He turns him around and then slaps him straight in the face. Blue blinks a couple of times. His eyes shrivel into two little bullets. Ossie hands his knife to Blue and points at Nizanna.

'Don't listen to the bitch; she's a witch, a proper one n'all. Don't let them things she says get inside your head, like I did. Them things she says and writes.'

Blue stands there looking down at the knife. Nizanna just sits in the chair stroking the dog's mane and staring up at both of them.

I look at Ninder, who's still standing next to me. Every bit of her body is shaking.

Eeny.

I let go of her hand.

Meeny.

I walk across the floor towards Ossie.

Miny.

I take a hold of his arm. He shapes as if to clout at me with his other one.

Mo.

I grab hold of his hand. Put both of me own hands around it; try and remember to say the right words, just like Watergate told me to.

'Healing hands, Mr Mingle, like you said in the museum, that's the real reason you came back to Ravenswood isn't it?'

I turn the palm of Ossie's hand upwards and nod at Nizanna.

'You came to heal her, didn't you? Her and yourself.'

Ossie's blue eyes fix right on me. His top lip is trembling a little bit. He reaches inside his jacket pocket and pulls out a clear plastic syringe filled with a thin yellowy liquid.

'Little bit of ketamine, young William, know what that's for?'

I stare at the syringe in his hand.

'Yes, I'm good at understanding stuff like that: what different types of chemicals will do.'

As soon as he injects Nizanna with the anaesthetic, she begins to fall asleep.

Chapter Thirty-Four

Nizanna's face has gone dead pale. She's lying on a green rubber mat on top of a metal hospital trolley in the electroshock room. Next to where her head is there's a big cabinet which has lots of handles and pulleys on it, and a couple of old-fashioned dials that look a bit like the ones she's got on that red Bakelite radio she keeps on her living room table.

I'm standing at the foot of the bed about two feet away from Ossie, in a dusty room with peeling green paint and mould everywhere. The carpet is covered with old medical records that are spilling out of brown folders. There's not much else in here except for a small table and chair, with a dirty white straitjacket hanging off the back of it, and a really massive green metal cabinet right next to the doorway.

Blue Tear and Ninder are standing in the main doorway of the room next to the green cabinet. In the background, we can hear JJ barking and howling away in the stone tower.

Ossie takes a couple of steps and hands Blue Tear his knife. Then he walks back to the bed and takes hold of a brown leather strap with a bronze buckle, and pulls it tight around Nizanna's waist.

'It's a very small dose, so she's only going to be out for about twenty minutes but that's all the time I need.'

There's another brown strap at the bottom of the rubber mat, near her feet.

Ossie points at it.

'Get that tied for me will you, young William. Nice and tight. Nurse Leech's little girls and boys tend to rock and roll like Elvis on a Big Dipper, once I put the volts through them.'

I shake me head.

'I can't...I can't help. Not with this.'

Blue Tear takes a step forward and boots me right up the arse.

Ninder jumps forward and tries to grab him by the neck. He swings back towards her and holds out the knife. Ninder takes a couple of deep breaths. Then she steps backwards out of the door.

'You killed my uncle you bastard!'

Blue Tear holds up the knife and steps towards her. Then he shakes his head.

'Not me, him.'

'Him?'

He spits out the words.

'Jimmy Segs!'

'You helped him though?' she says. 'Gave him the phosphorus.'

Blue Tear's lips curl upwards. A sneer-smile spreads across his face. He nods his head.

'Jimmy wanted a few quid off him, that Noor, a bit each week. "The usual," he calls it. It was an accident, though, that's why he used the phosphorus and not fucking petrol for a proper job. Jimmy only wanted to make him crap his pants so he'd cough up, he thought it would just start a little fire, so he'd be warned, but the fucking curtains around the back door went up. That's what he told me anyways, because me and Bino, we weren't there.'

Ninder stares at Blue Tear. Then she puts on a daft soppy lasses' voice. 'I love you, Blue,' she says, 'I really, really love you!'

She takes a step towards him. Stands on her tip-toes and pushes her face as close to his as she can.

Her voice goes all mocking and flirty.

'You and Bino, eh? Maybe you love him back?'

A thin blue vein, that snakes down from under Blue's shaved head near his temple, pulses slightly. His eyes go all dead hard and narrow.

He grabs Ninder by the throat and pushes her out of the door. He twists her left arm right around the back of her neck and starts to march her down the corridor, back towards the tower.

'Come with me, you Paki bitch' he says, 'I'll show you exactly what happened to your uncle.'

I make a move towards the door to follow them. Ossie grabs me by me ear and twists it, pulls me back.

'Not you, young William.'

He points down at Nizanna.

'Me and you are going to hold her.'

OSSIE PICKS UP A STRIP OF WHITE CLOTH WITH SOME RED electrodes sewed into it and attaches it to Nizanna's forehead.

'All them letters she wrote, here. All them fucking words. I couldn't help reading them. After a while, I felt like I was drowning. When I was walking around the wards, it was like they were whispering to me. My fever came back. I took a week off. Got myself some ampoules. Slept all the time, I wasn't on the juice. Felt better. Then it changed.'

Ossie is standing at the top of the bed. He fixes two red-and-black wires that lead to the buzzing, whirring metal cabinet with the dials on it, to either side of Nizanna's head.

I move a little closer to him.

'It?'

'My dream.'

I move closer still.

'Your dream?'

He looks dead pale now. Haunted.

'My dream of Germania, Albert Speer's Germania, it changed.'

'Changed how?

Ossie tightens a red wire on the left-hand side of Nizanna's head. He straightens up and looks straight at me.

'The sweet dreams I had, when I took them ampoules, stopped being sweet, young William. In this new dream, I was walking – same as usual – down the Avenue of the Splendours, to the Volkshalle, the people's hall. I stare up at that magnificent white dome that Adolf and Albert have built and then I see him.'

'See who?'

'Only a little dot, at first – he comes hopping and skipping toward me. Little kid, eight years old, maybe, with black hair, carrying a red hoop. He comes closer still. Gives me a long hard stare. Then smiles.'

Ossie's voice is going quieter and quieter.

'That's when I sense them.'

'Them?' Me voice sounds dead weird. Spooky, like it belongs to someone else. I have to lean forward to hear Ossie better.

'I turn around slowly,' he says, 'and there they are – the place is crawling with 'em.'

I let meself have a quick look across to the metal cabinet that's standing directly behind Ossie. Then flick me eyes back to him.

'Crawling with what, Mr Mingle?'

He points down at Nizanna's sleeping face.

'All them dead 'uns that are inside her. They're everywhere – mothers pushing prams, little nippers going to school, market-traders setting up stalls for the day's work. A grey-haired geezer with these beautiful polished shoes on. A woman in a pink hat standing waiting for someone... That's when I realise. That's when I start to shake.'

'Realise what?'

'I'm all alone in there. Trapped. All alone. Just me and them.'

I see the metal door of the green cabinet push open just a fraction more. Then I take another step towards Ossie. I'm standing right next to him now.

I point down at Nizanna on the trolley.

'But you were a nurse here? You could have injected her with something permanent and no one would ever have known – one of them ampoules? Why didn't you just do that?'

Ossie reaches across with his right hand to a metal lever with a black rubber handle that sticks out of the right-hand side of the monitor, next to a dial with the word Volts written on it in red. I can see his fingers are trembling a bit.

'What if my dream's like that story about that witch they burned in the tower here and them fucking ravens that left their caw behind? What about that, eh? If she goes, I'll never sleep again. She'll be gone and I'll be stuck with all these bleeding Kikes inside me bonce. They'll never let me be. Never...'

Ossie's right hand closes around the rubber handle.

Behind him the green cupboard door swings wide open.

'There's another way to break her spell though. It worked the last time. I just need to stop her writing. Once she stops writing, I'll finally get some fucking peace,' he says.

The handle jerks back an inch or so. There's a buzzing sound. The dials begin to flicker and glow. Then the cupboard swings wide open and Watergate steps out of it. He slips his hands under Ossie's armpits and jerks him back from the handle. I grab the bottle of chloroform and the hanky out of me Levi's jacket. I pull the stopper off the bottle and tip out some of the liquid onto the hanky. I ram the blue rag into Ossie's face.

Watergate whispers to him as his eyes begin to close.

'Let's hope you never stop dreaming.'

Watergate unhooks his arms. Ossie drops to the floor. Nizanna turns her head to the left slightly but she's still asleep. I grab hold of the brown belt that's tied around her waist and untie it. Watergate rips two white cords out of the straitjacket on the back of the chair, and hands one to me.

'Quick as you like, Billy, son. Let's get this sick bastard tied up nice and tight. Then go and find young Ninder.'

TWO SHINY BLACK DR MARTENS BOOTS ARE GOOSE-STEPPING down the centre of Alter Strauss. Everywhere I look I can see small curls of smoke floating up from the model's burning buildings. Blue arches his back and beats his chest with his hands. He stamps one of his feet down on a clump of trees.

Ninder's kneeling down on the other end of the trestle that Blue Tear's stamping on. She's got both hands held up in front of her face. He must have smacked her about a bit.

Blue Tear's laughing at his own piss-taking walk and gazing up at the glowing marmalade jar like it's the most beautiful thing in the world, as he marches up and down. Light from the burning white phosphorus inside the jar is flickering a lot which makes dead odd-shaped shadows run across the tear on his cheek and the rooftops of the model houses below him. JJ runs around at his master's feet – prowling around the little model streets.

Blue stands still and starts to unscrew the top. As more air gets into the jar, the phosphorus glows even brighter. He opens the lid and it flares right up. He tips the jar upside down. Three more burning lumps of phosphorus fall out of it. They fizz and crack in the air.

One of them lands on top of the little synagogue. Its tiny towers start to spark and burn. As each spark spirals through the air a different fence, tree or rooftop begins to catch fire.

Blue Tear lifts his right hand and hoys the empty jar against the roof of a tiny school.

Ossie's sleeping body is tied at the hands and feet. It's really knackering me hands having to carry him. Me and Watergate throw him on the floor next to an upturned hospital chair. Then we run towards the end of the table where Ninder's kneeling.

As soon as we get near it, JJ starts barking like crazy. Watergate heaves his fat gut onto one end of the trestle, taking out a couple of rows of little burning houses as he does.

Then he pulls his legs up after him.

Blue Tear takes a couple of steps back down towards the end of the trestle where Ninder is. Burning houses, cafés and lamp-posts smash to pieces under his feet. She pulls her hands away from her face and tries to get up. Her nose is bleeding. I climb up onto the table and stand next to her and Watergate. When Blue Tear sees me and Watergate a massive sneer-smile spreads across his face. He holds up Ossie's knife.

'Come on then...'

Right behind his head, a big bit of flame shoots up the curtain that's hung around the door to the next room. Pieces of it begin to shred and drop to the floor. Black ashes and burning embers fly up into the air. Me eyes are dead sore and starting to water from all the smoke. Now, tiny flames sprout up from the model houses and streets on the tables in the next room as well. JJ is standing directly between me and Watergate and Blue and Ninder. There's only about five-feet of table that's separating us all with the dog growling and slavering in the middle.

Suddenly, Ninder drops onto all fours between me and Watergate, and Blue Tear. There's a flash of green and yellow as her right hand stretches out towards the back of the dog. It closes around his balls and, then, makes a sharp twisting movement. There's a horrible strained barking sound. JJ jumps right up at Blue Tear and chomps his teeth into his arm. Caught right off balance, Blue tips back and drops sideways onto the main street; crushing loads of houses as he falls. The dog goes mental and jumps on top of him in a dead mad frenzy of snarling and biting.

Ninder pulls herself up on her feet. She swings her right foot back and boots Blue straight in the bollocks with one of her DMs.

'That's for me uncle.'

Then she boots him again.

Thick clouds of black smoke begin to fill the tower as Blue Tear clutches his nuts and screams in agony.

Watergate grabs me arm and points past Ossie's doped-up body towards the Fire Escape. Then he takes the chloroform rag from his pocket and takes two steps across the burning model towards Blue Tear. I swing me head around and look at the door that leads to the corridor where the Electroshock room is. A bit of red flame is already beginning to lick at the purple curtain that covers it.

Before Watergate can stop me, I'm running towards the room. Me eyes are stinging and watering even more now. I pull the collar of me shirt across me mouth to keep the smoke out.

The stink of burning is everywhere. I push the door of the electroshock room completely open with me right hand. The machinery is still buzzing and whirring. But the metal bed is empty. I look to me left. The curtain that leads to the Community Room is already on fire. The smoke is at its blackest in that spot. I pull me Levi's jacket around me ears and duck me head right down inside it to protect me ginger bonce from the flames.

Then I run into the blackness.

Everything goes dark. I put out me right hand and feel me way forward. I can hardly feel anything at first, then me fingers notice the change in the surface of the walls between the rough black stone of the tower and the smooth painted plaster of the Community Room.

I TAKE THREE BIG STEPS. THE SMOKE CLEARS A LITTLE BIT. Nizanna's standing in the middle of the room next to the big knackered telly.

Her letters are burning.

Some of them, the ones pinned near the very bottom of the walls, are already really sizzling. As I watch, a sheet of flame leapfrogs from one letter to another and, in seconds, moves all the way from the floor to the ceiling behind her. The smoke begins to thicken.

I hold out me hand and walk straight towards her.

She doesn't move; just stands there with her hands behind her back staring straight at me. I'm standing straight in front of her now with me right hand still stretched out.

I look into her eyes.

She smiles. Then steps away from me. Black smoke fills the room. I start coughing and spluttering again. I can feel it coating the inside of me mouth. I reach up with both hands and wipe me eyes.

I open them again. I see Nizanna take another step backward. She glances over to the wall to the right of her. A sheet of flame covers it. Big clouds of embers lift up and swirl and swerve like a swarm of little black insects through the air.

I hold out me hand again.

'We've got to go, Nizanna!'

She looks down at it. Then back up at me.

'The more I speak, the less I believe, Postman.'

She shakes her head and looks all around at the burning letters that cover the walls. 'They live in my silence.'

A big black cloud filled with cracking embers twists and turns in the air, just behind Nizanna, then it covers me and her. Me eyes fill with smoke again. So does me throat. I start coughing and spitting. I rub me eyelids with both hands.

When I open them again all I can see is smoky blackness. A hand grabs me shoulder. I swing straight around.

Watergate has ripped off his shirt sleeve and tied it around his mouth to keep the smoke out. He points in the direction of the broken fire doors that leads back to the tower.

'Come on, Billy, son. Get moving!'

I LEAN OVER ON THE GRAVEL AGAIN AND PUKE ME GUTS OUT for the second time. I feel like I've smoked more tabs than them experimental Beagles on the telly. I pull meself up onto me knees and put me hand out against the post office van to steady meself. Then I press the side of me face against the cool metal of the passenger door.

I watch as Ninder and Watergate drag Ossie's still sleeping body away from the bottom of the fire escape stairs at the back of the building. Two loud bangs come from the back of van where the metal mesh is. Watergate's already got Blue Tear tied up in there. He must be waking up. Somewhere in the background I can hear JJ barking madly in the wood behind me.

Ninder and Watergate prop up Ossie against the wheel of the van. He's waking up now too. He looks down at his hands and starts straining at the straitjacket cords around his wrists. He's tied good and tight though. He can't do nowt.

'She's still in there,' I say to Watergate. 'We've got to go back.'

Watergate stands up and shakes his head, he raises his hand and points up towards the back of the stone tower.

'No, she's not.'

Me, Ossie and Ninder look up.

There's a narrow ledge at the very top of the tower, about a hundred feet above our heads. It's sticking directly out from the rough stones of the building.

It can only be ten inches wide. Nizanna is standing on it.

Her hands are stretched out over her head. It looks as if she's trying to reach out and catch one of the thousands of stars that are twinkling above her head. She looks down towards me. I can't see her face properly, she's too far away, but she looks a bit like she did the first time I saw her. When she was staring down at me and me dad's whistling.

She pauses. Then looks up again. At all them stars above her head; out into the solar system – towards Mars, where Viking 1's lander is falling towards the red planet. I think I know where she's going now. Part of me wishes I could go with her.

Nizanna looks down at us all one last time.

Watergate shouts out a single word.

'No!'

Then she steps out into space.

Chryse Planitia
Thursday, July 29th 1976.
Viking 1's lander has landed

Chapter Thirty-Five

I'm sitting in the club with me dad, Ninder and Watergate. We're all wearing black because we've just come back from Nizanna's funeral at the crem. We've got a drink each and there's three cheese plates sitting in front of us: a big, a small and a middle-sized plate. An Eeny, a Miny, and a Mo. We asked the barmaid to set them up for us special, like, since it's not a Sunday.

There's no cheese on them though. We ate all that straightaway.

Watergate scoffed most of it. He pats his fat belly and then, with his other hand, stifles a belch.

He lets out a big sigh.

'She's left us.'

Ninder dabs her eyes with one of her "What are little girls made of?" hankies. She wearing pink mascara but it's running quite a bit.

'Yes.'

She's got big circles around her eyes because she was up dead late last night covering her first gig for the NME, an all-girl punk band called The Stroppy Bitches who were playing the Mayfair rock club in town.

I've bubbled a lot in the last week. Bubbled about mam, same as ever, and bubbled about Nizanna too. I saw Watergate coming out the bogs at the post office on Tuesday. He had streaky marks around his eyes. I reckon he might even have been bubbling too. But today, after the funeral, I feel a little bit better.

I reach across and take a last bit of cheese from the middle-sized plate. Stick the cheddar into me gob and swallow it. It tastes good.

I lick the last crumb from me lips and then turn to Watergate.

'What'll happen to Ossie and Blue, and Bino and this Jimmy Segs, Tommy?' I say.

'Plenty, that's all you need to know, Billy Quiz. I was with the coppers for a good eight hours after they'd talked to you and Ninder the other night. Everything we told them tied up with what Bino said to them when they picked him up, and what they found in the rest of the museum after the break-in. Them horrible bastards are all going down for a few years.'

Watergate leans across the blue Formica table a little bit and points at Ninder's hair. She's just dyed it purple.

'Hey, Ninder, Pet, I was in the library yesterday, getting a book out on Sir Isaac Newton's Alchemy for Billy Quiz here, since, thanks to you, he's still banned. Billy tells me that, even though he was one of the greatest scientists that ever lived, Sir Isaac spent loads of his life looking for something called the Philosopher's Stone and investigating all kinds of alchemy and magic. That when he died, more than anything else, he believed that the Universe was filled with many magical things that would always remain inexplicable to man and out of the reach of science.'

'So?'

He reaches across and ruffles me ginger bonce.

'I'm thinking Sir Isaac Newton might be right, and our lad, Billy, here, might have cast a bit of spell on you.'

I go a bit pink in me cheeks when he says it.

Ninder sticks her middle-finger in the air and wiggles it in front of Watergate.

'As if, feck off, donkey bollocks.'

Me dad folds his Daily Mirror in two and puts it on the table.

'I get most of it but the bit I don't understand,' he says, 'is how this Nizanna was in the museum at the same time you were, our Billy?'

Ninder butts in.

'Me mammy says they'd caught her three times before that already, trying to get at that model. Hanging around the ladies' bogs just before the museum closed, trying to hide away and then come out later. On that last night, they must have missed her.'

Dad takes a swig of his lager and smiles at me and Ninder. He looks happy. He was out with Brenda, Mrs Damoan, last night. She's had a word for him at the post office about the letters in the garage and she thinks things might be alright. She says that because of me mam getting knocked over and me dad's doctor's note, she'll be able to "Swing it with the higher-ups," so it all gets put down to me dad's nerves.

Dad puts his pint down near his Daily Mirror. The front cover says MARS: FIRST EVER PIC. Image reveals actual landing site on Chryse Planitia, the Golden Plain. It shows a close up shot of the real Martian surface taken by Viking 1. There's not much to see really. Just some rocks.

I take Nizanna's s cream envelope, the one she gave me at her flat, the only one she never posted, out of me pocket and rest it on me Vimto glass. The four of us stare at the address written on the letter:

Alter Oz,
Alter Strasse
Bezirk Veiundzwanzig.
Wein.

I take out a pen and write something else on it. I rest the envelope back against the Vimto glass.

Now it reads:

Lena Agnew and Alter Oz,
Alter Strasse
Bezirk Veiundzwanzig.
Wein.

I stand up and start taking me jacket off the back of me chair. Watergate stands up too and grabs his.

'I'll come with you, Billy Quiz, then shall I?'

'Come where?' says me dad. 'Come where?'

THE RED POST-BOX ON SCROGG ROAD IS ONLY ABOUT TWO-hundred yards away from where me mam had her accident.

I take the letter out of me pocket.

The one I wrote last night:

Dear Mam,
Ich Sehe Sie,

I've been sitting at me desk next to me telescope for ages but I couldn't think of anything to write. In the end, I thought a

Jaffa Cake might help so I went downstairs to our kitchen. Me dad was there. He was gluing up your Wilma Flintstone pepper-pot with a tube of UHU. We broke it, me and him, I'm sorry about that. (Dad is too, I expect.)

When I asked him why – Wilma's days of sprinkling pepper on Dad's rissoles are long gone – he said something again that he told me at the Hancock Museum once, about gravity and relativity not being the things that really stick the Universe together...That it's love that does that.

When he said that about the pepper-pot I came straight back to me desk because I knew exactly what I wanted to say to you

It's this:

I've thought about you every day, Mam, every single day for two years.

And I know now, I'm never ever going to stop.

I'm sorry what I said about the church and God and Jesus and that. I still don't believe in them things, not really, but it wasn't because of science that I said them.

Right then, in the middle of us shouting and bawling, I just wanted to make you feel bad.

Not as clever as me because being clever with facts, and that, is the only thing I've got.

I love you Mam. I'll always love you. And I know, in spite of me saying all them daft things back then, that, wherever you are, you'll always love me right back.

Ich Sehe Sie, (That's German for "I see you" by the way, just in case you were wondering.)

Billy

PS: I'm thinking I might stop being a postman, soon. All the walking has been giving me sore feet and it's started to wear away the soles of me Polyveldts.

There's a college up the Coast Rd that Ninder Lally goes to. I rang them yesterday and I'm going to see one of the teachers, who does Physics and Chemistry, next week. I'm not sure I'll make as good a scientist as Sir Isaac Newton but they've got a machine at the post office called the AirSteam 750. They use it to open letters, and that. I think I'd like to be the sort of bloke who invents the next one of them.

PPS I've stuck something in this envelope for a wife called Nizanna. If you see her around can you give it to her? I think it's the last thing she needs to get everything in her dad's house back to exactly how she likes it.

I fold the letter in two. Ninder hands me the cream envelope

I put the letter inside it, next to the one Nizanna wrote to her brother and the drawing she did of her Uncle Rudy's ice-cream house. Then I take the white bead that Nizanna left behind on the Martian surface at the museum and put that into the envelope she gave me too.

I lick the gum on the back and seal it.

I step towards the post-box.

'Hang on a minute, son.'

Watergate holds out his palm.

There's a stamp in it.

'She believed, Billy son. The Letter Lady really believed. That's why she always stuck a stamp on them.'

I take the stamp from him and lick it. Stick it on the envelope. There's a little picture of a bloke with wings on his feet on the front of it.

'Hermes, Hermes the Messenger,' says Watergate. 'The post office did some special "Greek Myth Collector's Edition" covers a few years back. You could get Apollo, Aphrodite and

Zeus as well, but I know that man there is your favourite, Billy Quiz.'

After I finished writing last night, I had a look up through me telescope and began to imagine something. It was Mr Pontefract's patent-leather driving gloves slowly unscrewing a silver lid on the Viking 1 lander. Then I saw him stepping down out of the space probe on to the dusty surface of a dead mysterious red planet.

I hold the envelope up and kiss it.

I give it to Watergate and Ninder and they do the same.

Me dad puts his lips together and starts to whistle a tune.

It's one of "Just a Mo" Morovitz's favourites.

I drop the letter inside the red metal slot.

I'm a man of science, like I said, but I've a got a feeling – just a daft imaginary feeling – that, right now, somewhere up there, amongst the stars, Mr Pontefract is carrying a postbag on his shoulders. In the distance, he can already see all them chimneys, spires and towers – and maybe a white cupola too – that Nizanna's dreamed, that Nizanna's built, in District Twenty-Four on Chryse Planitia, as he walks towards Alter Strasse across the golden plain.

Geordie for Beginners

Mam – Mum/Mother

Me – My, as in: 'me mam,' meaning 'my mum'

Dead – General term for 'very,' as in: 'dead good,' meaning 'very good'

Canny – Generally, meaning 'good' as in: 'a canny night,' meaning 'a good night.' But, also, sometimes replaces 'very' as in: 'canny good,' meaning 'very good'

Deek – 'Look,' as in: 'give me a deek,' or, more commonly, 'give's a deek, like'

Like – Added gratuitously into almost any sentence, as in: 'How's tricks, like?' or 'Thanks, like, but I'm alright' (Normally pronounced: alreet)

Hoy – 'Throw,' as in: 'If you don't shut up, I'll hoy you out'

Or something/and that – As 'like,' gratuitously added to the middle, or end, of almost any sentence in ways calculated to outrage the grammar police

Bairn – 'Child,' usually quite young

Pet – General term of endearment used when addressing someone you may not know that well, as in: 'Alright, pet?'

Them – Often used to replace 'those,' in a sentence. As in: 'Them facts,' instead of 'Those facts'

Bog – A fixed receptacle into which a person may urinate or defecate

's – Somewhat confusingly, this can mean 'us,' or 'me.' So, in Geordie, 'Give's a deek,' can mean 'give me a look,' or 'give us a look.' The exact meaning needing to be deduced from the context of the sentence

Scran – Food, a meal

Hockle/greb – Two onomatopoeic words used to describe spit, or the act of spitting

Rissole – Pressed meat and spices, coated in breadcrumbs and deep fried. Usually round, and served with plenty of chips. A popular form of scran, especially during the 1970s.

About the Author

Chris Rickaby lives in Newcastle upon Tyne. He has spent most of his professional career working in advertising as a copywriter; eventually going on to set up his own advertising agency. He has written scripts for television and is also the author of an award-winning experimental novel. This is his debut novel in print.